SARAH ALDERSON

In Her Eyes

MULHOLLAND
BOOKS
HODDER

First published in Great Britain in 2019 by Mulholland Books
An imprint of Hodder & Stoughton
An Hachette UK company

1

Copyright © Sarah Alderson 2019

The right of Sarah Alderson to be identified as the
Author of the Work has been asserted by her in accordance
with the Copyright, Designs and Patents Act 1988.

A CIP catalogue record for this title is available from the British Library

Paperback ISBN 978 1 473 68184 2
eBook ISBN 978 1 473 68185 9

Typeset in Plantin Light by Hewer Text UK Ltd, Edinburgh
Printed and bound in Great Britain by Clays Ltd, Elcograf S.p.A.

Hodder & Stoughton policy is to use papers that are natural, renewable
and recyclable products and made from wood grown in sustainable
forests. The logging and manufacturing processes are expected to
conform to the environmental regulations of the country of origin.

Hodder & Stoughton Ltd
Carmelite House
50 Victoria Embankment
London EC4Y 0DZ

www.hodder.co.uk

To Theo and Clarissa

PART ONE

I

DAY 1

A sledgehammer slams into my chest, splintering my ribs. In its wake comes a lightning bolt of pain.

'Ava!' Someone is shouting my name over and over, but I can't see who. The fog deepens, darkens. Cold, bony fingers are snaking around my throat, sliding over my mouth, clamping my lips together – and I start to panic. I can't breathe. But the harder I fight, the more tightly I'm held. What's happening? Where am I? Where's June?

June. Her name rises up in front of me and I snatch for it, grasp it tightly, as though it's a flashlight that will light a path out of the fog. June. Not just a name or a promise of summer. A face too; dark hair, deep blue eyes, freckles scattered across her cheeks – one on her lip that looks like a chocolate sprinkle. She's smiling. She's always smiling. I reach for her, but she vanishes. I try to scream her name but I can't open my mouth. Fear surges through me. I need to reach her and so I start to fight – kicking and punching with every ounce of strength left in me, trying to get free, but it's impossible.

It hits me then that June's dead. And if she is, then I want to be too. I stop fighting and let the fog pour into my ears. It kills all sound and then it rams its fists into my

3

eyes and blinds me. It's a darkness so complete I might as well be encased in lead, free-falling to the bottom of the ocean.

Gratefully, I let myself sink.

2

DAY 1: Earlier

'An affair?'

Laurie hands me the olive from her martini and nods.

'You honestly think Dave's having an affair?' I ask her, shaking my head in astonishment. I can't believe it for a moment. It's absurd. It would be easier to believe he was Grand Wizard of the KKK.

Laurie downs her drink in one swallow. 'He's been acting shifty for months, working late, refusing to open up and talk to me.'

'How's that any different to normal?' I ask, and immediately realize I shouldn't be making light of it. Laurie's serious. I reach across the table and take her hand. 'I'm sorry, I'm just finding it hard to imagine.'

She forces a terse smile and signals the waiter for another martini.

Now I get why she sounded so tearful when she called and begged me to meet her. I was meant to be having dinner with Robert. He'd arranged a special date night for our anniversary completely out of the blue (admitting to me that Hannah had reminded him). But given the last time he asked me out was about three hundred years ago, I had been looking forward to it. He wasn't at all happy when I postponed. But Laurie has been there for me through so many ups and downs; I couldn't not be there for her in her hour of need.

'Do you have any proof?' I ask Laurie, still incredulous.

'What? Lipstick on his collar? Credit card receipts for a Motel 8?' She shakes her head. 'No. I just know there's something going on.'

I take a big gulp of my wine and try to process what Laurie is telling me, but I just can't. Dave's Dave. If the *Jeopardy* answer was 'Dependable', the question would be 'What is Dave?' He and Laurie have been together for fifteen years. I was maid of honor at their wedding and I'm godmother to their son, Cory, who has just started college.

There are lots of our friends' husbands who I'd lay money on playing away from home – in a small town like ours rumors fly like the winged monkeys in Oz – but not Dave. No way. It took him two years to pluck up the courage to ask Laurie out, and even then he made it a double date with Robert and me because he was worried he'd be too nervous to talk to her if he was on his own.

'Are you sure you're not just jumping to conclusions?' I ask Laurie. 'It doesn't sound like the Dave I know.'

She snorts. 'How well do we ever really know anyone?' she asks, arching an eyebrow.

I ponder that.

'He's acting different,' Laurie goes on. 'He's started taking care of himself. He gets up every morning at the crack of dawn and does this seven-minute workout thing.'

I stare at her blankly.

'Siri barks orders at you as you do jumping jacks,' she explains. 'It's some mid-life crisis app that someone out there is getting extremely rich off of.' She glances my way for a beat, almost apologetic, before shrugging it off and moving swiftly on. 'And the other day I found all these bottles in the bathroom cabinet – pills and oils and ointments.'

'Pills?' I ask.

She taps her head and automatically I think she's talking about anti-depressants. I know Dave was on them before, but these days who isn't? Doctors are handing them out like candy.

'For his hair,' Laurie clarifies. 'To make it grow back. We're broke and he's pouring money away on snake oil to make his hair grow back. He's been bald, Ava, for half his life. There are billiard balls more hirsute than him.'

I stifle a smile as the waiter lays a fresh martini in front of Laurie.

'What did you think when I said pills?' Laurie asks, glancing at me over the rim of her glass. 'That he was taking Viagra?'

I give a tiny, non-committal shrug.

'I wish!' Laurie spits. 'I can't even remember the last time we had sex. I think it was my birthday. So when was that? Six months ago? And believe me, I think I exerted more effort blowing out the candles on my cake. And the cake was way more satisfying. And it was a *vegan* cake. Take a minute to think about that.'

I take a sip of wine and try not to think about that. Instead I think about Robert. When was the last time we had sex? Last week? No, last month. That's right. It was after June's school play. And it was good, definitely better than cake, vegan or otherwise. It's always been good, if a little sporadic recently. We've been together for twenty-two years though, since I was a young and naive nineteen-year-old, so I suppose it's no surprise that our sex life is in decline. The fact we're still together and still having sex (albeit occasionally) and don't hate each other's guts feels like success to me, given how many of our friends' marriages are hitting the dust and then the divorce courts. Besides, everyone's sex life takes a nosedive after forty, doesn't it?

I switch my attention back to Laurie. 'So, Dave's getting in shape, how does that equate to him having an affair? Maybe he just wants to be on a par with you.'

Laurie is forty-one, like me, with jet-black hair and an angular face that most people would call striking, if not outright beautiful. She's tall and slender and has never had to work out in her life to stay that way. Unlike me. I have to work harder than Beyoncé at the Super Bowl to keep the weight off, which could be why I'm never going to get back to the size I was before I had kids. I've had to let that ambition go, along with a million others.

Laurie swallows half her martini in one go and then sets it down. 'I overheard him the other night in the bathroom. He thought I was asleep. I get up to pee and I hear him in there, whispering, on the phone to someone, telling them he'll be there, promising them, he just has to make sure I don't find out.'

'Maybe he was arranging something for your anniversary.'

Laurie scowls. 'At three in the morning?'

OK. She has a point . . . but still. 'Why didn't you just ask him what he was doing?'

'I did.'

'And?'

'And he told me it was a missed call. At three in the morning. What? I'm some kind of idiot now? I checked his phone the next day.'

'And?'

'He'd cleared his call log. Who does that? A guilty man! That's who.'

Laurie huddles closer and casts a furtive glance around the bar. We live in a small town and everyone knows everyone, but The Oak mid-week is half-empty so we're safe. 'I think it's someone from work,' she tells me. 'He keeps coming home smelling of perfume. Something cheap and nasty too, like a Vegas stripper might wear.'

I pull back to study her. Is she serious? Dave's the manager of a local wine-tasting room. I know there are a couple of girls in their late twenties who work there; LA hipster types who've migrated north to our idyllic little valley and who all dress like they're extras in *Little House on the Prairie*, but I can't imagine for a moment that Dave has seduced any of them. Not that Dave doesn't have a certain appeal – he's got a brilliantly droll sense of humor – but he's not exactly Brad Pitt. More William H. Macy.

Laurie digs in her glass for the stray olive and starts stabbing it violently with the toothpick. 'I thought about hiring a private investigator.'

I almost choke on my drink. 'Are you serious?' I ask, assuming she can't possibly be, because it sounds far too Hollywood noir to be something people actually do in real life.

Laurie doesn't smile back. 'Absolutely.' She stabs the olive again, this time so viciously its pimiento guts spill out. 'But I can't afford it,' she sighs.

My face warms, and I take another sip of my drink. Money has always been a contentious issue and I try not to bring it up when I'm around Laurie. I know she and Dave have been struggling financially but I've learned my lesson about offering to help. Not that I would ever offer to pay for a private investigator, because I can't for the life of me believe Dave is doing the dirty. The evidence Laurie has laid out isn't exactly a slam-dunk for the prosecution.

Laurie slips off her stool and heads to the bathroom, swaying a little as she goes. I ask the waiter to bring two glasses of water, and while I wait for Laurie to come back I think about what she said about never really knowing anyone completely. Is it true? No. I would know without a shadow of a doubt if Robert were having an affair, though I also know I'm probably echoing the words of every woman who's ever been cheated on in the history of the world.

But there's barely room in Robert's life for the kids and me. When would he have time for an affair? He shuts himself in his study every day, emerging like a vampire when it's dark to eat dinner with us, before returning to his study to work late into the night. So, unless Robert's locked in there all day every day watching porn . . . I laugh to myself, but then I abruptly stop, recalling an article I read a while back about a man who was addicted to porn. He re-financed his house, basically bankrupted himself paying for cam girls – not even in-the-flesh girls, but girls performing on a camera, which seems like a monumental waste of money to me – and then the wife found out when she used his computer to check her email one day and got an eyeful of waxed vagina. But you couldn't help reading the article and rolling your eyes at the wife's stupidity for not knowing what was going on right under her nose. I'm not that wife. I'm not that stupid. I feel confident that I would know if Robert was having an affair.

I doubt he could say the same about me, however. Ever since June was first diagnosed with cancer six years ago, Robert's become increasingly insular and uninterested in what's going on around him. It's as if he can't trust the real world anymore, so he's withdrawn into a realm of binary numbers instead; a virtual reality where no surprises exist, where there's no uncertainty, and where there are no rugs that can be yanked from beneath his feet.

He spends his time working on his world-building app for kids; a world, I like to joke, in which he gets to play both architect and God. He's so involved in it that I could have swinging-from-the-chandelier sex with Javier the gardener right outside his study door and he wouldn't notice. Not that I would. Javier is about sixty and has hands like antique shovels.

My phone buzzes in my bag. I pull it out. It's June. I answer it, feeling the usual gnawing anxiety I always feel whenever I think of her. 'Hey sweetie,' I say.

'Mom,' June blurts. 'I'm sick.'

'Oh no, what's up?' I ask, immediately looking around and signaling the waiter for the check.

'I feel like I'm coming down with something. I've got a headache and I think a fever.'

Laurie reappears, weaving her way through the tables towards me. She waves at the waiter, holding up an index finger. One more martini. Damn.

'Did you try your dad?' I ask.

'He's not answering,' June says, and I can hear the sigh in her voice.

Anger flares inside me. I bet he's at home with his phone switched off, sitting in front of his computer. It's always the same with him. Laurie's had to drive me to the hospital both times I've gone into labor.

'OK, I'm on my way,' I tell June, just as Laurie sits down opposite me. She frowns at me questioningly. *June*, I mouth, pointing at the phone.

'Thanks, Mom,' June says, hanging up.

'She's not feeling well,' I tell Laurie. 'I said I'd pick her up from her sleepover.'

Laurie gives me a smile that fails to hide her disappointment. I slip my credit card to the waiter, hoping that Laurie's too drunk to notice.

'I'm sorry,' I tell Laurie as I slide off my stool. 'It's really bad timing. How about we pick this up tomorrow? Brunch?'

'I've got to prep for work tomorrow,' Laurie slurs. I forgot. She's a teacher and spends most Sundays preparing for the week ahead. 'Work,' she adds, grabbing her bag off the back of her chair, 'that thing some of us don't have the luxury of avoiding.'

I sign the credit card slip and take the receipt, glancing at Laurie as I do and trying to shake off the jibe, which I put down to her being drunk. I link my arm through hers and lead her out the back to the parking lot.

'I think I need to eat something,' she announces, resting a hand on her stomach and swallowing queasily. 'Do you have to pick up June right now? Can we get a bite to eat first?'

I shake my head. 'I can't, I'm sorry.'

Laurie's lips purse as if someone is pulling a drawstring bag shut. I know she thinks that all I do is go running whenever the kids call, but I can't help it, especially not where June's concerned. It irks me that she's even making a point about it. I fish out my car key. 'Come on, I'll drop you home.'

Reluctantly, Laurie gets in the passenger side, and I spy her surreptitiously eyeing up the interior. The car's brand new and still has that chemical smell to it – a smell that Robert joked made his eyes water even more than the price of the car. When I press the button to turn on the engine and the dash lights up like a space ship, I notice Laurie's raised eyebrows. I cringe, waiting for a comment. She doesn't say anything though, so I put the car in drive and pull quickly onto the street.

Laurie flips the visor down and looks at herself in the mirror, grumbling under her breath at her reflection and swiping at her smudged lipstick.

'Thanks for telling me I look like a two-bit hooker,' she jokes. She flips the visor back up. 'What time is it?'

'Ten thirty.'

'Why don't you come back to mine?' she says. 'Bring June too. We can order pizza and watch a movie. There's that new Jennifer Aniston one on Netflix.'

I shake my head. 'I think it's best I get her home to bed. She sounded really sick on the phone.' As I say it, though, I catch myself questioning it. Did she sound sick? She may have just got into a fight with Abby and wanted an excuse to leave. She knows she can pull the sick card any time with me and I'll drop everything. Maybe Laurie was right to give me that tight-mouthed look a moment ago.

We drive for a few minutes in silence until I pull up outside Laurie's house, a small craftsman bungalow in the east end of town. The lights aren't on and Dave's car isn't in the drive. Laurie frowns. 'Where is he? He said he'd be home.'

'Maybe he's working late.'

Laurie doesn't answer me. She just gets out the car, pulling her phone from her bag.

'Call me tomorrow,' I shout after her. 'Let's go for a hike or something. If you're not too busy,' I add, remembering she has to work.

Laurie's not listening. She's dialing a number – probably Dave's. 'Good night,' she says to me, slamming the car door and hurrying up the path.

On a whim I pull a U-turn and decide to drive by the tasting room on my way to pick up June. I'm hoping I'll spot Dave through the window sitting at the till, tallying receipts.

But the lights are off, the closed sign hanging crooked on the back of the door. It doesn't mean anything, I tell myself firmly. There's no point in jumping to conclusions – that's what the doctors used to tell us after June's diagnosis. We need all the facts before we can determine the correct path of action.

3

June must have been waiting for me, looking out the window, because I haven't even put the car in park before the front door flies open and out she runs, head down, bag flung over her shoulder. She's wearing a pair of gym shorts with Hannah's NYU hoodie over the top. Abby – a friend of June's since pre-school days – is leaning, scowling, against the door-post. I wave at her and smile. She gives me a perfunctory wave back before slamming the door shut. Charming.

June gets into the passenger seat, slumping low, and grunts hello at me. At least I think it's *Hello*. It could also be *Drive*. I step on the gas. Sometimes I feel like all I am is a glorified chauffeur, but I don't say anything. She's twelve, I remind myself. I need to make the most of it. She'll be gone before we know it, flying the nest just like Hannah did before her. And then what?

Her hood is pulled up and she turns away from me to stare out the window. I know that I have to let her come to me, not try to push, but the silence eventually gets to me and I cave. 'How are you feeling?' I ask.

'I'm fine,' she mutters. I catch a glimpse of her face as she says it – that beautiful, heart-shaped face that I used to spend hours staring at as she slept on, oblivious, webbed by tubes and wires. She looks pale, her eyes red-rimmed. *Is* she sick? That familiar sense of dread creeps through me and I struggle to shake it off. *Don't go there, Ava.*

15

'You have an OK time with Abby?' I ask.

She grunts again and I sigh. She used to be so eloquent that adults would often mistake her for being older than she was. It was all that time around doctors and hospitals. I'm not sure switching her to a private school was worthwhile; her linguistic skills seem to have regressed to pre-verbal days.

We could have bought a Caribbean island with the money we've spent on June's education, not to mention the cash we've bled to pay for Hannah's college tuition. But how can I resent it? They're both happy, healthy, bright, going places. I want their lives to be glorious. I want them to achieve more than I ever did, to be successful and fulfilled and to reach their potential in ways that I was never able to.

As we head up the winding road to our house, I glance surreptitiously across at June, trying to resist reaching over and laying my hand on her forehead to check her temperature.

She's frowning, her hands working at the cuffs of her hoodie, fraying holes in them. What's going on in that head of hers? I suppose she's just entering that awful early teen phase, and I steel myself, knowing what's coming. Hannah was just the same, though I think I'll take it worse with June because we have a much closer bond than I ever had with Hannah, who was always so aloof as a child, so self-contained and independent, that at times I felt redundant. I used to long for her to be like the other kids at kindergarten refusing to let go of their mothers. She'd push me out the door and march off to her desk without so much as a bye or a backwards glance.

I've often thought that if our family was a circus, I'd be the plate spinner, Hannah would be the ringmaster, Robert would be an illusionist (for his skill at creating invisible worlds that people spend millions of dollars buying unreal real estate in) and June would be the clown. Gene would be the hanger-on who doesn't earn his keep and who has to sleep under the big top at night.

June always made others laugh. Even when she was throwing up what looked like all her internal organs, the ulcers carving craters into her mouth, she could still somehow find a way to crack a joke. She had a book of them, *10,001 Jokes for Kids*, and she'd memorize as many as she could. Every time she saw us looking sad she'd pull one out, and she'd keep pulling them out until we smiled again.

So now, when I see clouds scudding across her face, gathering like an ominous storm front, I worry. I can't help it. Fear entered my life when the children were born but it fused with my DNA when June got sick. Now I live with it constantly. It whispers into my ear most nights, keeping me awake, seeding nightmares that the cancer will come back and this time we won't be so lucky.

'What's black and white and red all over?' I ask.

June rolls her eyes and keeps glaring out the window. 'A newspaper,' she grunts.

O-kay, that didn't work.

Normally June talks ten to the dozen, bombarding me with so much information about her teachers and school and who said what and who did what and who has a crush on who that I often have to get her to slow down. The silence now is disconcerting.

She's had an argument with Abby, I'm guessing, most likely about the choice of movie to watch. Abby's parents – buttoned-up evangelical Christians who preach God's love and forgiveness while campaigning vigorously against transgender bathrooms at the school and regularly posting pro-life propaganda on Facebook – don't allow Abby to watch anything rated over a U. They even pulled the poor girl out of sex-ed class last semester. Later Sam, Abby's mother, called me up in a rage to complain that June had taken it on herself to explain to Abby the ins and outs of how babies are made. You would have thought from her reaction that June had forced Abby to build an altar and worship the devil.

I apologized, of course, and then took June out for ice cream and talked to her about consent, choice and Planned Parenthood, hoping she'd find a way to leak the information to Abby. Because otherwise that girl is very likely going to go the way of Bristol Palin – abstinence spokeswoman and teenage mom.

I glance across at June again. She's pulled back her hood and is still staring out the window, lost in thought, and I realize she's no longer an open book. She's keeping secrets from me. Laurie's words echo loud in my head. *You can never really know anyone completely.*

She's right, isn't she? I reach forwards and turn the heat up in the car. I know that better than anyone.

4

Even after five years of living here I still get a thrill as I pull in through the gates. I used to look up at these houses on the hill when I was a kid and wonder about who lived there and how they could possibly afford it.

Sometimes, when I walk through the rooms at night, I find myself tiptoeing and looking over my shoulder like a burglar. You're supposed to put a stamp on a home but I feel like other than my paintings, which are dotted around the place – more at Robert's insistence than mine – we've failed to do so. It feels too big, too vault-like, too grand. I wanted something more modest but Robert insisted nothing but a big house in the hills would do. So I went along with it, even though it meant having to drive into town rather than walking and having to hire a gardener and housekeeper as the grounds were too expansive and the house too big to take care of on my own.

After all those years of living hand to mouth, relying on my parents a lot of the time to bail us out, when Robert's business finally hit the big time he wanted to make a statement, show the world he'd made a success of himself at last. And I get that, I do, and it's hard not to fall in love with the place. It's a beautiful old ranch house on one hundred acres, with the Topa Topa mountains rising up majestically behind us and the valley tumbling away below.

As soon as I pull into the garage, June jumps out of the car and runs through the side door into the house. I follow her, frowning at the thumping music coming from overhead. Gene's home. Of course he's home. He's always home. He's like an obnoxious foot wart that we've tried treating but which refuses to go away, so now, utterly defeated, we just hope it will one day vanish of its own accord. Though there are times I wish we could squirt liquid nitrogen on him and watch him fizz.

I know plenty of twenty-six-year-olds live with their parents these days, given the state of the economy and the outrageous size of college debt, but Gene has no college debt (he also has no college degree either, having dropped out in his sophomore year) and the state of the economy doesn't really affect him, since Robert and I provide him with free bed and board.

If Gene were my son he would not be living over the garage. He would be a successful graduate, in his first, maybe second job by now, living in his own house and dating someone normal, not one of the many dubious-looking, sleeve-tattooed females who shuttle through his apartment on a high-speed conveyor belt.

Gene isn't my son though. He's Robert's son from his first marriage. He was eighteen months old when I first met him and lived with his mother on the other side of the country. He only moved in with us when he was twelve, after his mom married some guy she met at the bar where she worked and who, it turned out, hated children. She drove across the country and dumped him on our doorstep unannounced. She said she'd be back for him but never returned.

Gene barely scraped through high school, not because he isn't bright, because he is – he takes after his father in both brains and looks – but because he kept skipping class to hang out at the skateboard park or to go surfing. I think his mother abandoning him was a major factor in his teenage rebellion.

But that was also around the time that June got sick, so we weren't paying that much attention to his attendance, or to anything to be honest, except for cancer treatments and prognoses. I think the guilt about that and about leaving Gene with his mother for the best part of his childhood is why Robert's so soft on him now.

Gene moved back in with us after he flunked out of college. When we argued with him he told us college educations were worthless. *Hell, look at Ava* were his exact words – something to which I frustratingly had no comeback. He moved into the apartment we had converted over the garage and for a time he just stayed in all day watching TV, apparently on a mission to win the world record for most amount of weed to ever be consumed by a human being in one sitting.

Given how much he smoked – the garage resembled a giant hot box most days – it was amazing he was even sentient. When Robert and I sat him down to talk about his habit and how it might be contributing to his lack of ambition, he pulled out his medical marijuana certificate, signed by a real MD, and told us he needed it to deal with stress, which, I told them both, was like the Pope claiming he needed a prescription for Viagra. Gene's comeback to that was that the Pope, like most Catholic priests, probably did need a prescription for Viagra. Maybe he should look into a career in improv.

Robert finally gave him an ultimatum. Either he quit smoking and got a job, or moved out, as we were no longer going to fund his drug habit and didn't want June exposed to it. Gene took the ultimatum to heart, or maybe he was just scared he'd end up homeless, because the very next day he got a job working behind the bar at the Bison Lodge in town, and we never again smelled the heady aroma of weed wafting from the apartment.

Maybe he goes somewhere else to smoke, I'm not sure, but he doesn't seem like quite so much of a space cadet as he used to; he's up before ten most mornings, he puts out the trash, cleans the leaves from the pool, takes June to soccer and basketball at the weekends and occasionally wanders into the house with a cake he's baked and flops on the sofa to watch *American Crime* with me.

When he lost his job two weeks ago (he said they were laying people off but I suspect he was fired for being unreliable) I started talking to him about turning his talent for baking into a career as a chef. I thought he'd laugh at me like he usually does when I offer him ideas for a career path that requires getting out of bed before seven each morning, but he actually took the idea seriously. Yesterday he showed me some culinary courses he'd bookmarked on his iPad, so maybe there's light at the end of the tunnel. Maybe he won't still be living with us when he's sixty, although perhaps by then we won't mind so much as we'll likely be senile and grateful for having someone to lift us out of bed, change our diapers and spoon-feed us baby rice.

'Always look for the silver lining,' my dad used to say, and that's what I'm trying to do.

As I head inside the house behind June I think I hear a raised voice over the top of Gene's music. I stop. Nothing. Maybe the TV is on. It better not be *American Crime* – he promised we'd watch the last episode together.

In the kitchen, June's left the milk on the side and the refrigerator door ajar. I put the milk away and wipe up a spill, set the alarm by the back door, and then wander over to the other side of the house to Robert's study. The door is shut. I press my ear to it. Not a peep. Silently, I try the handle. It's locked. That's unusual. I try to ignore the first thought that flashes into my mind, which is that he's in there watching porn. I knock and call his name. There's the sound of a filing cabinet slamming shut with the force of a guillotine, and then I hear Robert clearing his throat before the door jerks open.

'You're back,' he says, surprised.

He seems flustered and his shirt is half hanging out of his pants. I frown at him and try glancing over his shoulder to see if I can see his computer, but he's angled the screen away from the door. 'I had to pick up June, she wasn't feeling well,' I say, eyeing him with suspicion.

'June's home?' Robert asks, looking mildly alarmed.

'Yes, she's gone up to bed. She's fine, I think, don't worry.'

Robert rubs the bridge of his nose and glances at his watch. He hasn't shaved and I notice the flecks of white in his beard now far outnumber the black, but it only makes him look more handsome. Men have it so much easier than women, I think, making a mental note to make an appointment with my hairdresser.

'Did you eat already?' I ask, hoping to salvage something of this evening.

He nods.

'Do you want to come to bed?'

Robert shakes his head. 'No, no,' he says, distracted. 'I have some things to finish off.'

I really hope he's not being literal, but he doesn't look like a man caught with his pants down. He looks more like a man in the final moves of a challenging chess match.

'Oh,' I say, trying not to sound disappointed, 'OK.' I kiss him on the cheek. 'Well, goodnight then. I'm sorry again about our plans. Maybe we can do it tomorrow night?'

'Maybe,' Robert says, hurriedly closing the door. A hissing voice in my head tells me he's just not that into me anymore, but I try to ignore it.

I cross the living room and draw the blinds. As I'm doing that I see someone rushing down the stairs from Gene's apartment. Whoever it is is dressed all in black and is wearing a dark sweater with a hood covering their face. Adrenaline shoots through me before I realize that it's not a burglar at all. It's Gene. I'm just not used to seeing him move that fast. And I'm not used to seeing him wearing actual clothes. He usually lounges around the house in his ratty old college athletic shorts and a pair of Adidas sandals with tube socks – a fashion look that doesn't seem to deter the girls.

I watch him jog right past the carport where his Highlander is parked and take off down the drive, sticking to the gloomy shadows cast by the trees. He glances over his shoulder up at the house and I instinctively edge behind the blinds. Where is he going at this time of night and why isn't he taking his car? We're three miles out of town so it's a little odd to go anywhere on foot.

Halfway down the drive, just where the road curves and disappears into the orange grove, a set of headlights flash on, giving me a start. They briefly douse Gene in a halo of light and I watch him dart to the passenger side and jump in. The car – a dark SUV – takes off down the drive and I lose sight of it. Who was that? And what's with all the cloak and dagger?

I go and pour a large glass of Pinot, a gift from our neighbor's private vineyard, and carry it with me upstairs, pausing to straighten a painting in the hallway (my wedding present to Robert – a sketch I'd drawn from memory of him on our first fateful meeting). I stop again on the landing outside June's room. The wall here is covered in photographs that I've taken over the years. There's a black and white one of Robert and me on our wedding day. I look like a child bride, albeit one glowing with happiness, and Robert looks as dashing as a movie star. There's another of me – taken a few months later, visibly pregnant with Hannah – with my arm around a smiling, chubby-faced Gene. I was younger than Hannah is now, just nineteen, and every time I pass that photo I feel a pang of something – an ache – for the girl I was. I was so stupidly young. If Hannah got pregnant now, I'd strangle her.

I knock on June's door and turn the handle but I'm stopped by her shouting from the other side for me to hold on. I hear her scrambling around, opening and slamming a drawer, and a few seconds pass before she finally wrenches the door open. She's pulling her robe on and she's a little out of breath. 'Yeah?' she asks, using her body to try and block my view of her room.

What is with my family tonight? Everyone has secrets all of a sudden.

'I just wanted to see how you were feeling,' I say. Her room is a mess – clothes strewn all about, her desk overflowing with books and drawings, the hamster cage looking like it hasn't been cleaned in weeks. I think about speaking out, at least about animal welfare, but as usual I bite my tongue.

'I'm fine. Better,' she adds quickly.

I give her a long, hard stare and place my hand on her forehead. She jerks out of my way. 'Mom,' she moans. 'I'm fine, honestly. It's just a headache. I took an Advil. You don't have to worry about me all the time.'

'It's my job to worry about you,' I say, kissing her on the top of her head.

She doesn't pull away this time, but lets me hug her. 'I love you,' I tell her.

'I know,' she sighs, 'I love you too.' There's a pause and I smile to myself. Here it comes.

'Mom?'

'Mmmm?'

'Should you always tell the truth?'

'Of course,' I say.

'Well, what about that time you told Dad you loved the earrings he bought you for Christmas?'

'I do love them.'

'Then why do you never wear them?'

I hesitate.

'See!' June pounces. 'You just lied. You said you liked them and you don't.'

Hmmm. She's got me there. They're great big diamond drop earrings and when I wear them they make me feel like a chandelier.

'And remember when you told me that I was only a little bit sick and there was nothing to worry about?'

I make a sound in the back of my throat, knowing where this is going.

'And it turned out I had cancer and was probably going to die?'

'You didn't, though, did you?'

'But you and Dad didn't tell me the truth.'

'No, we wanted to protect you. And how would it have helped you knowing?' I kiss her forehead. 'There are times when telling the truth isn't always the right thing to do.'

She's silent for a bit. 'But how do you know when it's right and when it's wrong?'

'Do you want to tell me what it is? Did Abby do something?' I know last semester June caught her going through another girl's bag in the locker room at school, something Abby denied when confronted – probably because if she'd admitted it, her parents would have sent her off to the Christian reform school they often threaten her with.

'It doesn't matter,' June mumbles.

'OK,' I say, trying not to pry further. If she wants to tell me she will. 'If you need anything let me know.'

She gives me a smile and I feel a sharp tug on my heart-strings. She's in that beautifully awkward in-between space – half girl, half young woman; long limbed and gangly, with pink-colored braces on her teeth, but her face is losing the softness of childhood and she's starting to fill out her training bra. Maybe that's why she didn't want me to come in while she was getting undressed.

I think about how I used to fear never seeing her grow up and before I can stop them, tears start to well up.

June rolls her eyes at me. 'Mom,' she says, laughing, 'I'm not dying, OK? Good night.' She pushes me out of her room and I go, laughing too.

I didn't want June. When I found out I was pregnant I seriously considered an abortion. Hannah was ten and I'd just got my life back, had finally graduated from college – the oldest in my class at twenty-nine – and had scored my first job working in a museum, helping to run the arts program for school kids. Those two blue lines showed up like little daggers and slashed my dreams to pieces. I didn't tell Robert at first. I wrestled with it on my own, and then with Laurie, even booking an appointment at Planned Parenthood, before I finally told him and he convinced me that we could do it, that we could find a way to manage. But, of course, when it came to it we didn't have the money for childcare and I couldn't go back to work.

I waited five years, until June started kindergarten, and after applying for a dozen jobs I managed to find one working part-time on a terrible salary as an assistant arts educator for the Board of Education. I saw it as an entry position, worked my butt off and within six months was put forward for a promotion. On the day of my interview we found out June had cancer. Clear cell sarcoma of the kidney, to be precise. So that nixed that plan. The only thing I was

27

promoted to was full-time nurse, mother and carer for the next four years – becoming an unpaid expert in the right angle to hold a cardboard bowl when your child is projectile vomiting and what to say to someone who is bald as an egg and asking you how they look.

Not that any of it matters now. I'd give up everything, even my own life, for June – for any of the kids. In a heartbeat.

I wander into our en-suite and turn the shower on, stripping out of my clothes and dumping them in the laundry bin. Once June was in the clear a career didn't seem so important. We didn't need the money by then and it felt like it was far too late, despite what all those articles in women's magazines like to preach. But recently I have to admit I've been feeling the itch, the need for something more than bi-weekly yoga, managing the gardener, mind-numbingly dull PTA meetings, and watching back-to-back episodes of *American Crime*.

I step into the shower and let the hot water sluice over me. Maybe tomorrow I'll take that walk down to the gallery in town with my portfolio. But even thinking about it makes me squirm. Just uttering the word *portfolio*, even in my head, makes me feel like a fraud. No one wants to look at my paintings.

I reach for the shampoo and start washing my hair, and I'm just rinsing out the suds when I hear a scream.

5

My heart slams into my chest like an axe into a block of wood. I turn the shower off and stand there, dripping. Did I imagine it? I strain to hear but there's only a buzzing silence and I'm about to turn the water back on, putting it down to faulty pipes, when another scream tears through the house.

June.

I wrench back the shower door, skidding in my haste. I grab my robe, pulling it on as I race out into the hallway. The door to June's room is wide open, the bedside light on, but she's not there. I'm about to call her name – shout it loud – when I hear another scream from downstairs; a sound so gut-piercing that for a moment I can't reconcile that it's June, that it's even coming from a human, because it sounds like an animal caught in a trap. I follow it, my legs elastic, my heart constricting tighter with every beat.

Adrenaline flooding my body, I'm about to leap down the stairs three at a time when I hear Robert yelling, the words slurred and twisted: 'Leave her alone!'

I freeze instantly, gripping hold of the bannister. From this angle I have a partial view of the kitchen. A man in black is standing in the doorway with his back to me, holding June by the arm. She's sobbing, trying to pull away from him. At first I think it's Robert and wonder what on earth he's doing but then the cogs turn and I realize it's not Robert. It's a stranger. In our house.

What's happening? I don't understand. My brain goes blank, as though a plug has been pulled. But instinct takes over. I want to throw myself down the stairs and hurl myself at this stranger who has my daughter, who's hurting her. I stop when I hear another voice – a second man's – demanding: 'Where's the wife?'

There are two of them. The one holding June looks up towards me and I let out a strangled cry. A monster with razor-sharp teeth stares back at me, blood dripping from his eyes. It takes a second before I realize it's not a face, it's a mask.

Seeing me standing there, frozen at the top of the landing, the man lets go of June and lunges towards the stairs. My brain takes another second to kick in and he's already halfway up before I manage to turn and run towards the bedroom. I can hear him behind me, his boots pounding, and when I glance over my shoulder he's already reached the landing. Not looking where I'm going, I slam into a side table, grunting as pain explodes in my hip, making me stumble like a drunk.

I throw myself, limping, into the bedroom and turn in panic to slam the door but I'm not fast enough. He's there, right behind me, and he throws his whole weight against the door to stop me from shutting it. My bare feet slide on the carpet as I push back but I'm not strong enough. His foot wedges into the gap, prying it open. He's wearing gloves – black leather gloves – and he's holding a gun in his hand. It's the sight of the gun, its blunt nose an inch from my face, that makes me let go and fall backwards.

The door flies open and smashes into the wall, throwing him off balance, and I leap across the bed, towards the phone, thinking that if I can just reach it and dial 911 everything will be OK. But a hand grabs hold of my ankle, jerking me roughly back. He drags me off the bed and I land with a thump on the floor, smashing my head against the frame. I kick out blindly, stunned by pain, and try to crawl away, but the touch of cold metal to the back of my neck paralyzes me.

'Get up,' the man snarls right next to my ear. He's breathing hard, and I'm hit with a blast of musky aftershave or deodorant mixed with the sour, sharp tang of sweat.

Terror grips me. I can't stand, can only cower with my hands over my head.

'Move!' he yells.

He drags me to standing and pushes me ahead of him out of the bedroom. I pad down the hallway, unsteady, blood thundering in my ears. This isn't happening. How can this be happening? Halfway down the stairs I start shivering violently and look down. My robe is hanging wide open. I draw the belt tight and knot it with shaking hands as the man prods me impatiently to keep going.

Everything was so fast a moment ago – but now time has slowed to a viscous crawl. As I make my way down the stairs I feel as if I'm dragging my limbs through quicksand. What are they doing in my house? What do they want? How did they get in? I locked the garage door, didn't I? And I set the alarm.

I try turning towards the man, thinking I'll reason with him. Surely this is some kind of mistake, this can't be real, it's something you read about in the newspapers, something that happens to other people in other places. But he jabs the gun hard into my shoulder blade until I turn back around.

'Please,' I whisper, trying and failing to hold back tears. 'What do you want? Please, just leave us alone.'

He doesn't answer.

In the kitchen I find the second man pointing a gun at Robert's head. He is wearing a mask too. It's a decaying skull.

June is pressed up against the refrigerator, tears streaming down her face, and as soon as she sees me she throws herself on me, clinging tight, her body wracked with sobs. I hold her close, wrapping my arms around her, wishing there was some way of shielding her. My fear turns to anger before morphing back into plain, heart-pounding terror.

The man with his gun trained on Robert is shorter, more wiry, than the other one. He's vibrating with energy, pulsing with it, reminding me of a coyote we once found trapped in my parents' garage. I see him glance over in June's direction, down at her bare legs, and I push her as far behind me as I can, trying to block his view, even as panic crawls up my throat, strangling me.

'You,' the man shouts. 'Come here.' He points at June.

'No!' I shout as June cries out, clinging to me even harder.

'Leave her alone!' Robert yells – though it comes out as a splutter and when I look at him I see that his lip is split and bleeding.

The man responds by pressing the gun between Robert's eyes.

'Come here,' the man repeats. An order, not a request.

June shakes her head and buries her face in my shoulder.

'I won't hurt you,' he says, quieter now, wheedling. 'I promise. I just want you to come with us.' June still doesn't move. 'What's your name?' he asks.

June can't answer him. She's started crying again.

'What's your fucking name?' he yells.

'June,' I hear myself say. 'Her name's June.'

'June,' he says, sounding it out. A shot of pure hatred pumps through me. I want to snatch her name back, rip it out of his mouth, tear it off his tongue.

'OK, June, get over here.' He says get like *git*. 'Your dad's going to open the safe, and you're going to come with us to help.'

Why do they need her to help? Will they threaten to hurt her if Robert doesn't comply?

June shakes her head at them.

'Please June,' I whisper in her ear. I make her look at me, force her away from my shoulder and take her face in my hands. 'Just do what he says. OK?' I can't believe I'm telling her this, making her go to him. What kind of a mother am I? But what else can I do?

June nods at me, her eyes brimming with tears, her bottom lip wobbling, and then she moves to stand beside Robert.

'OK, lead the way,' the man in the skull mask orders. He looks at the other guy, the one in the monster mask, and jerks his head at me – telling him to stay with me here.

I catch Robert's eye as he and June are frog-marched out of the kitchen – he looks terrified, blood painting his face into a mask as frightful as the ones the men are wearing.

After they're gone I stare at the man who's stayed behind. He catches me looking at him and takes two fast steps towards me, bringing his gun up to chest height. I flinch backwards and stare at the floor – at the drops of blood from Robert's lip – and press my own lips together to stop the whimper escaping. What do they want? Are they going to kill us?

The man looks out, checking the hallway, and I glance up and scan the kitchen quickly. There's the phone by the back door – but it's out of reach. The knife block is within reach, just an arm's stretch away. But then my gaze falls on the man's gun. What good would a knife be against a gun?

A scream from June makes my heart leap. The man takes a step out into the hallway to see what's happening and I move towards the knife block. But then I stop short, catching sight of June out in the hall. She's being pushed at gunpoint towards the stairs by the short man in the death mask. She's crying hysterically but the man doesn't care. Where's he taking her? Where's Robert? June trips on the first step and the man hauls her to her feet and shoves her forwards and up the stairs.

'What are you doing?' the other one yells.

'Never you mind,' the shorter one answers, pushing June up the stairs.

Before I know it, my hand is closing around the hilt of a knife. I draw it out. It's the biggest one – the carving knife.

'Where's your bedroom?' I hear the man in the skull mask ask June as they reach the top of the stairs.

June sobs so loudly I can't hear her answer.

I take a step towards the man in the doorway, who still has his back to me. I bring the knife up, about to slash it down and bury it into his back, but he senses me and turns. His arm swings up – the arm holding the gun – just as I drive the knife down with all my strength. He ducks but I manage to strike the top of his arm. The knife slices through his sweater like warm butter and he lets out a cry, dropping his gun. I jab at him once more and he stumbles and falls to his knees.

I slash again, aiming for his face, and he jerks sideways to avoid me, smacking his head into the corner of the wooden island in the center of the kitchen. While he's dazed I bring the knife down like a dagger, aiming for his chest, but he rolls out of the way just in time, kicking out with his legs and slamming me into the cupboard behind. The knife goes flying out of my hands, landing with a crash in the sink.

He reaches for the gun on the floor. Somewhere in the back of my head I register that my hands have landed on the wooden chopping board – the one I bought just a few months ago at the farmer's market and which Robert laughed was heavier than a gravestone.

I'm not sure how I manage to lift it, but I do. It seems to weigh nothing and I swing it like a baseball bat and smash it into the man just as he levels the gun at me, catching him around the back of the head with a dull clunk.

He goes down like a sack of lead and I drop the board with a clatter to the floor beside him. I stand over his body for a few seconds, shaking so hard my teeth rattle. June. Her name punches its way through the fog in my head. I make my way unsteadily to the kitchen door before remembering the gun. I turn around and go back for it and I'm out in the hall, almost at the stairs before I remember Robert. Where is he? What have they done to him? But I don't have time to look. I keep moving forwards, towards the stairs, towards June. There's a phone on the console table by the front door and I grab it and dial 911. A disembodied voice on the other end of the line asks me what my emergency is.

'Help,' I whisper. 'There're people in my house. They've got guns.'

'What's your address?' the woman asks. 'Ma'am?'

I whisper our address as fast as I can and then lay the phone face up on the table.

'The police are on their way,' I hear her say, her voice tinny and far away. 'Can you get somewhere safe until they arrive?'

I don't answer. I'm already halfway up the stairs. The adrenaline hits me in another wave, making me light-headed. I look down at the gun in my hands. It's heavy. Heavier than I thought it would be. An alien object. I don't know how to fire a gun. I slide my finger over the trigger.

At the landing I take a step down the hallway towards June's room. I can't hear anything. Oh God. I whisper a prayer. Please don't let him have touched her. If he's laid a finger on her . . .

I bring the gun up, hold it in both hands like I've seen them do in the movies, my finger clamped over the trigger.

My chest feels hollow, my heart rattling around in it like a loose ball bearing. I take a deep breath and step forwards into June's room.

June is on her knees.

He's standing in front of her.

I don't think. I just aim.

6

Lightning jolts through me and the reverberating shock of it disperses the fog. I can breathe again. Light pours in. Color too. A UFO of dazzling, spinning flashbulbs hovers above me. The voice calling my name is no longer muffled but crystal clear, and a face emerges to go with it – a man, in his thirties or thereabouts, Asian, clean-shaven.

'Ava, can you hear me?' he shouts right by my ear.

Yes, I want to shout back, *I can hear you*, but the words won't come.

'I've got a pulse. Blood pressure seventy over forty,' he calls.

'What have we got here?' A woman's voice this time. Out of breath, clipped, professional. She reminds me of Laurie.

'Female, forty-one years old, brought in by paramedics,' the other doctor tells her.

Are they talking about me? They must be. But how did I get here? *Why* am I here?

'Head wound, possible fractured skull.'

Skull? And like that, I remember. The images pop fast and furious on the back of my eyelids. The gun in his hand. The blast of it. The bullet slamming home. The look on June's face; her eyes widening in horror, her mouth opening in surprise.

'She's losing pressure.'

'What happened?' someone asks.

What did happen? I can only recall snatches. *Remember, Ava, remember!* There were men. Masks. They were wearing masks. The house. They were in the house. They had guns. Robert. Oh God. Robert. What happened to him? Where is he?

'Burglary went wrong,' someone says.

The beeping right by my ear gets louder and more urgent.

'Blood pressure's falling. Possible intercranial bleed.'

'Prep for an MRI,' the doctor shouts. He seems to have lost some of his calm. 'Let's get her sedated.'

No. No. I need to know what's happening. June. I whisper her name, murmur it like a prayer, but no one seems to hear me, they're too busy yelling over the top of me. Where's June? Where's my daughter? And my husband? Where's Robert?

'OK, on three.'

They count down. Three. Two. One. I'm lifted, suspended, dropped and now I'm moving again, flying down a brightly lit corridor, people in blue scrubs flanking me on all sides.

There's a sudden blast of cold air. I twist my head. Paramedics are rushing through a set of doors, pushing a gurney ahead of them. Doctors in white coats descend on them, calling out a barrage of questions. The flashing lights of an ambulance illuminate them in bright Fourth of July colors. I catch a brief glimpse of the body on the gurney, lying on crimson-soaked sheets. A face, pulped and unrecognizable; a mound of glossy, matted dark hair. Then we're gone, away, banging through another set of doors. We stop. There are more UFO lights spinning above me, and faces pulling in and out of focus as though someone is twisting a camera lens. A young woman leans over me, not much older than Hannah. She lays a cool hand on my forehead and gives me a reassuring smile.

And then there's a sharp sting in the back of my hand and the darkness comes again, but this time it's instant, like someone flicking off a light switch.

I'm there one moment and gone the next.

7

DAY 2

The sound of a car reversing. I wish it would stop. Surely you can only reverse for so long before you have to go forwards?

'Ava?'

A beam of light spears my brain. It's an ice-cream headache times a thousand. I wince and try to squeeze my eyes shut but I can't get away from it. Someone is prizing open my eyelids and stabbing my eyeballs with an electrified fork.

'Mrs Walker?'

A brown blur swims in front of me. Slowly he comes into focus. It's the doctor from before. 'Hi,' he says.

'June,' I say. My lips are dry, my throat so sore it feels as if it's been sandpapered, but I force the word out.

'Let's get you some water,' the doctor says, and places a plastic straw between my lips.

Frustrated, I try to push it away, but my arms are heavy and tangled up. Wires holding me down; wires and tubes leading to machines that beep. Not cars reversing. The straw is forced between my lips again and this time I sip. It feels like the only way I'll get an answer, and the water is so good, so cold and pure that it cuts through the fuzziness in my head.

'I'm Dr Warier,' the man says. 'I'm an ICU physician. You had us worried for a moment there.'

'June,' I say again, making sure I enunciate the word properly. 'Robert.'

A shadow passes over his face. He swallows. 'I'm sorry . . .'

Sorry? What does that mean? Oh God. Please not both. Please not either of them. The beeping sound to the left crescendos. Dr Warier is on his feet.

'Ava? Ava?'

He punches a button on the wall behind the bed and suddenly people wearing scrubs rush into the room. Dr Warier starts rattling off some numbers and words I don't understand. Why can't they speak in English?

A man's voice cuts through it all. 'Is everything OK? Can we speak to her?' It's a voice I recognize. A man's voice. Not Robert's.

'Sir, if you could just leave the room,' someone says to him.

Darkness starts to blot the edges of my vision. A shadow looms over me.

'Ava.'

I'm falling backwards, slipping off the deck of a ship into icy waters below, nothing to grip on to. I don't even try.

'Ava?'

Gone.

8

'Ava.'

Nate? I wake, confused. Where am I? I turn my head. Robert is sitting in the hospital chair beside my bed. His face is puffy and shiny, like an overripe eggplant that's on the verge of splitting its skin. One eye bulges obscenely as though an egg has been laid beneath the lid.

'Oh God,' he says the moment he sees my eyes flicker open. 'I thought I'd lost you.'

'What happened?' I ask.

'You were hit around the head. You lost a lot of blood and they were worried about the possibility of a cranial bleed, but it's OK. You're going to be OK. How are you feeling?'

I groan. It hurts to open my eyes. My head pounds. I try to remember what happened. My hand creeps upwards to the back of my head where I feel a strange tingling and tightness on the scalp right where the painful throbbing is worst. My fingers brush a bandage of some kind, about an inch behind my ear.

Robert snatches my hand away. 'Don't touch,' he says. 'They had to give you stitches. After the MRI. Do you remember what happened? They think he must have hit you with the barrel of the gun.'

Gun. Everything rushes in as though a dam has been blown, images piling on top of one another, clamoring to be

42

the first I see. The house. The men. Those masks. June walking up the stairs. June on her knees. The man in the skull mask turning to me with the gun in his hand.

It's a silent question. There's no way I can voice it. But he hears it anyway. *Is she alive?*

His one good eye is shining – but not with excitement or happiness. With pain. It's bright with it, alive with it. His hand is squeezing mine so hard the bones crunch. He bows his head. His shoulders shake.

I know what he's going to say before he says it and I don't want to hear it so I turn my head away, wishing I could slip overboard, fall back into the ice-cold water again and this time let it pull me under forever.

June's face in my head. That look in her eyes when she turned and saw me standing in the doorway with the gun. I was going to save her. I didn't. I failed her. It's my fault. I remember the man's gun going off. I remember June's eyes widening and the frown passing over her face, a question forming on her lips that I never got to hear because a red rose was blooming rapidly across her chest.

Pain blindsides me. It comes out of nowhere – a thousand punches landing on my body at once – and a scream builds inside my chest, so immense I think it might rip a hole on its way out.

'She's out of surgery,' I hear Robert say.

I jerk towards him, eyes flying open. What's he saying? She's alive?

'But,' his voice cracks, 'she's critical. The doctors say we just have to wait . . . wait and see . . .' He stares down at our interlinked hands, then up at me, his eyes bloodshot. 'They don't know if she's going to pull through, Ava.' A choked sob erupts out of him and he starts to cry. 'I'm so sorry.'

I lift a hand and stroke the back of his head. *She's alive.* That's all I can think. She's alive. And she's a fighter. We know that. She'll make it through. She has to.

'What about Gene?' I whisper. 'Is Gene OK?'

'He's fine,' Robert says, wiping his nose with the back of his hand. 'He's with June. Hannah's on her way home. Dave and Laurie have gone to pick her up from the airport.'

I swallow, feeling the reverberation through my bones as I recall the thwack of the chopping board as I smashed it into the man's head. Did I kill him?

'Did . . .' I start to ask, then stop. How do you ask that question? Did I kill someone?

'They got away,' Robert says, intuiting what I was about to ask.

I blink and stare at him. What? Panic starts to build – tiny bubbles of it trapped in my bloodstream, making their way to my heart. What does that mean? Are they still out there? They must be. What if they come back? What if . . . 'I need to see June,' I say, trying to swing my legs out of the bed. Robert stops me.

'No, you can't get up.'

'But I have to see her,' I shout. 'I need to see her.'

Robert pushes me back into bed. 'I know. I'll talk to the doctor.'

'What time is it?' I ask, looking around for a clock.

'It's two in the afternoon.'

I blink, trying to put it all together. It must have been around eleven o'clock last night that it happened. I've been unconscious for over twelve hours.

'When can I get out of here?' I ask, struggling to sit up. I can't stay here in this bed while June needs me.

'The doctor said you'd be on your feet in a day or two. But you should try and rest—'

A soft knock makes me jump. The door opens and a man puts his head around it. 'Can I come in?' he asks.

Robert nods and the man enters the room. He's tall, broad-shouldered, with dark hair and startling blue eyes, the color of a summer sky.

'Hi,' he says.

I knew I recognized that voice earlier. My heart stumbles into my mouth. What's he doing here?

'This is the Sheriff,' Robert explains to me. 'He's in charge of the investigation. I'm sorry,' he says, turning to the man, 'I forget your name.'

'Nate. Nate Carmichael,' he answers, not taking his eyes off me.

9

'Nate,' I say, in shock. My voice is a rasp and my heart rate has jumped into the stratosphere, a fact recorded by the beeping machine to my left.

'Ava,' Nate answers.

'You two know each other?' Robert asks, looking between us and frowning.

'Nate and I went to school together,' I explain, feeling the blood rush to my face.

'It's been a while,' Nate says with a warm smile as he walks towards me.

I nod, but actually it hasn't been that long at all and I know he's only saying it to protect me.

'You're in charge of the investigation?' I ask, eyeing his uniform in confusion.

Nate rocks back on his heels and points to the silver star pinned to his shirt. 'Yep. Sheriff's department's got jurisdiction on this one.' His expression turns serious all of a sudden, businesslike. He gestures at a chair and I nod. He pulls it over so he's sitting on the opposite side of the bed to Robert and I'm sandwiched uncomfortably between them.

'I'm sorry to have to do this now,' Nate says, leaning forwards and resting his elbows on his knees, 'but the quicker we can get statements, the greater the chance we have of finding the men who did this to you and your family.' He glances at Robert and I'm probably imagining it but it feels

46

as if there's an atmosphere brewing between them. Does Robert know? I swallow drily at the thought. No, how could he? I'm being paranoid. But, oh dear God, why is Nate the one in charge? Why couldn't it be someone else? Anyone else?

'I've already taken a statement from your husband,' Nate says, 'but I really need to get your version of events too.'

'Of course,' I say, though panic sweeps through me at the thought.

'I'm not sure this is a good time,' Robert interrupts, his voice rising. 'My wife's in a lot of pain. She has a head injury. And our daughter is currently fighting for her life.'

'It's fine,' I interrupt, squeezing Robert's hand. 'I want to help.' I can't just lie here and do nothing. Robert glances down at my hand and then pulls his out from under it.

'Great,' says Nate, who's noticed and is looking between us curiously. 'Thank you. I'll try to keep it short.'

I nod and Nate turns to Robert. 'If you could just step out of the room please, sir.'

'What?' Robert asks.

'We like to take statements with witnesses on their own,' Nate explains. 'It's standard procedure.'

Robert starts to protest but I cut him off. 'It's fine, Robert,' I say, nodding at him. 'Go be with June.'

Reluctantly, Robert gets to his feet. He kisses me on the forehead but I don't miss the glance he throws Nate's way and the suspicious look he gives me before he walks out.

There's a silence after the door bangs shut.

'How are you doing?' Nate asks softly.

Tears spring to my eyes and I try to blink them away, though even blinking feels like an axe chopping through my skull. 'I don't know,' I tell him, because it's the truth. I can't stop worrying about June, thinking about what happened. I look at Nate, jarred by the sight of him sitting by the bed. 'I can't believe you're here. That you're in charge of the investigation.'

'I'm glad I am. I was worried about you—' He breaks off before adding, 'When I heard.' His hand brushes the back of mine. I draw in a sharp breath at the unexpected yet familiar touch. 'I swear to God I'm going to find the people who did this to you.'

My lip trembles and all I can do is nod. He smiles at me reassuringly then withdraws his hand to pull a small notebook and a pencil from his pocket. I feel the loss of his touch keenly. I've missed it. I study his face as he flips pages in his notebook. Things weren't left well between us. Do I need to clear the air with him first? 'It's not going to be a problem, is it?' I ask tentatively. 'I mean, you and me.'

He glances up, a slight frown on his face. 'Don't worry, we're good. Everything's in the past.'

I nod and he lifts his pencil and holds it over the page.

'Can you walk me through the events of last night?' he asks.

My mind goes suddenly blank. Whether it's the blinding terror of being forced to go back over it or because the head injury has knocked my memory, I couldn't say.

'Ava?' Nate says gently. 'There were two men, yes? That's what your husband told us.'

I nod.

'Did you see either of their faces? Can you give a description?'

I shake my head and force myself to concentrate. 'No,' I say, frustrated. 'They were wearing masks.'

'What kind of masks?' he asks, pencil poised.

'Like something from a horror movie. Um, a skull . . . one of them was a skull and the other was . . . a monster or

48

something.' I frown, trying to remember, but they're fragmented images, nothing whole, like a puzzle missing pieces from the center. 'I could . . . I could draw them maybe.'

'OK,' says Nate. 'That would be great.'

'What did they want?' I ask. 'Why us?'

'They wanted what was in the safe, we think. They're usually after jewelry, cash, anything they can turn over fast.'

'But we hardly have any jewelry or cash in the house. The safe is just where we keep important documents.'

Nate nods thoughtfully and jots something down. 'Look, let's go back to the beginning. Tell me about your evening. Had you been out?'

I nod. 'Yes. I was at The Oak – the bar in town – with my friend Laurie.'

'And was this something you'd arranged in advance?'

'Um, no, Robert and I had plans that night. He was going to take me out for dinner, but Laurie called me around five and asked if we could meet, so I cancelled with Robert.'

Nate looks up. 'Was he annoyed about that?'

I shake my head. 'You'd have to ask him. He was busy with work anyway.' I look away, hearing the bitter note in my voice.

'Why did Laurie want to meet with you?'

'She wanted to talk to me about some stuff.'

'Stuff?' Nate asks.

'Relationship stuff,' I say, frowning at him. Why is what I talked to Laurie about important? It won't help catch these men and I feel uncomfortable breaking a confidence. Then I realize with a shock that there is no privacy anymore. Those men invaded our home. Now the police are going to invade our lives.

'And Laurie and Dave – they've been friends of yours a long time?' Nate presses.

I nod. 'Why are you asking?'

'Just some background,' Nate says, smiling at me. 'How long have you known them?'

'Well,' I say, thinking. 'I've known Laurie since I moved back here twenty years ago, and Dave I've known for around the same amount of time. He was a friend of Robert's.'

'Was?' says Nate, latching on to the past tense like a terrier onto a bone.

'Is,' I correct myself. 'They were in business together, a while back.'

'Were?'

'Yes, years ago, when Robert was just starting out developing apps. Dave has a degree in business, you see. But they made no money and so Dave went off and got a real job, you know, one that paid the bills and covered his health insurance.'

'And then Robert, your husband, got very successful. Made a lot of money.' There's a pause. Nate knows this, of course. Everyone knows this. Robert's been profiled in the *Washington Post* and *Wired*, as well as in all the local newspapers. He gave a TED talk a few months ago too.

'You can't think Dave has anything to do with this,' I say. 'That's absurd.'

'I didn't say that,' Nate answers. 'I'm just making the point that you and your husband are well off. That probably made you a target.'

Damn TED talk. Yes, we're rich, I want to say to Nate, but there are many people richer than us. The bloody Rothschilds have a home here and God knows how many A-list actors. Why did they choose us? All at once the shock of it, the realization of what's happened, that my daughter is lying in another room on life support, hits me with the force of a bullet. I let out a sobbing gasp, which reverberates through my head.

Nate takes my hand and squeezes it. 'It's OK,' he says gently. 'We're going to find these people. I swear to you.'

I stare into his eyes, and he fixes me with a look of such certainty and reassurance that the pain in my head subsides a little and I find myself believing him. Nate waits until I've gotten a hold of myself and then starts up again with the questions. 'What time did you get home?'

I think back. Everything is so fuzzy and unclear. 'I dropped Laurie home, then picked up June . . . About eleven, maybe a few minutes before? I don't know.'

'When you got home were you aware of any cars in the drive or parked on the street, or anyone following you?'

'No, not then,' I say, shaking my head, 'but later . . . yes, there was a car in the drive. Gene . . .' I stop. I don't want to get Gene into trouble.

Too late. 'Go on,' Nate presses.

'Well, just that I was closing the blinds . . .'

'Where? In the living room?'

'Yes. I saw Gene leaving his apartment. It's over the garage.'

'What time would this have been? Do you recall?'

'I don't know, a few minutes after I got back. Maybe just after eleven? I saw him get into a car that was parked halfway down the drive.'

Nate's pencil stops scratching and he looks at me. 'The car didn't pull up to the house?'

I shake my head.

'And did you get a look at the car? Make? Model? Color?'

I shake my head again. 'It was too dark. I think it was an SUV but I couldn't swear on it. Why don't you just ask him? I'm sure he'll tell you.'

'I've spoken to him already. He didn't mention it but I'll check with him again.' He looks back down at his pad and underlines something.

Why didn't Gene tell him he went out?

'So, Gene left the property,' Nate goes on, 'and you don't know where he was going and you didn't see him return?'

'No, but I wasn't watching out for him. He lives his own life. Comes and goes as he pleases. I went upstairs and took a shower.'

'And you were in the shower when you heard the break-in?'

I nod. A shudder runs up my spine and I have to close my eyes to stop the room from spinning. June's scream echoes around my skull and the pain is so great, for a moment I think my head is going to explode.

'Ava?'

I'm pulled back into the present by Nate's hand on top of mine. 'Are you OK?' he asks me. I open my eyes and I nod, an action I instantly regret.

'Are you sure?' Nate asks. 'Do you want to take a break?'

I shake my head, careful to keep my movements to a minimum, the pain settling to a low thrum. I just want this over with.

He lifts his hand and once again my body betrays me by pining for his touch. 'OK, so what happened next?' he asks. 'Do you remember?'

I start to tell him and as I do I can feel my heart beginning to race, adrenaline piston-pumping into my system. As I describe every detail it's as if I'm there, reliving it all over again. I can feel the bump as I fly into the side table, the vice-like grip of his hand around my ankle as he drags me across the bed. The bruises on my body start to throb.

When I finish, Nate waits a beat then asks, 'Is there anything else? Can you remember what they were wearing?'

I try to picture the men but it's a blur. 'Just black. All black.'

I watch Nate write that down.

'The first one was about five foot ten or eleven maybe.

Shorter than you. Medium build.' I try to remember the details but they're all fuzzy and indistinct. 'The other one was smaller – maybe five eight or five nine? He was the one who took June upstairs.'

'Why did he take her upstairs?' Nate asks, suddenly alert.

I close my eyes and try to remember. The pictures are so out of focus. 'He . . . um . . .' My heart pounds. 'I . . .' The pain in my head crescendos and I fall back onto the pillow, squeezing my eyes shut.

'OK,' Nate interrupts gently. 'It's OK.' He waits a minute, until I've opened my eyes again. 'Let's go back. Did you hear either of them speak at all?'

'Yes.'

'Can you tell me anything about the way they spoke? What did they say? Did they have accents?'

'The taller one he didn't really say much. I don't know. He just sounded normal.'

Nate looks frustrated. 'Could you tell if he was white? Hispanic? Black?'

I shake my head. 'No. I'm sorry.' I feel like I'm failing a test somehow. Why couldn't I have remembered more? Is it the head injury? Has it affected my memory?

'And the other one?'

'He spoke more.' *What's your fucking name? Which way's your bedroom?*

'Ava?' Nate presses.

'Um . . . he sounded maybe, I don't know, southern? There was a kind of twang to his voice but it was hard to tell, because of the mask. It was muffled.'

Nate nods. 'You're doing great. This is all really helpful.' I look at him and he smiles encouragingly. Our eyes stay locked for a while before he drags his gaze back to his notebook. 'OK,' he says, flipping back through the pages.

'You said he had a gun. Do you remember what the gun looked like?'

I shake my head. 'I'm sorry. I don't know anything about guns. It was a handgun, small – I guess.' I glance at the gun holstered on Nate's waist. 'A little like that one,' I say, pointing.

'Like this?' he says, taking the gun out of its holster and showing it to me.

I cringe back against the headboard. Oh God. Just seeing a gun again makes my hands start to shake. Nate sees my reaction and quickly reholsters the weapon.

'I think so. I can't really remember though.'

'And when you got to the kitchen, Robert was already there with June?'

I nod. 'The other one, he was holding a gun to Robert's head and he . . .' I struggle to remember the order of it. 'June was crying. And . . . and he, um, he made her come over to him and then he said that they were going to go and open the safe.'

'Were those his exact words?' Nate asks.

'I . . . I think so. I don't remember. It was all so fast. He told her to lead the way.'

'So the shorter one took Robert and June to the study? To open the safe?'

I nod.

'And you were left in the kitchen alone with the other gunman?'

'Yes.'

'How long were they gone for?'

'I don't know. It felt like forever but maybe a couple of minutes? Then I saw the short one with June, pushing her towards the stairs.'

'Why were they going upstairs, do you know?'

I can't suck enough air into my lungs and my vision starts misting.

'Where was Robert at this time?'

I shake my head. 'I don't know. I didn't see him. His study?'

I look at Nate hoping he can tell me where Robert was. Until now I've not given it any thought. Nate holds my gaze for a moment.

'He was beaten, knocked out.'

Poor Robert. That at least explains the bruises on his face.

'What did you do next, Ava?' Nate presses.

'I grabbed a knife – a carving knife – from the block and . . . the man had his back to me and I . . .'

Nate looks up at that. 'Did you stab him?'

'I think so.'

'Where?'

'Here,' I place my hand on my shoulder to show where I sliced him.

Nate nods and makes a note.

'We fought. And I grabbed hold of the cutting board on the side. It's wooden. And I hit him with it.'

Nate looks up through his lashes at me and there's a trace of a smirk on his lips. 'That must have hurt.'

'I thought maybe I'd killed him.'

There's a part of me that feels relief that I didn't kill him but there's another part of me – a bigger part of me – that feels disappointed.

'Ava?'

I look up, startled. Nate's watching me carefully and it strikes me again how surreal it is that he's here but at the same time how glad I am, even after everything. 'What happened next?' he asks.

'I took the gun, *his* gun, and I went upstairs.'

'Into June's bedroom?'

I nod.

'And then what happened?' I hear Nate ask.

The room turns to static and the hammering in my head gets louder and louder. Everything turns black at the edges, my vision shimmers.

'Ava?'

'I . . .'

'Did you fire the gun?' Nate asks.

'It was so fast. He shot June. And then . . . and then I don't know what happened . . . maybe the man from the kitchen came up behind me and hit me.' The static roars to life in my ears, obliterating everything. 'I don't remember anything after that.' As if on cue the pain in my head ratchets up three notches and I hunch over, squeezing my eyes shut. The tears leak out.

'It's OK.' Nate is on his feet, standing beside me, and I'm suddenly sobbing against him, and he's holding me, his arm around my shoulders. 'It's OK,' he whispers, one hand stroking the back of my neck. The tears won't stop and Nate's other arm wraps around me, strong and reassuring and protective. He's soothing me, saying my name, and I cling to him like he's a life raft. I'm so glad it's him here, even though I know I shouldn't be.

'Excuse me, Sir?'

Nate steps backwards, away from the bed, and I glance towards the door as I wipe my eyes. There's a police officer standing there. He glances my way and gives me an apologetic smile. I swipe my hand over my face, feeling hot with embarrassment.

'Sorry to interrupt but I just had a call from ballistics.'

Nate nods. 'I've got to go,' he tells me. 'But thanks for this.' He waves his notebook at me.

I nod at him.

'I'll come back later. In the meantime, get some rest.'

I watch him head to the door. 'Nate,' I call just as he's about to disappear.

He turns.

'What if they come back?' I ask.

10

June looks so tiny lying in her hospital bed that I'm immediately thrown back to the days when we lived on the cancer ward with her. The rage inside me swells as I sit by her side in my wheelchair and hold her hand, feeling as impotent as I did back then, and just as angry – maybe angrier because I have a focus for my anger this time, I'm not just raging at a bunch of out-of-control cells.

'June,' I whisper over the slow, steady beeping of the machines keeping her alive. 'It's Mom.' I fall silent. I don't know what else to say. What is there to say? Can she even hear me?

They said that the first twenty-four hours are critical and it's been almost twenty and so far there's no change.

Please God, I say as I stroke June's hair. It must be the thousandth time I've thought the words in the last hour. She beat the odds before. She'll beat them again. I have to believe that. But looking at her lying there, lifeless and pale as a corpse, her chest rising and falling shallowly as a machine forces air into her lungs, I can't help but feel like the game is already up, that every breath is a countdown.

I turn and catch a glimpse of the police officer standing guard outside our door. When Nate came back an hour ago to finish our interview, I asked him again about the men returning to finish the job. He reassured me that we had nothing to worry about, but that he'd also arranged a police guard – two seemingly contradictory statements that I didn't call him on because I was afraid to. He must think there's a risk and that terrifies me.

The door suddenly flies open.

'Mom!'

Hannah bursts into the room. She's wearing jeans and an oversized sweater and carrying a small backpack over her shoulder. I wince as she hugs me and she pulls back, face aghast, at the sight of my IV and bandaged head.

'I'm OK,' I tell her, reaching up to stroke her face. 'I'm OK.'

She turns to June and her face pales. 'When will she wake up?' Hannah asks, staring down at her sister.

'Soon,' I hear myself answer.

She sits down on the other side of the bed from me. Her hair – lighter brown than June's, and wavy like mine – is tied up in a messy ponytail and she looks exhausted, circles ringing her cornflower-blue eyes, her face pale and stark without her usual lashings of makeup. She strokes the dyed blue ends of June's hair, her bottom lip starting to tremble.

'She dyed her hair blue,' she stammers, tears spilling down her cheeks.

My throat constricts, tears welling in my own eyes. 'Did Laurie and Dave pick you up?' I ask, trying to turn the focus from June because it's too much.

Hannah nods. 'Laurie called me this morning. I got the first flight I could.'

The door opens again. This time it's Gene, looking exhausted, with a day's worth of stubble, still wearing the clothes I saw him in last night. He's carrying a cup of coffee. 'Hey,' he says when he sees Hannah.

He puts the coffee down on a side table and shuffles towards her, but she doesn't get up and so his intended hug becomes a pat on her shoulder. He frowns and backs away, picking up his coffee and coming to stand behind me.

I would have thought the animosity between them might have softened given the circumstances but it's still there, going strong. Hannah has had an issue with Gene ever since he moved into the apartment over the garage, since before that really. She's had it out with me on more than one occasion – she thinks he's spoiled and gets away with everything. She's the one who got a 4.0 grade point average, she's the one who scored an academic scholarship, she's the one who's worked the hardest, so why is Gene the one who gets rewarded all the time?

It's classic jealousy between siblings and I get her point of view. But it's not a competition. We bought her a car. We pay for the tuition that isn't covered by her scholarship as well as her accommodation, and NYU is one of the most expensive colleges in the country. She's not exactly getting a bum deal.

'Where's your dad?' I ask Gene.

'He's in with the insurance person – I think there's a problem with the paperwork.'

I sigh. For God's sake. We were victims of a burglary. Our daughter is in a coma fighting for her life. And they're expecting us to fill out forms? The whole healthcare system in this country is insane.

'I'm telling you, we should have moved to Canada years ago,' Gene says.

It's something we joke about a lot – given the backward state of healthcare and the rising number of gun-toting crazy people in the US.

'Why don't you move there?' Hannah asks. 'Oh, that's right, you wouldn't be able to live rent free if you did.'

'You gave a statement to the police?' I ask Gene, trying to change the subject.

He glances my way, distracted. 'To that Sheriff guy.'

'Where were you last night?' I ask, trying to keep my tone neutral.

'I went out with a friend.' He swallows hard as he stares at June.

'What friend?'

Gene shakes his head. 'No one you know,' he mumbles, then his eyes fill with tears. 'I'm sorry. I should have been home. I could have . . .'

'I'm glad you weren't,' I say, taking his hand, and hearing Hannah sigh loudly in the background. She's got it into her head that Gene's my favorite, which is frankly ridiculous. I don't have favorites. That should be clear to all of them.

Gene brushes his hand over his face to force back the tears.

'I'm going to find Dad,' Hannah says, getting up and rushing out of the room, letting the door bang shut angrily behind her. Gene takes her empty chair and slides his hand into June's and we sit there in silence, locked in our own thoughts.

The doctor, a woman a couple of years younger than me, comes in a few minutes later and runs some tests on June. I wait, biting my tongue, hoping that she'll turn to me smiling and tell me that June is showing signs of improvement, but when she does finish writing up her notes, her expression is grim.

'Is there any change?' I ask.

She shakes her head. 'I'm afraid not, Mrs Walker. We'll let you know the minute there is.'

'She'll be fine,' Gene says to me when the doctor leaves.

I don't answer. It used to infuriate me when people told me that while she was going through chemo and it infuriates me just the same now. He's not clairvoyant. How could he know she's going to be fine?

'You remember the time her hair started to fall out?' Gene asks quietly.

I nod. All her beautiful hair. How can I forget that moment when she screamed at me and I came running, terror making me fly so fast my feet barely touched the ground? We knew, of course, it was a side effect of the chemo. But June hadn't fully understood what would happen to her; how sick she was. Not until then.

'She was so upset,' I whisper, stroking her hair back from her face, remembering how fair and straight it used to be.

'Yeah,' says Gene, smiling.

I smile too. June woke up the next morning and declared she was going to shave all her hair off for charity. Gene and Robert both shaved their heads too, in solidarity with her. I would have done mine as well, but June made me promise I wouldn't because she said I'd look ugly if I did.

She didn't flinch or cry when the clippers got to work and her hair started to drift in clumps to the ground, her lip didn't even tremble – and she was only six years old. I had never felt so proud in my life as I did that day.

'She's going to be fine,' Gene whispers again.

11

A nurse comes to get me a few minutes later to take me back to my room. The doctor wants to check my stitches and make sure I'm healing properly. I try to protest but there's no arguing and Gene says he'll stay with June, which makes me feel better because I can't stand the thought of her being alone, not even for a minute.

I catch Hannah in the hallway outside talking to the Sheriff on duty at the door to the ICU.

Hannah sees me and breaks off her conversation, heading straight over. 'Why are there police on the door?' she demands, a flash of fear in her eyes.

'It's nothing to worry about,' I reassure her. 'It's just a precaution.'

'What for?' she asks. 'Is June in some kind of danger?'

'No, of course not,' I say, though I can tell she's not buying it. 'Where are you staying tonight?' I ask, changing the subject so she can't dwell too much on it.

'I don't know,' Hannah answers. 'Not in the house though.' She shudders at the thought, wrapping her arms around her body.

'It's still a crime scene,' I tell her. 'We can't go home until the police say we can. Why don't you and Gene stay with Laurie and Dave? They spoke to your father and said you could.' *You'll be safe there*, I think, but don't say. Despite Nate's reassurances I can't help but worry that the men will

63

return to the house. It's stupid – I mean, why would they risk it? But still I can't shake the fear. I don't know how I'll ever feel normal again, how I'll ever get rid of the terror gnawing away on my insides.

'What about Dad?' Hannah asks.

'He's going to stay here so someone can be with June.'

Hannah walks me back to my room and waits while the nurse records my blood pressure and the doctor shines a little light in my eyes and checks all my responses.

'How's the pain?' he asks me. 'Still have a headache?'

'It's getting better,' I tell him. It's now just a dull ache interrupted by the occasional savage spear of pain, usually if I move my head too fast.

'The scar won't show. It'll be covered by your hair,' he says and I snort. As if I care about what I look like.

'How much longer do I need to be here?' I say.

'I'd like to keep you in for observation for one more day, just to make sure there are no complications.' He makes a move for the door.

'Oh my God,' Hannah says as he leaves, pointing out the window. 'Have you seen how many news crews there are outside?'

I shuffle to the window and look down. Below us, outside the main entrance to the hospital, are dozens of news crews and vans.

Hannah moves to the bedside table to pick up the television remote and before I can argue she's flicked the TV on. CNN comes up and my jaw drops open as I see a picture of our house. It's film footage shot from a helicopter. You can see Gene's old green Highlander parked in our drive alongside a dozen police cars, yellow tape crisscrossing the front door and the entrance to the garage. People in white jumpsuits, like you see in the movies, are walking in and out of the house and Gene's apartment over the garage. It's on mute but the scrolling headline across the bottom blares: INTERNET ENTREPRENEUR'S DAUGHTER SHOT IN HOME INVASION ... DAUGHTER IN CRITICAL CONDITION.

'Turn it off,' I whisper.

Hannah clicks it off. 'This is insane,' she whispers back.

There's a pause while I wonder how we'll ever go home after this. I can't imagine stepping foot in the house again, let alone spending a night there.

'Do you think they'll catch them?' Hannah asks, looking at me, terrified.

'Yes,' I tell her, wanting to erase the look of fear on her face, but the truth is I don't know.

12

DAY 3

Something wakes me in the early hours of the morning. I burst into consciousness with my heart pounding, sweat pasting my hair to the pillow. Disorientated, I glance around, relaxing a little when I see Robert slumped in a chair fast asleep and the reassuring shadow of the police officer standing on duty outside. But then I become aware of the pain in my head. What did I just dream about? Something niggles at me. There was something I needed to remember.

'Are you OK? Do you need something?' It's Robert. He's awake and on his feet, hovering over me.

'No, I'm OK,' I tell him. 'Why aren't you with June?'

'They needed to run some more tests and I was in the way, so I came to check on you. I must have fallen asleep.'

I reach over and take his hand. In the dim light I can see the bruises on his face are turning a mottled blue and purple color and he has pouchy bags beneath his eyes. 'You look tired,' I say.

He shakes the comment off and reaches over to the light switch, turning it up so he can see to pour a glass of water. The gesture triggers a memory.

'How did they get in?' I ask.

Robert doesn't answer. He busies himself pouring the water.

'Why was the house alarm off?' I press.

'I turned it off,' Robert says quietly, handing me the glass.

'Why?'

'I took the trash out and forgot to reset it.'

I frown. The alarm came with the house and the first time I saw it I laughed. I mean, why was it needed? We live in a place where the crime rate is so low it often wins accolades for being the safest town in southern California. We have a police department of two.

Robert's head is bowed. He's waiting for me to say something but I bite my tongue. I want to yell at him, scream at him. Why did he forget to reset the alarm? None of this would have happened but for one stupid mistake – a mistake that might cost us our daughter. I grind my teeth but I know if I let my anger out, there will be no reining it back in. How can I blame him? I'm looking for a scapegoat, that's all – someone to hurl all my anger and grief at in the absence of a culprit. It was a mistake. He didn't mean to do it. How many times have I left the alarm off or gone to bed and remembered as I climbed under the covers that I hadn't set it but then rolled over and gone to sleep anyway because I was too lazy to go back downstairs?

With a monumental effort I slide my hand over his. He looks up, his eyes filled with tears and relief that I'm not blaming him. We stay like that for a while until he pulls his hand out from under mine, ostensibly to wipe at his nose.

'You and the Sheriff, then?' he asks. He says it lightly but the words feel weighted. 'You went to school together?'

'Mmm,' I say, my heart rate accelerating, wondering how much I should admit to, and why Robert's chosen now to bring it up. Does he know something? I need to stay calm, monitor my reaction and choose my words carefully.

'Didn't you used to date him in high school?' Robert asks. How does he know? My surprise must show in my face.

'He told me,' Robert says.

I stare at him astonished. Nate told him? Why?

'He did?' I say. 'It was only for a short time.'

'You haven't seen him since school then?'

'God no,' I say quickly, probably too quickly. I feign sleepiness, wanting to put a stop to the conversation. 'Can you go and check on June?' I add hastily. 'I don't like her being alone. What if something happens and neither of us is there?'

They told me last night that she's through the most critical stage but she still isn't breathing on her own. The bullet collapsed her lung and nicked an artery. She lost so much blood before the ambulance arrived that she suffered two cardiac arrests before she made it to the hospital. The paramedic who brought her in came to see me earlier and told me it's a miracle she's even alive.

Robert gets up slowly and makes his way over to the door and for the first time ever I see him as old; someone's stooped-over grandfather, not the young, dashing man I fell in love with, not even the greying but distinguished man I kissed goodnight the other day. He's aged a decade or more overnight and it makes something in my heart ache anew.

'Robert,' I call just as he's leaving.

He turns.

'I love you,' I say.

Robert gives me a grim smile that fades as fast as it appears, and then shuffles out of the room. With an effort, I stretch and turn off the light and lie there in the semi-darkness, staring up at the ceiling, my mind racing. Every time I close my eyes the man in the skull mask appears in front of me, leering at me, his tongue lolling out between his tombstone teeth.

13

18 MONTHS AGO

Hannah kicks her feet up onto the dash and I glance over at her long, flawless legs, feeling a pang of loss for the child she once was and for the days I used to carry her everywhere on one hip. There's a hint of envy too, of the smooth perfection of her skin, along with annoyance at how wasted youth is on the young. She has no idea how gorgeous she is, nor how quickly that bloom will fade, hopefully not as fast as mine did . . . but then, hopefully she won't get pregnant as young as I did.

As we crest the mountain and spot the ocean glittering with promise in the distance, my phone rings through the car's audio system, interrupting the thumping godawful music Hannah insisted we listen to. She huffs as some rapper singing about hos being messy gets cut off. The number on the screen says unidentified.

'It's just spam,' Hannah says. 'Don't answer.'

I answer, if only to give my ears some respite from the caterwauling misogyny.

'Hello,' I say.

'Ava?' Gene's voice comes booming through the speakers so loudly I have to spin the volume dial way down.

'Gene, where are you?' I ask. 'Where are you calling from?'

Hannah pulls her legs off the dash and sighs melodramatically, as is her wont when it comes to Gene.

'Um . . . I'm kind of in jail.'

'Jail? What for?' I ask, realizing my foot has come off the gas and I'm veering across the lane, onto the hard shoulder. I right the car.

'What did you do?' Hannah asks, her tone a little too gleeful.

'Could you come and pick me up?' Gene pleads. 'It's the county jail in Ventura.'

'Yes,' I say, already signaling to take the southbound entrance onto the freeway. What the hell has he done? Is it another DUI?

'No,' interrupts Hannah. 'We can't come and get you. We're on our way to Santa Barbara to go shopping.'

'No,' I say over the top of her, 'of course we'll come and get you.'

Hannah gives another loud sigh and crosses her arms over her chest.

'Do I need to call a lawyer?' I ask in a panic as I merge onto the freeway.

'What did you do?' Hannah asks again.

'Were you driving under the influence?' I ask, thinking that's the most likely situation, but the call drops before I get an answer.

'Damn,' I hiss. If he's been caught driving under the influence I am going to kill him.

'I bet you it's drugs,' says Hannah smugly. 'He was probably driving stoned. I mean he's always stoned.'

'He's quit.'

'Yeah, right. It could be sex with a minor.'

'What?' I shriek, glancing at her.

She shrugs. 'Some of those hos he brings back are like, sixteen.'

'What are you talking about?' I say, turning to face her. 'And don't call women hos. You're listening to too much of that music. It's rotting your brain. And what are you saying anyway? Gene doesn't date sixteen-year-olds.'

'You think he bothers to check their IDs before he bones them?'

I open my mouth, then shut it. The truth is, though I try to sneak glimpses at the women who trail in and out of his apartment, it's usually at night. Is Hannah right? Is he sleeping with underage girls?

Shit. Maybe I should call the lawyer. Or at least Robert. I decide to wait until I know the charges, but Hannah's incessant speculation about Gene's crime makes me wonder if that's wise.

By the time I find parking I'm wound so taut with worry that I snap at Hannah to stay in the car. I don't need her endless snarking commentary accompanying me inside. But, of course, she doesn't listen and follows me in.

The deputy behind the bulletproof window in reception tells us to wait and so we do, sitting down on a row of bolted-together plastic chairs, opposite a board papered with Most Wanted and Missing posters. How can so many children be missing? Where do they all go? I turn my attention away from all those sad little faces and glance at Hannah.

She's on her phone, texting. I've no idea who. She's always on her phone, texting, posting, taking selfies. The narcissism of her generation never fails to shock me. June seems to have grown up with a more sensible and objective view of social media, refusing so far to dip her toe into a world she considers superficial and vain.

Hannah is the opposite. She's always been conscious of the way she looks. Even when she was seven years old she had to have the right sneakers, the right hair ties, and the right backpack for school. At fifteen she started her own YouTube channel, giving makeup tutorials, teaching people to apply the perfect cat eye and how to contour. When she went to college she shut it down, obviously realizing that a future as a Kardashian wasn't on the cards. She still posts to Instagram, and I'm secretly quite glad because unlike June, who tells me everything, Hannah has always kept the lid on her private life. Her posts are the only window I have into her life in New York. Recently, though, her Instagram has become less fish pout-y and more Proust-y. She doesn't post selfies so much as obscure quotes about life that veer from the clichéd to the confounding, as though she's pulling them from poorly written fortune cookies. Maybe that's it. Maybe she's being ironic. It's so hard to tell with Hannah. Her beauty hides a brilliant mind, but you'd never know because she disguises it so well.

I pull out my own phone and contemplate calling Robert to tell him about Gene. But he's at June's basketball game and I don't want to take him away. He and June rarely spend time together as it is.

A shadow falls over me as I sit there figuring out what to do, and I look up at the sound of my name.

'Ava?'

There's a man standing in front of me. 'Nate?' I stammer, astonished. I get to my feet unsteadily. Oh my God. Nate Carmichael. It is him. I stare at him in wonder and he stares right back at me, grinning.

'It is you,' he says, his gaze falling the length of me, taking me in. 'You haven't changed at all.'

A rush of blood to my face feels like a menopausal hot flush. 'Neither have you,' I mumble, self-conscious and wishing to God I'd put on more makeup or looked in the mirror before I came in here.

I'm not lying or being polite like he is. He's taller and broader than I remember, that's all, but he's lost none of his rugged athlete's build or good looks. The only other change I can see are the crows' feet scored around his eyes, which suit him far more than they do me. I run a hand through my hair, wishing I'd washed it, and that I'd worn something less frumpy than these old leggings. I flush some more under his scrutiny, aware that I'm at least twenty pounds heavier than I was at eighteen. But Nate shakes his head and smiles at me. 'You look great.'

'Thanks,' I mumble, feeling like I'm still that shy, bookish teenage girl being chatted up by the best-looking boy I'd ever seen. I'd forgotten how his smiles and the piercing blue of his gaze used to launch butterflies in my stomach.

Nate's smile becomes a frown. 'What are you doing here?' he asks.

'What are *you* doing here?' I say at the same time, taking in the uniform he's wearing in a confused daze. Nate's the last person I'd have imagined becoming a Sheriff.

'I work here,' he says, grinning, and revealing a dimple in his right cheek that I'd clean forgotten about. 'I was in Long Beach for ten years, just moved back to Ventura six months ago.'

I nod politely, my eyes automatically flicking to his left hand to check for a wedding ring, before scolding myself for being so damn obvious. There is no ring.

'Of all the places in all the towns . . .' Nate continues. The spark in his eyes triggers something inside me. I'm tongue-tied just looking at him.

'This your daughter?' Nate asks, glancing in Hannah's direction.

I nod, flustered. She's staring up at us both, frowning. 'This is my eldest, Hannah,' I stammer.

Hannah stands up slowly and shakes Nate's hand.

'Nice to meet you,' Nate says. 'You look just like your mother.'

Hannah scowls, clearly not taking it as a compliment. *Thanks, thanks so much.*

'Your mom and I knew each other when we were your age,' Nate explains, his eyes settling back on me in a way that makes my pulse pound loudly in my ears.

'Nate was high school football champion,' I say, trying to pull myself together.

'And your mom was the girl everyone wanted to date,' Nate adds with a smirk.

He's lying about that, trying to pay me a compliment, but my cheeks heat anyway at the flattery.

'And I was the lucky one she said *yes* to,' Nate continues blithely on.

Hannah's jaw drops and she looks at me open-mouthed as a fish before turning her attention back to Nate. 'You guys dated?' she asks, wrinkling her nose at the thought.

'Yep.' Nate is still grinning at me, and I'm thrown back to that heady summer when Nate, a high school football god from neighboring Ventura, took an interest in me – a quiet, insecure girl whose goal in life was to not be noticed. He started talking to me at the library one day between the history and self-help stacks, asked me out for ice cream and became my first boyfriend.

I get a sudden flash of blistering days spent hanging out at the beach, his head resting on my sun-burned stomach, me sketching him as he lay in my backyard hammock snoozing, the first time he ever kissed me, under an oak tree in the park during the July Fourth parade, Nate stripping naked in such a hurry he stumbled against my mother's antique sideboard and broke one of my grandmother's dishes . . .

'How long did you date for?' Hannah asks.

'Not long,' Nate says. 'She dumped my sorry ass when she took off for college.'

I flush bright red and start shifting foot to foot. 'It wasn't like that.'

He cocks an eyebrow at me and laughs. 'Yeah it was, but you were right to. You were going places and back then I was going nowhere.' He notes my awkwardness and gently nudges me with his elbow. 'Don't worry, all's forgiven.'

I cringe some more, remembering the details of our break-up. How I went over to his house the morning of the day I was leaving, how I let him pull me into bed, and how, afterwards, lying there naked in each other's arms, I told him I thought we should have a break. He swung his legs over the bed, stood and walked naked to the door, then opened it for me. He didn't say a word. I gathered up my clothes in silence, tears falling down my cheeks.

'I'm sorry,' I said to him as I scurried past.

'Have fun in New York,' he muttered.

I wonder how long it took him to get over me? Not long, I imagine. Still, I don't want to make him dwell on our break-up.

'So you finished college and then moved back here, huh?'

'Yes,' I nod. 'So, what about you?' I ask quickly, trying to change the subject. 'Do you have any children?'

His face lights up. 'Two. Girls. Twelve and fourteen. I'm divorced so I see them every other weekend. They live in Long Beach with their mom.'

I nod, trying to picture the kind of woman Nate might have married and what might have happened to break them up.

'You?' he asks.

'Oh, um, yes, I'm married.' I hold up my left hand, as though needing to prove it by showing off my worn wedding ring.

'No,' he clarifies. 'I meant, any other kids?'

'Oh, yes, I've got another daughter – June – she's almost eleven. And a stepson, Gene, he's twenty-four.'

I wonder if he already knows some of this about me. It would be easy enough to discover by searching online – there are several articles featuring Robert that mention me, but he wouldn't necessarily have known my married name and perhaps he's never been curious about what happened to me. I would never admit it but every so often I've looked up Nate, but his Facebook profile was always set to private and I didn't want to friend him – it seemed too stalker-ish.

'You're at college?' Nate asks Hannah.

She nods, her back straightening with pride. 'I'm a sophomore,' she says. 'NYU.'

Nate takes that in and I see him frown a little as he does the math on her age. He turns to me and to cut him off before he can ask, I shrug, embarrassed. 'College dropout!' I laugh.

Nate studies me curiously and I realize that he's probably the only person who truly understands how much college meant to me. How much I'd dreamed of New York and being an artist. It's why we broke up. I wonder if he feels smug that it didn't work out. 'I'm sorry,' he says somberly. 'That's a real shame.'

I'm surprised by his reaction. I would have thought he'd have reveled in my downfall, but I suppose I'm thinking of him as the swaggering teenage boy I used to know and he's not that person anymore. He's a grown man.

'Anyway,' Nate says, looking between me and Hannah, 'you still haven't told me what you're doing here. Can I help at all?'

'Um, well, we're actually waiting for my stepson,' I say, grateful for the change in the conversation. 'He's ... I think ...'

'He's been arrested,' Hannah cuts in.

Nate looks at me and I shrug in embarrassment. 'What's his name?' he asks, walking over to the counter and grabbing a clipboard from the cop sitting behind the desk.

'Gene . . . Gene Walker.'

Nate scans the list. His finger stops at a line and his eyebrows rise.

'What?' I ask, my heart sinking. 'What did he do?'

'Failure to stop for a police officer after a minor traffic misdemeanor. He was driving erratically.'

I latch onto the word *minor*. 'Is that bad?' It doesn't sound too bad and at least it's not a DUI.

'Well . . . it depends,' Nate says. 'He eventually pulled over and they found 30 grams of marijuana on him.'

'Told you!' Hannah crowed.

I glare at her.

'Is that a lot?' I ask Nate.

Nate grimaces. 'The legal limit is 28.5 grams. Anything over that and he can be charged with possession.'

'What does that mean?' I ask.

'Six months jail time,' Nate answers. 'Or a fine.'

'Oh God.'

Nate hesitates a second, clearly weighing something up. 'Come with me,' he finally says, nodding his head towards a door that leads beyond the waiting room.

'Wait here,' I tell Hannah, and follow Nate.

'Don't you dare pay his fine,' Hannah hisses after me. 'Why should you always bail him out? He'll never learn his lesson!'

Nate leads me through a set of double doors, down a corridor, and into an office. There are framed photographs on the wall of Nate in dress uniform shaking hands with someone covered in medals, and on the bookshelf is a snapshot of two girls – both exceptionally pretty, with Nate's dark hair and blue eyes.

'Your daughters?' I ask.

He glances at the photo and nods. 'Yeah, they're great. Though they only have two activities: shopping and finding everything I say or do mortifying.'

'Sounds just like Hannah,' I laugh.

If I've ever stopped to think of Nate these last twenty-two years it's been only occasionally and never with regret, but now, seeing him again, it's like the past has collided with the present and atoms are splitting inside me. It's discombobulating. Unwelcome.

Well, possibly unwelcome.

Clearing some papers off a chair, Nate gestures for me to sit. I do. Nate leans against the edge of his desk. I eye his gun, holstered at his waist, and his crotch, which is right at eye-level, then look away, flustered. I'm bombarded with memories of us having sex in the way that only teenagers have sex, with total abandon and excitement and terror and curiosity.

'OK,' he says. 'I can probably get the first charge dropped. I just need to have a word with the officer who pulled him over. The second one – the drug charge – is going to be harder. But he doesn't have any priors on record, and he has you to vouch for him.'

'Absolutely,' I say, nodding madly, wondering how he doesn't know about Gene's prior DUI. I wonder if I should mention it but decide not to.

'So,' Nate continues, 'I can make this disappear just this one time.'

'You can do that?' I ask him, relieved.

He nods.

'Nate, that's . . . I don't know what to say . . . how to thank you . . .'

'Just buy me coffee sometime,' he says.

'OK,' I say, swallowing. Is there something in his smile or am I imagining it? Does he really mean it or is that just something people say?

A knock on the door blasts me back into the moment. A uniform cop pokes his head in and tells Nate someone is looking for him. I stand up and Nate ushers me out of his office with his hand resting on my lower back, and I feel it there, imprinted, even after he moves away.

I find Hannah in the waiting room, flirting with the police officer behind the desk.

I glare at the officer, who's happily flirting right back at her. He's at least eight or ten years older than her. There's a line of disgruntled citizens waiting behind Hannah, but neither of them appears to have noticed.

I clear my throat and Hannah looks up and runs over. 'So?' she asks. 'Is Gene going to jail?'

'No, they're letting him off without pressing charges,' I whisper.

'Seriously?' Hannah asks, scowling at me as though she's disappointed. 'What did you have to do? Sleep with that cop dude?'

I whack her on the arm.

'No, I'm serious,' she answers, laughing. 'He was totally into you. I could tell. And he's hot, you know, for an old guy.'

I whack her again. 'Hannah,' I hiss.

'What?' she asks. 'You dated him, didn't you?'

I nod, blushing.

'When did you break up with him? Or should I ask *why*?' she says, elbowing me in the ribs and laughing.

'Before I went off to college,' I mumble.

I glance up and see Nate behind the counter, talking to the deputy – the guy Hannah was just flirting with. Maybe he's the one who pulled Gene over. He's frowning and shaking his head and I panic that maybe he's refusing to drop the charges. But Nate says something – clearly pulls rank – and the cop, though still scowling, finally nods.

Nate gives me a thumbs-up. Victory.

Ten minutes later Gene's free.

14

Dr Warier discharges me with all the usual caveats and paperwork and I promise to return if I experience any sort of symptom at all, reassuring him that I'm not planning on leaving the hospital, not while June is still here. She's being stubborn, refusing to wake up, though they've taken her off the critical list and the doctors are saying she's stable. Stable but unresponsive.

I've tried talking to her. Gene's tried singing to her. Hannah's tried reading to her from a joke book. Robert sits quietly by her side, holding her hand, not saying much.

'She'll wake up,' Laurie tells me, squeezing my arm as she helps me pack my things into an overnight bag. Robert's with the insurance person again, handling the paperwork for June and me – God knows how much this stay in hospital will be costing our insurance company, but based on the final bill for June's cancer treatment, I can only guess it's close to a million already. Hopefully our insurance will cover it all again.

There's a knock on the door and we look over to see Nate entering. 'I heard you're being released,' he says to me, nodding hello at Laurie.

'Yes,' I say. 'Robert said you'd told him we could go home?'

Nate nods. 'Yeah, forensics have released the crime scene.'

I swallow hard. I don't want to go home. I can't bear the thought of it, but Robert says that we have to. I gave up arguing with him, reasoning that it doesn't matter much anyway, as I'll be at the hospital with June most of the time. I'm only going back there now to grab a change of clothes.

'It's a mess, I'm afraid,' Nate says with a grim smile. 'I tried to get forensics to be as tidy as possible and clean up after themselves but they're beholden to no one, those guys.'

'It's OK,' I say.

'I'll organize a cleaner,' Laurie says to me.

'Good idea,' Nate says. He pauses then asks, 'How's June doing?'

At the mention of June I feel wobbly and overcome. 'She's the same,' I croak.

'The docs say anything more?'

I shake my head. 'They don't know when she'll wake up,' I tell him.

What I don't say is that they refused to answer me when I asked if she would *ever* wake up. 'Have you got any leads?' I ask, hopeful.

'We're investigating a few lines of inquiry.'

I have watched enough *American Crime* to know that means they've got squat.

'I actually came by to ask you to come down to the police department later, if you can.'

'OK,' I say, surprised. Maybe I spoke too soon. 'When?'

'Now?' Nate says. 'Or later this afternoon? Whenever is convenient.'

'Um, OK,' I say, thinking of June and calculating how long we'll be away from her. 'We should be able to come now.'

'Just you,' Nate says quickly. 'Robert doesn't need to be there.'

I'm about to ask why when a nurse enters with my medication and before I know it Nate's walking out the door, telling me that he'll see me shortly for our interview.

'Interview?' Laurie says, bewildered. 'Hasn't he inter-viewed you already?'

'Yes,' I murmur, taking the bag of prescription painkillers from the nurse.

'I wonder what he wants?' Laurie asks.

'God knows.'

15

'Ava?'

Looking at Nate now, I find it hard to reconcile him with the swaggering ex-football player I used to know. On paper Nate and I were complete opposites. I had a 4.0 grade point average, a scholarship to college, a firmly middle-class upbringing and had never drunk, smoked or dated. Nate, who lived with his single mom, had never had a grade higher than a C, had read only about three books in his life, lived to play football, and had dated a dozen girls before me. Yet the attraction was so intense between us the differences didn't matter, at least at first. When a knee injury took away any college scholarship ideas he might have entertained, though, Nate had gone into a spiral. He drank and partied his way through the final semester of school and by the time I left for college he was working construction jobs and I was relieved as hell to be getting away from him.

'Ava, do you recognize any of these items?' he presses me.

I startle, and it takes me a few seconds to come back to the present. He's laid out a dozen plastic bags on a table, each sealed and tagged with an evidence label. I peer closer.

'Yes,' I say, pointing at the diamond bracelet and a pair of earrings – the chandelier pair. 'Those are mine.' I look up at Nate. 'Where did you find them?'

'Is there anything else?' Nate asks, avoiding my question.

I scan the table, peering closer at all the items. 'Yes, that's my grandmother's engagement ring,' I say, pointing at an art deco diamond ring. 'But I lost that about a month ago.' I look up at Nate. 'I don't understand. Where did you find all of this?'

'I'm afraid I can't tell you.'

'What?'

'I'm sorry, Ava,' Nate says softly. 'It's an ongoing investigation. I'll need to ask you to sign an affidavit that these items belong to you, and we're going to have to keep it all for evidence for the time being. You won't get any of it back until after the trial.'

'Trial?' I ask, stunned. 'Does that mean you have a suspect?'

'I mean *in case* we get to trial,' Nate says quickly, gathering all the bags and dropping them into a plastic crate.

I study him. What isn't he telling me? Why's he avoiding my eye? And why can't he tell me where he found my things? Surely I have a right to know? Nate leads me out of the room and then, to my surprise, into a small room next door with a bolted-down table in the middle and two scarred plastic chairs. He gestures for me to take a seat. I glance around. There's a mirror on one wall, which is clearly two-way. My blood runs cold. This is an interrogation room. Why am I in an interrogation room?

'I just need to ask you a few follow-up questions,' Nate says, sitting down and pulling out his battered notebook.

I frown, and he must see the expression on my face because he smiles at me as though to reassure me. 'Nothing to be concerned about,' he says lightly. 'I just need to check some things from the witness statement you gave after the incident.'

'OK,' I say, slowly lowering myself into the seat opposite him. My pulse starts to skitter and my lips are suddenly so dry that I reach for the jug of water on the table. My hand shakes when I pour it and I spill some.

Nate looks up from his paperwork. 'You said that when you got home you set the alarm on the back door.'

'Yes,' I say, taking a sip of water.

'And your husband told us he disarmed it later when he put out the trash.'

I nod.

'Was that something he normally did?'

'What? Disarm the alarm?'

'No. Put out the trash.'

'When I nagged him enough.'

Nate smirks. 'I hear that. I think my wife used that when she filed for divorce as evidence of my unreasonable behavior. *He never put out the trash.*'

I smile, but distractedly. Why is he asking questions about Robert? And why did he ask me to come alone?

'And did you always set the alarm at night?' Nate asks next.

'Well, no. But recently people have been posting on the local Facebook community page about car break-ins on our road, especially near the trailhead, and we're not far from there, so we figured better safe than sorry.'

Nate nods thoughtfully and writes something down, then he flips back through his notes until he finds what he's looking for. I wish I could read his mind, know what suspicions he has. 'And I just wanted to check – you mentioned you hit one of the intruders with a wooden chopping board and that you used a carving knife to stab him.'

I nod.

'We haven't been able to locate either of the items in your house.'

'Oh,' I say, bewildered. 'What do you think happened to them?'

Nate shrugs, studying me like he thinks maybe I had something to do with their disappearance. Or am I being paranoid? 'Likely guess is that they took them, knowing that otherwise they risked leaving DNA evidence we could use to trace them. If that's the case, they're smart.'

'What about blood?' I ask. 'Did they find any traces of blood? I hit him. I stabbed him. There must have been blood on the floor. Can't they try to match the blood? Don't you have a database or something to do that?'

'There weren't any traces of blood found in the kitchen.'

I shake my head, confused and bewildered. My head still feels foggy, patches of memory are blank. I was so sure I'd managed to cut his arm. I can still remember the way the knife felt slicing through his jacket and then through the flesh, like it was made of warm butter. Surely there was blood?

'We've been trying to trace the masks – thanks for the drawings by the way – but so far no luck. A lot of those masks are sold by companies in China via eBay and Amazon, so it's hard, but we're trying.'

The masked faces flash in front of me. It keeps happening. I'll be in the middle of a conversation when BOOM, one of the masks appears in my mind's eye. Each time, though, new things are being revealed. I just wish I could see the whole picture now. I know I'm missing something vital and Nate seems to be probing to find that missing piece. What does he know that I don't?

'OK ... one more thing,' Nate says. 'When you went upstairs with the gun and entered June's bedroom, can you tell me in more detail what you saw? Have you managed to remember anything else?'

The breath leaves my body in a whoosh. I reach for my glass of water and nearly knock it over.

'I'm sorry,' Nate says quietly. 'I have to ask.'

'No, no,' I say, gripping the glass as I'm assaulted by the memories. '*I'm* sorry. It's just . . . it's hard to remember. It was so fast. Everything's a blur.'

June's face flashes in front of me. The man's too. His gun coming up. Why didn't I manage to shoot him?

'It's my fault, isn't it?' I say suddenly.

'No,' Nate says, and he sets his notepad down and reaches across the table. Without thinking, I reach forwards too and put my hands in his. He squeezes tight.

'Ava, this is not your fault at all. And I promise you I'll find the people who did this. They're not going to get away with it.'

My face crumples and I bow my head again, so grateful for the words even if I don't fully believe him. He strokes the top of my hands with his thumbs and out of nowhere I feel a shudder of desire travel up my spine. It's so completely out of the blue and disturbing that I find myself leaping to my feet.

'I need to get back to the hospital,' I stammer, throwing my bag over my shoulder and turning for the door.

How can I be feeling desire at a time like this? What is wrong with me?

Nate gives me a fleeting smile and stands slowly from the table. 'Let me see you out,' he says and, with his hand on my back, he ushers me out of the room and towards the exit. That hand, that same imprint. Just one touch. It's all it took the last time and I find myself slowing my pace, leaning back into his hand, feeling it like a metal brace giving me strength and support.

When he says goodbye there's an awkward moment where we stare at each other and it looks like he wants to say something but before he can, I turn and rush off.

I hurry over to the Tesla. Robert's in the driver's seat, waiting for me.

'Everything OK?' he asks me, as I gingerly get in beside him.

I hesitate, feeling the imprint of Nate's hand like a branding iron on my back. 'Yes. They . . . they found my jewelry.'

Robert turns to me. 'They found it? Where?'

'He wouldn't say.'

Robert frowns. 'What do you mean, he wouldn't say? Why not?'

I shake my head. 'I don't know. Something about it being an ongoing investigation.'

'Why wasn't I allowed to come in with you?' Robert asks, narrowing his eyes at me.

I think about Nate's questions about Robert putting out the trash and failing to set the alarm. What was he getting at? Does he think Robert is somehow involved? 'He wanted to ask me some more questions about my statement,' I say. 'Verify something.'

Robert looks annoyed. He runs a hand over his face, which looks almost as rumpled as his shirt. The bruise from where he was hit is turning a vivid, grotesque puce color. How can he be in on it? It's a ridiculous thought. Look at what the men did to him. I'm being paranoid. All the stress and anxiety are taking a toll and God knows what all the drugs I'm on are doing to my mind.

'So, if they've found the jewelry does that mean they've got a suspect?' Robert asks, and I wonder at the forced casualness of his tone. It's as if Nate's laid little maggots of suspicion in my brain and they're starting to burrow. 'Are they going to arrest anyone?'

I shake my head, studying him. 'I don't know,' I say.

Robert purses his lips. 'Did he say anything useful?' he asks irritably. I shake off the horrible thoughts popping into my head. He's as tired and stressed as me, probably more tired as he's been sleeping in a chair by June's bed for the last three nights.

'No,' I admit. 'But he promised me he'd find the people who did this to us, to June . . .'

Robert huffs in a way that reminds me strangely of Hannah, and then puts the car in drive and tears out the parking lot.

16

The fingerprint ink on the kitchen counters won't come off. I'm scrubbing it with a scouring pad, understanding how Lady Macbeth felt with her damned spot, when Robert walks in.

'What are you doing?' he says, grabbing the scouring pad out of my hands. 'You don't need to do that.'

'It's stained the counter,' I tell him.

'It doesn't matter, Ava,' he says, throwing the scourer onto the side and taking both my hands in his.

'Laurie said she'd organize cleaners.'

'I told her not to,' Robert admits.

'Why?'

'I don't want any more strangers in the house.'

'Have you seen upstairs?' announces Hannah, storming into the kitchen, a horrified look on her face. 'The carpet's covered in blood. Someone's stepped in it and trailed it all over the hallway. There's no way I'm staying here.' She shakes her head, her eyes wide as saucers, almost hysterical.

'You can stay with Laurie and Dave,' I reassure her weakly.

Hannah starts to cry, quietly.

'Where's Gene?' I ask, looking around.

'He's in the apartment, clearing up,' Hannah says with a sniff, seemingly pulling herself together. 'It's been trashed too, by the way. Not that you can tell the difference. It was always a shithole. Now it's just more of a shithole.'

I didn't know Gene's place had been robbed too. Did they go in there before they entered the main house?

'Where's Gene's car?' I ask, glancing out the window and realizing it's not there.

Hannah shrugs. 'How should I know?'

'Oh my God, the hamster.' My hand suddenly flies to my mouth. 'We forgot about George.'

'I'll sort it out,' Robert says, putting his arm around me. 'You get back to the hospital.'

I nod, distracted. Yes, he's right. I need to get back. We've agreed that one of us should be with June at all times. Laurie appears in the kitchen, holding my weekend bag in her hand. 'I think I've got everything,' she tells me.

'Thanks,' I say. I sent her up to my closet to pick out some clean clothes. I didn't want to have to deal with seeing June's room, or the blood.

'Shall we go?' Laurie asks, smiling at me like I'm some ancient, mentally frail aunt.

I nod and hurry to the front door, snatching the bag from her hand. I'm not that frail.

'Don't worry,' Robert says again, as he follows us. 'I'll sort everything out here and I'll see you back at the hospital later.' He doesn't kiss me, just waves me absently off, before hurrying back inside.

'Don't forget the hamster,' I yell after him. June would never forgive us if she woke up and George was dead.

In the car Laurie looks over at me. 'Do you want to stop for some food?' she asks.

I shake my head.

'You need to eat.'

'I can't.' My stomach is so twisted up there's no way I can force anything down and besides, we need to get back to June. She's all alone.

'What did the handsome Sheriff want to talk to you about?' Laurie asks as she drives.

I glance at her. 'They found my jewelry.'

'What?' Laurie says. 'Where?'

'He wouldn't say.'

'Why not?'

'I don't know.'

Laurie mulls that over then reaches across and pats my leg. 'They'll catch them soon. Maybe that means they know who it is.'

Maybe, I think to myself, staring out the window. But maybe the men just chucked the jewelry in a dumpster some-where or took it to a local pawnshop, and it doesn't explain my grandmother's ring.

Laurie has stopped at a red light and my thoughts trail off. Right beside the car is one of those blue newspaper vending machines. The headline of the weekly paper is screaming: LOCAL GIRL IN COMA AFTER BRUTAL ATTACK IN FAMILY HOME.

June's smiling face shines out at me. They've chosen a photograph they must have found in the archive – of the time her basketball team came second in the local tournament – and they've obviously zoomed in on her. She's wearing her basketball shirt and is red in the face from the game she's just played.

The light turns green and Laurie drives off, leaving me to crane over my shoulder, trying to keep June in sight.

Twenty minutes later we pull into the hospital car park and Laurie swings around to the front to drop me off, but as we get close to the main entrance we see three TV vans festooned with satellite dishes blocking the way. A small crowd of news presenters holding mics mills around.

'What the . . .?' Laurie whispers under her breath as she spots them.

The camera crews set up camp here immediately after the attack, peddling stories that they seemed to pull out of thin air, or more like out of their asses. But they drifted away after the first day, bored by the lack of news to report. So why then are they back?

Laurie steps on the gas, meaning to go past them before they can notice us, but too late. They've spotted us and are already swinging their cameras in our direction. As we drive by the murder of journalists (is that the right collective noun? If it isn't, it should be) questions are hollered at me through the windshield, but I can't make out what anyone is saying. Laurie is sitting on the horn, trying to make them move out the way.

'What do they want?' I ask, shrinking in my seat. 'Why are they here?'

Laurie doesn't answer. She keeps honking the horn and pushing through the crowd until she's able to hit the gas and speed out of the parking lot.

'What's going on?' Laurie asks.

The only thing I can think is that something has happened to June and the media have somehow found out before me.

I pull out my phone, my heart hammering wildly. I'm expecting to see a missed call from the hospital but there's nothing from either the doctors or from Robert, or from Nate either. If they'd caught the guys I'm sure he would have called me. I glance at the radio dial, fighting the urge to tune in to the news. If something has happened, the last thing I want is to find out about it from a stranger on the radio.

Laurie pulls up by a side entrance to the hospital. 'Get out here,' she tells me. 'I'll throw them off by doing another spin around the parking lot. I'll see you in there.'

I get out the car and hurry inside, pushing through a set of double doors that bring me into a giant industrial kitchen. I weave my way among the shining metal stations, ignoring the curious glances of catering staff, before I exit through some double doors and head down a series of long corridors that lead, I think, in the direction of the lobby, though the hospital is vast, like some dystopian nightmare, all concrete and glass, built in the '70s, and I could be going in entirely the wrong direction.

I glance over my shoulder as I walk, and when I hear footsteps behind me, echoing through the empty rooms, I up my pace to a jog, even though the pain in my head becomes an ululating throb and makes me feel nauseous and dizzy. The footsteps behind me speed up too and I'm almost sprinting by the time I burst through another door and finally stumble into the lobby.

Sweating, and still glancing over my shoulder, I hurry towards the closest bank of elevators. Am I imagining things? Am I just being paranoid? I punch the call button and wait for the elevator to arrive, bouncing on the balls of my feet and glancing back towards the door.

A man wearing dark jeans and a black sweater enters via the double doors I just came through and I watch him scour the lobby, looking for something or someone. I jab the button again, earning a sideways glance from a group of nurses waiting alongside me.

The elevator doors take an eternity to open but as soon as I can I dart inside. The man breaks into a jog. I stab at the button to close the door and then hide behind the nurses who have piled in after me, thankful for the barrier they're providing. The doors start to close – slowly, so slowly – and I'm holding my breath, panic starting to scratch at my throat, when the man appears suddenly in the gap between the closing doors. His eyes dart over the nurses and fall on me, cowering in the back. One of the nurses reaches to open the doors for him.

No, I almost yell at her but I'm too paralyzed to speak.

But it doesn't matter because the man smiles and takes a step backwards. 'No worries,' he says, holding up his hands and smiling. 'I can wait.'

His eyes hold mine as he says it and they stay locked on me right until the moment the doors finally slide shut.

I'm still shaking, my heart racing as if I'm being chased by a machete-wielding maniac, when I make it to the sixth floor and the dimmed lights and hushed atmosphere of the ICU. I walk as fast as I can manage the whole way down the corridor towards the pediatric unit, looking over my shoulder so often I almost run straight into the police guard posted outside June's door.

I think about saying something to him, mentioning the man I saw down in the lobby, but when I start to phrase it in my head it sounds absurd. *A man wanted to get in the elevator. He looked at me strangely. He didn't get in when he had the chance*. Yes, I sound like a lunatic.

He was the same height and build as one of the men who attacked us – but so are a good percentage of the population. And besides, why would either of those men come back? I didn't see their faces. I'm no threat to them.

But what if June did? an insistent voice in my head pipes up. What if they think she saw something? What if she could identify them? I hadn't considered that before now but maybe that's why Nate has arranged for the police protection. Maybe that's what he's worried about. He just didn't want to tell me in case he scared me.

'Mrs Walker?'

I jump but it's just Dr Warier coming out of June's room.

'Ava, please, call me Ava,' I say, smiling in relief at seeing a friendly face.

'How are you feeling now?' he asks. 'How's the head?'

'Fine,' I say, looking past him anxiously. 'June? Is she OK?'

'No change, I'm afraid,' he answers. 'I just came to check in on her.'

'It's not good, is it?' I blurt.

He pauses before answering. Never a good sign. 'Her blood pressure has stabilized so that's one good thing . . .'

'But?' I say, because it's clear from his tone that he's holding something back.

He pauses again, takes a deep breath and then exhales with a sigh. 'Her brain isn't responding to stimuli. And . . . well . . . She isn't able to breathe on her own. She's being kept alive by machines.'

'Just be straight with me,' I cut in. 'I'm tired of all the crap. I want the truth. Is she going to be OK?'

The doctor studies me, weighing his answer. 'Unless a miracle occurs . . .' he finally says.

I suck in a breath, reeling backwards, and he catches me by the elbow and steadies me. 'Mrs Walker.'

His voice sounds distant and far away. I fall with a bump and realize I've collapsed into a chair that he's steered me towards. He's standing over me, his brow furrowed with worry. 'I'm sorry,' he says. 'Are you OK?'

I shake my head. How can I be OK? How can I ever be OK again? Why won't people stop asking me that question? It feels like a dozen bullets have been fired into my body at point-blank range.

'I shouldn't have said that,' he says, frowning unhappily.

'No,' I whisper through the pain. 'I'm glad you told me.'

He kneels down in front of me, his hand resting on my shoulder and for a while neither of us speaks. Finally, I look up at him. 'Do you believe in miracles?' I ask.

17

Has she already had her one miracle? I wonder as I sit beside June half an hour later, stroking her fingertips. Did she use up all her luck beating cancer? I can't believe she won that battle just to fall at another hurdle so soon after. How can that be allowed? How is that fair? Whatever the doctors say, I'm not giving up on her. I can't. I have to believe in miracles.

'Can you hear me?' I say to June.

The machines answer. Beep. Beep. Beep.

Well, fuck them.

'Fuck you,' I say out loud, before pressing my hand over my mouth and glancing at June. I never swear in front of the kids. But can she hear me? Does she even know I'm here with her?

It's a while before I realize that Laurie hasn't appeared. And then I remember the press. What was that all about? What did they want? And that man downstairs who tried to get in the elevator. Who is he? Was he really following me or was I imagining it? Where's Laurie? Anxiety gnaws at me.

They don't allow calls inside the ICU so I stumble past the police officer stationed on the door and walk through the fire escape at the end of the corridor. It leads into a quiet emergency stairwell. I pull out my phone to dial Laurie and notice I have a voicemail from Nate. He left it five minutes ago.

'Hey, Ava, it's me. Call me when you get this. It's urgent.'

His tone is ominous and it sounds like he's walking somewhere in a hurry. Oh God. What's happened? I'm about to call his number, steeling myself for the news, when I hear the squeak of a shoe on the stairs below me.

I lean over the railing but can't see anyone and the footsteps stop. I turn towards the doors to the ICU – feeling suddenly exposed out here in the stairwell – and it's then, out the corner of my eye, that I catch a blur of movement as someone starts bounding up the last two flights of stairs towards me. It's the same man – the one who tried to follow me into the elevator. He's launching himself up the steps three at a time, and he's holding something black, something metal, in his hand – a gun!

I fumble in terror for the door handle. But it won't open. It's locked from the inside. There's a small electronic card reader beside it that I hadn't noticed before. I pound on the glass panes but the hallway is empty. Where did the cop go? Glancing back, I see the man has reached the top of the stairs. I think about making a run for it – trying to get to the next floor up – but he's almost on me. All I can do is shrink back against the door, legs giving way.

The man slows, seeing that I'm trapped. He takes a step towards me and I let out a sob. 'Please,' I say weakly, despising myself for pleading. 'Don't hurt me!'

He's out of breath and as he takes another step forwards I see the victory in his eyes. He points his gun at my chest. A tear slips down my cheek. I don't want to die like this.

'Did you know your husband is bankrupt?' he says.

What? My brain takes a moment to compute the question, then my gaze drops to the gun in his hand.

It's not a gun at all. It's a small, black voice recorder.

'Euan Shriver,' the man says, thrusting the recorder in my direction. '*Santa Barbara Herald*. Can you tell me, Mrs Walker, did you know about your husband's debt?'

'What?' I whisper, my heart still hammering. 'What are you talking about?'

'His company has gone bust. He owes over a million dollars to creditors. Did you know?'

Over a million dollars? That's ridiculous. How can that be? Where's this man getting his facts from?

'How is your daughter doing?' he asks. 'Has she woken up yet? Did she witness anything? Can she identify her attackers? Can you comment?'

'Here's a comment. Fuck off!'

I jump. Nate has appeared behind me in the doorway to the ICU. He's purple-faced with fury and looks like he just ran a mile to get here. He rushes past me and the journalist scuttles backwards, stumbling against the railing. Nate snatches the voice recorder out of his hand and tosses it over his shoulder into the stairwell. I hear it smash as it lands floors below us.

The journalist lets out a cry of protest. 'You can't do that!'

Nate grabs him by the collar and hauls him so he's leaning over the same six-story drop his voice recorder plummeted into. 'Looks like I just did,' Nate snarls. 'And you'll be lucky if you don't follow after it. How the hell did you get inside?'

'It's a public hospital,' the man cries. 'I'm not breaking the law.'

'I could arrest you for harassment.'

'And I'll press charges for criminal damage. That was a four-hundred-dollar piece of equipment.'

'You won't be able to press charges if you can't speak or write.' Nate twists the journalist's arm behind his back until he howls with pain. 'And who's going to believe you anyways? Who do you work for?' Nate demands.

'The *Herald*,' the guy grunts, his face contorting with pain, sweat beading on his brow.

I'm about to put my hand on Nate's arm to get him to stop when the doors to the ICU fly open and Laurie and the cop who was standing duty in the hallway come rushing into the stairwell.

'Is everything OK?' the cop asks, glancing at Nate and the man he has dangling over the railing.

Nate drops his arms to his sides and takes a step back. 'Everything's fine. This gentleman was just leaving.'

The journalist staggers in disarray towards the steps, clutching his injured shoulder and glaring at Nate, though there's fear in his eyes too.

'And if I see your face anywhere near here again,' roars Nate, making the man jump in fright, 'I'll arrest you. Go on, get lost!'

The man vanishes, rushing down the stairs like he's got a rocket up his tail.

'Damn press,' Nate spits, as he turns around to face us. His shirt is rumpled and his hands are shaking. 'Are you OK?' he asks as Laurie rushes over to me and asks the same thing.

'Is it true?' I ask. 'What he said about Robert . . . about him being bankrupt?'

Nate nods. 'That's what I was calling about. I'm sorry, Ava.'

I glance at Laurie. She knows too. Maybe she heard from the reporters outside. She looks at me pityingly and I have to turn away, shoving past them both and heading back inside the ICU.

The linoleum floor shimmers in front of my eyes. All these puzzle pieces I never even knew were puzzle pieces start to slot into place, the picture becoming clear: the insurance troubles here at the hospital; Robert's increasing stress over the last few months; the way he's been locking himself away every night in his study; the fact that last week Javier approached me about not having been paid for two months ... I dismissed it, putting it down to Robert just being forgetful, being caught up in work. I've been so goddamn blind. And so damn smug at the same time. Thinking I knew everything that was going on in my family – that everyone told me everything. Why did I think I was the only one who had secrets?

18

Robert looks up at me, hunkered over himself like a child being scolded. 'I'm sorry,' he says.

'Sorry?' I say blankly.

'I didn't want to worry you.' Robert bows his head, dropping it into his hands.

I collapse down onto the sofa opposite him. I can't bring myself to sit anywhere near him, rage bubbles through my veins so hot that I can almost see the steam rising off my skin. The whole way home in the car I tried not to let my anger get the better of me. I told myself to stay calm but now I'm confronting him all that goes out the window. 'You didn't think I had a right to know?' I shout.

He glances at me through the slits between his fingers. 'I thought I had it under control.'

I can't look at him. If I look at him I might launch myself across the coffee table and start pummeling his already injured face. I look around the living room instead. 'The house. Are we going to lose the house?' I ask.

I am surprised at how calm I sound. I think it's because it all feels so unreal. It's like trying to understand basic math and then being told to wrap your head around quantum physics. I was struggling to deal with the break-in and what's happened to June. Now this on top . . . it's too much to process. I press my hands to my throbbing temples.

'The bank already owns the house,' Robert mutters. 'It's not ours anymore.'

'But we paid cash for it,' I stammer, wondering how on earth someone can fritter away close to three million dollars, which is what the house is worth.

'I had debts. The business . . . The app I've been working on. I poured a lot into it. And . . . I made some stupid investments.' He mumbles this last part.

'In what?' I ask, anger giving way to stupefaction.

'In some start-ups.'

I groan and rub a hand over my eyes. I'm trapped inside a nightmare. Who is this man sitting opposite me? This man with the haggard expression, livid bruises and pouches under his eyes isn't familiar to me at all. He's a complete stranger, I realize with a shock. I can't even remember the last time I really looked at him, let alone the last time I really spoke to him, about anything beyond the children or everyday nonsense. When did it get like this? How did I not notice the giant fissure between us?

But deep down I know the answer to that question. It's been at least eighteen months that we've been drifting apart and I'm surely to blame, at least for half of it. But not for this. What Robert's done is unforgivable.

'Surely there's something left,' I say.

He doesn't reply.

'Our 401s?' I ask.

He shakes his head.

'You gambled away our pensions?' I hiss.

'Yes,' he mumbles.

I try to gather a breath but the room tilts violently on its axis.

'My inheritance?' I ask quietly.

He gives a shake of the head.

'The kids' college funds?'

He shakes his head again.

Rage spirals up inside me and I have to clamp my jaw shut to stop it corkscrewing its way out.

'I'm sorry,' he mumbles.

Sorry?! That inheritance was *my* money, gifted to me by my grandparents after they died. Not much, but I'd been setting it aside, hoping to use it one day to help the kids get their feet on the property ladder, or to pay for an extravagant family holiday when I turned fifty . . . or to start a new business, maybe open my own art gallery in town. I don't even know. But the point is, it was *my* money. Not his. And if he's spent the college fund, what will happen to Hannah? How will we afford to pay for her tuition? Or June's?

'How could you be so damn stupid?' I shout. I stand up. Bone tired, with every muscle in my body aching as if I've done twelve rounds in a boxing ring, I walk towards the door because I cannot be in this space with him for one more second.

'Where are you going?' Robert calls after me.

'Back to the hospital.'

'We need to pack,' he says.

I wheel around. 'Excuse me?'

'The bank is foreclosing on the house.'

I close my eyes and take another deep breath. Keep calm. Keep it all inside. There's no point in losing it. It's beyond that now. 'Did you talk to them?' I ask. 'Did you explain? How can they expect us to move with everything else that's happening? Where are we supposed to go?'

'They've given us an extra week. But we were meant to be out months ago.'

I stare at him. 'Months ago?' Is he joking? He looks at me with a hangdog expression. Apparently not. All that time. And he never once thought to tell me what was going on. 'You got us into this mess,' I finally say and walk out the door.

Laurie is waiting for me outside.

'Are you OK?' she asks when I climb in her car.

I shake my head. Laurie thankfully doesn't say anything more. She starts driving, slowing to navigate her way through the cluster of news crews gathered at the gate to the house.

I close my eyes as we inch our way through them. I'm getting used to the near constant throb of pain in my head, like a nagging headache that won't go away, but every time the stress increases, the pain flares and I have to sit quietly with my eyes closed until it passes. A fist lands on the window right beside me, making me jump, and my eyes fly open.

'Did you know?' one of the reporters yells at me, the snout of his camera pressed up against the glass. I cringe away from him, automatically scanning the crowd, remembering the journalist from the hospital. I can't see him among the dozen or so reporters. I wish Nate could do the same thing to all these ones, make them all leave us alone.

Laurie leans her palm on the horn until the news crews back grudgingly away and we're able to squeeze past.

'We have to leave the house,' I say finally to Laurie, when I can't keep it in any longer. 'The bank is foreclosing. We have one week to get out.'

Laurie stares at me, her mouth falling open. 'What are you going to do?' she asks.

'I don't know,' I say with a shrug, and it's true. I have no idea.

And what about the medical fees for June and me? Has he been paying our health insurance premiums? If not, then we're even more screwed. The ICU is thousands of dollars a day. I grimace and shake my head. I can't think about that right now. The only important thing is June. The rest will have to wait.

I find Hannah at the hospital, sitting with a tear-stained face beside June's bed.

'Is it true?' she asks, jumping to her feet the moment I enter.

I nod. This is the worst of it, having to face my child and admit to her that her future has just been wiped out because her father is an idiot. I lay a hand against my stomach to still the boiling anger brewing there, which feels like it might spill over and scald anyone in the vicinity.

I put my hand on Hannah's shoulder. 'I'm sorry,' I say, wondering why I'm the one apologizing to her. I should have kept a better eye on our finances yes, and maybe I've been too blithe with my spending but for God's sake, he never gave me a single indication of the debt we were in.

I scan June for any sign of change but there's none. If anything, she looks paler, the shadows around her eyes bluer, her cheeks more sunken. The machines beep their relentless tune and I suddenly feel like screaming, like punching holes in the walls and yelling until all the howling rage and spitting anger and utter desperation is purged. Right now, with it trapped inside me, it feels corrosive, as if it's eating me alive from the inside out.

'What's going to happen?' Hannah asks, looking up at me, eyes wide.

I shake my head and press my lips together even harder

and somehow, though God knows how, I force a smile. 'It'll all be OK,' I say.

She nods at me and I can see she believes it, or at least she's trying hard to. I turn away.

The lies we tell.

19

DAY 4

I still have no idea what we're going to do the next morning. I spent an uncomfortable and sleepless night twisted like a pretzel in a chair beside June's bed. Now I'm sitting with the hospital's insurance liaison in her office, my eyes blurring from the staggering sums I'm being asked to review. I've never seen so many zeroes in one place. It's almost laughable. A buzzing noise breaks through the haze. It's my phone. Gene. Damn. He must have heard. I can't talk to him right now. I'll have to call him back.

Robert apparently signed something saying that we would be personally responsible for the medical bills given our lack of health coverage. Even if he hadn't lost all our money, these kinds of sums would bankrupt a small nation. And what was he doing signing anything? He knew it meant nothing. But then again what was he going to say to the people trying to save his daughter's life? 'No, we can't actually afford it. Turn the machines off'?

The door bursts open behind me.

'Mom?'

I spin around in my chair. Hannah is in the doorway, her face a horror mask.

'What is it?' I ask, rising out of my seat, the papers scattering around me in a snowstorm flurry. 'Is it June? What's happened?'

Hannah shakes her head. 'No, but you need to come. Now.'

She grabs my hand and tugs me out of the room. 'What is it? Where are we going?' I ask, dread making my legs feel like they're encased in concrete.

She drags me into a waiting area where exhausted families sit awaiting news of loved ones. A muted flat-screen television is mounted on the wall and Hannah halts in front of it.

I glance up. Not more news. I can't face seeing any more news reports. I'm about to turn away when the word 'ARREST' flashes on the bottom of the screen and captures my attention. The image it's blasted over is helicopter footage – and it's a bird's-eye view of our house. I clutch Hannah's arm and gasp. They've arrested someone! Finally.

The camera zooms wonkily in on the front door of the house and I see two policemen leading someone out in handcuffs. Wait. What's happening?'

'Why are they arresting Dad?' Hannah cries.

I don't answer her. I'm already walking towards the nurse's station. I yell at the orderly sitting at the desk to pass me the TV remote and then snatch it out of her hand so I can pump up the volume. I don't care that the people in the waiting room are all staring and that Hannah has started crying hysterically.

'And news is just in that Robert Walker has been arrested,' a woman's voice intones as the image captured from the helicopter fills the screen. 'We're crossing right now to Diane Washington who is outside the Ventura Sheriff's Office where we're expecting a press announcement any moment from the Sheriff in charge of the investigation.'

The camera cuts away from the studio to a woman with a helmet of hair who is standing outside Nate's office along with a small army of other reporters.

'Mom?'

Hannah is pulling on my arm. I turn to her impatiently, noticing as I do that everyone in the room is now gawping openly at us, a few of them exchanging whispers and nods at the television. Hannah jerks her head to the left and I glance in that direction to see a woman filming us on her phone with absolutely no subtlety whatsoever. She even stands up to get a better view.

'Let's go,' I say, taking Hannah by the hand and pulling her towards the elevators.

As we pass the television I catch a glimpse of Nate on screen, striding out of the building and heading towards a podium. What's he doing? How could he arrest Robert without telling me? I drag my feet, wanting to stay and listen to whatever he's about to say, but the heat of all those eyes on us, and the awareness of the woman filming us, makes me turn and quickly usher Hannah into the elevator.

The doors close on us and once we're sealed inside Hannah starts to cry even harder, shaking. 'It's OK,' I say, putting my arms around her. 'It's just a stupid mistake. That's all. Just a stupid mistake.'

It has to be. What else could it be? But then I realize that it isn't Hannah who is shaking so hard her teeth are rattling. It's me.

20

'Solicitation.'

'What?' I say, blinking at Laurie in shock.

She shakes her head and keeps on reading from her iPad. 'I don't think it means what you think it means. I think it means he solicited help to commit a crime.'

'I don't understand.'

'There's more,' Laurie continues. 'Conspiracy to commit insurance fraud. Conspiracy to commit burglary. Aiding and abetting . . .'

'Stop,' I shout. I can't handle it, can't begin to understand what is happening. How can they have arrested Robert? How can he be guilty of all these things?

Laurie sits down beside me and puts her arm around my shoulders. The relatives' room in the ICU is empty and for that at least I'm grateful. I drop my hands away from my ears. 'It can't be true,' I whisper, feeling like one of those cartoon characters that walks into a wall and then stands there twanging like a plucked guitar string. Laurie doesn't answer and I whip my head around. 'You don't think it's true, do you?'

She shakes her head firmly but perhaps a beat too late. 'Of course not. Look, we need to get down there to the station and find out what's going on.' She pauses. 'And maybe you should think about calling a lawyer?'

I pick myself up from the sofa. 'With what money?' I ask tersely.

★   ★   ★

It turns out that we don't need to hire a lawyer. They've appointed a public defender; a disheveled man called Horowitz, who has tufts of hair sprouting from his ears like succulents and who is wearing what I think is a polka-dot patterned tie at first, until I realize the dots are splashes of coffee.

'They'll set bail at around half a million dollars,' he tells me when I arrive at the police station and he's shown me into one of the interrogation rooms.

'What? We don't have that sort of money,' I splutter. 'We don't have any money.' Has he not been watching the news?

The man sniffs and shrugs his indifference.

'I don't understand the charges,' I say, indicating the sheet of paper they've given me.

The lawyer sighs. 'Your husband has been arrested for conspiring to commit a robbery.'

'But he can't have,' I say plainly. 'He wouldn't.'

'You're in significant financial difficulty. Three weeks ago your husband pawned some jewelry of yours.'

'What?' I gasp.

He opens a folder and spreads some photographs across the table.

'What are these?' I ask, picking them up.

'These are CCTV images from a downtown Oxnard pawnshop, taken three weeks ago.'

I snatch up a photograph. It's pixelated but it's still obvious to anyone that it's Robert in the photograph, handing something over to the man behind the counter.

'He was pawning these items.'

Horowitz lays out images of my stolen jewelry one after the other like cards from a winning poker hand.

'They weren't stolen in the burglary then?' Laurie asks.

'No.'

'I don't understand,' I stammer.

'You didn't know that he was pawning the items then?'

I shake my head indignantly. 'Of course not. I didn't know anything was missing. I don't wear jewelry all that often. They're heirlooms, not things you'd wear every day.'

He takes umbrage at my tone and sniffs. 'I'm not suggesting you were aware of what your husband was doing, Mrs Walker.'

'I don't believe this. It's just . . . unbelievable. He wouldn't do this.'

Horowitz sighs and then hands me a photocopy of something.

I take it. 'What is this?'

'It's your home insurance policy. If you look at where it's highlighted – that's a request for a policy increase, made just a month ago.'

I glance at the highlighted area.

'Your husband increased your insurance specifically for those items. He stood to make over two hundred thousand dollars if those items were stolen.'

'But he didn't make a claim, did he?' I say, trying to muster some defiance. 'I told the police, there were some car breakins happening in the neighborhood. Robert wanted to make sure we were properly covered. And those are my most valuable pieces of jewelry.'

'But the intention was clear, they'll argue. They'll go before the judge, lay out your financial situation, show them those photographs and the insurance paperwork and make a case that your husband arranged for some as yet unknown men to break in so you could benefit from a fraudulent insurance claim that would clear all your debts and bring you back into the black.'

Oh my God. All the puzzle pieces fit together. Is that why Robert wanted to take me out to dinner on the night of the break-in? Did he think we'd all be out and it just went badly wrong? I think about how he cried at the hospital when he told me about June. Was it sorrow or was it guilt?

Horowitz starts to gather up his papers. 'Listen, if I were you I'd speak to your husband and get him to admit it. If he does we can plea bargain, especially if he gives up the names of the men he hired to carry out the burglary. He might get ten years, maybe less, but the conspiracy charges, they're likely going to stick.'

He clicks the locks on his briefcase shut as though to signal the conversation is over.

'Ten years?' I stammer.

He swings his bag off the table and walks to the door. 'I'm due in court,' he says, glancing at his watch.

'But . . . What will they do to him?' I ask. 'What happens now?'

'They'll arraign him in the next twenty-four hours and then he'll be transferred to the county jail to await trial.'

'Jail? He's going to jail?'

'Yes, unless you can make the bail payment.'

I turn around, feeling dizzy, the walls closing in. All I can think about are the crime shows I've watched. How will Robert survive even five minutes in prison?

'How long until the trial?' I ask.

Horowitz draws in a breath and shrugs again. 'How long's a piece of string? If he pleads guilty, then it'll just go to sentencing, so it'll be quicker. Maybe a couple of months. If he doesn't, then you're looking at a year to eighteen months before it comes to trial.'

I collapse onto the nearest seat. It's a dream. A nightmare. It has to be.

'I'm sorry,' he says. 'If you need me, here's my card. Office hours are on the back, otherwise I'll be in touch as soon as I have news.'

I put my head in my hands. This can't be happening. I can't believe it. I know Robert. He wouldn't do this. He pawned my jewelry though. He lied to me about our finances. He stole money that was rightfully mine. He did so much behind my back. Maybe he is capable of this. I always thought of Robert as a gentle, honest man, but, looking back, weren't there signs?

What about how he dealt with that person who tried to claim the idea for his app was stolen? He left him penniless. Even when the man dropped the case and offered to pay costs, Robert insisted on suing him for slander and emotional trauma. He can be ruthless when it comes to business.

But I saw how scared he was during the break-in. I saw him cowering in terror. He was smashed in the face and hurt. He didn't do that to himself. God, I don't know what to believe anymore.

'Ava?'

I look up. Nate is standing in the door to the interrogation room. At least he has the good sense to look sheepish. 'Do you mind?' he asks, stepping into the room and shutting the door behind him.

I glare at him as I swipe at my tears. How could he not have warned me this was coming?

'How did it go with the lawyer?' Nate asks.

I shake my head.

Nate grimaces. 'Yeah, public defenders vary. You pulled a dud, I'm afraid.'

I glare at him, my eyes burning. 'How could you?' I ask.

'I'm sorry you had to find out the way you did,' Nate says, sitting down opposite me. 'It did not play out how I wanted it to at all. Someone leaked the news to the press, someone inside my department, I'm looking into who, but it meant we had to move faster than we had planned.' He sits down at the table opposite me. 'I wanted to be the one to break it to you. I'm sorry I didn't have a chance to before you heard.'

I purse my lips, anger building. I want to scream, punch something. 'How long have you suspected Robert?'

His eyes flash hurt. 'When we discovered the truth about your financial affairs. We did a little more digging after that and . . .'

My face flushes. I'm not sure if it's due to embarrassment or anger and I find myself leaping to Robert's defense. 'Just because we're broke doesn't give him a motive. How could he be involved anyway? You saw him. Is he supposed to have done that to himself? Did he punch himself in the face? I was there, Nate. You weren't. I saw how scared he was. I saw! And God, if he wanted to make an insurance claim, if this is what you think it's about, then why not just set fire to the house when we were all out? Why not just fake a break-in?' I take a deep breath. 'This is crazy. Why would anyone do this to their family?'

Nate studies me for a beat, his lips pressed together into a tight line, then finally he exhales softly. 'Ava, I'm afraid it's not all. We're about to file another charge. I wanted to make sure you heard about this from me, now.'

I can hear my heart starting to thud louder and louder. 'What do you mean? What other charge?'

Nate takes a breath and swallows. 'The prosecutor's given us the go-ahead. We've got enough evidence to charge him with conspiracy to commit murder.'

I have to play the words over in my head a few times. 'Wait, what are you talking about? Why would Robert have wanted June dead?'

He shakes his head slowly. 'Not June. We're charging him with conspiracy to commit *your* murder.'

I stare at him blankly and then I laugh. 'What? But ... that's ... oh my God. You think he was trying to kill me? Why would he want to kill me? That's the most ridiculous thing I've ever heard.'

Nate opens a manila folder and hands me a sheaf of papers. It's the same insurance policy Horowitz handed me but with a separate part highlighted.

'Robert made a request for cover in case of a home invasion.'

'OK,' I say, trying to grasp at something, something that will prove Nate is wrong, has to be wrong, but the words are jumbling on the page in front of me.

'I don't know anything about this,' I hear myself say. 'Maybe it was part of the policy, something they offered as an extra.'

When I look up at Nate he looks like he's wincing, in pain. He shakes his head at me. 'We spoke to the insurance broker. Robert was asked if he'd like to add the home invasion cover.'

'He was asked if he wanted it or he specifically requested it?' I snap back.

'Either way he said yes,' Nate answers. 'Per the terms of your policy you're entitled to half a million dollars compensation in the event of a home invasion, half a million more for a life threatening injury, up to five million in medical costs incurred as a result of any injury and ten million dollars for any death resulting from said home invasion. That's a lot of money. A lot of incentive.'

He points at the figures on the piece of paper so there's no way I can deny them. 'I'm sorry, Ava. I know this must be difficult.'

I look at him. 'No, it's not difficult. It's absurd. It's crazy. You really think Robert would arrange to have me killed just so he could collect on a life insurance policy?' I burst out laughing again. 'You have no idea what you're saying. This is Robert. He wouldn't . . .'

'There's more.' He reaches for another sheaf of papers from the folder.

A shiver of dread rides up my spine.

Nate pulls out some photographs. I think at first they'll be the same ones that Horowitz showed me of Robert in the pawnshop but they're not. These aren't CCTV images but surveillance ones, each of them large format and glossy. The images are fuzzy, as though they've been taken at night without a flash. The first thing I recognize is our car in the corner of one shot. And then I make out Robert, though he has his back half turned away from the camera. He's talking to two men on a street corner, handing them something. I don't recognize the men. They're in their twenties, I would guess. One looks like he might be Hispanic, the other white.

'What is this?' I ask. 'Who are they? Where was this taken?'

'These two men,' says Nate, pointing at the men, 'are Raul Fernandez and James Hill. Oxnard have had them under surveillance for months. They're drug dealers. Rap sheet a mile long between them. Aggravated burglary, sexual assault. Both of them have done time before for dealing as well as robbery. Fernandez was charged with homicide eight years ago and stood trial twice but was acquitted after the jury couldn't reach a unanimous verdict.'

'OK,' I say slowly, staring at the photo in horror. 'What was Robert doing with them?'

'Soliciting their help. We believe he's handing them cash – these photos were taken on the same day Robert visited the pawnshop three weeks ago, two and a half weeks before the break-in. The DEA had Fernandez under surveillance, which is how we have these photographs.' He points at the item in Robert's hand. 'We think this is Robert handing over the five thousand dollars he made from pawning the jewelry earlier. That it was the down payment on the job.'

'No.' I can't help smiling. This is all a joke. It has to be.

'You'd like to hazard a guess then,' Nate says. 'What was Robert doing at two a.m. talking to two of Oxnard's least upstanding citizens?'

He's got me there. I stare at the photograph. 'I don't know. Have you tried asking him?' I shake my head, tears welling. 'He didn't do it,' I whisper, but there's a plaintive note in my voice.

'Ava,' Nate says gently. 'Robert specifically asked you to go out for a date night, something you admitted in our second interview was not something you regularly did. In fact, you said it had probably been three or four years since the last time Robert instigated a date.'

'It doesn't prove anything,' I argue. 'And you're contradicting your own argument. You claim Robert was targeting me but if he was why would he have planned for us to be out having dinner?'

Nate shakes his head. 'He wanted to make sure he knew what you were doing that night so there could be no surprises. And it gave him an excuse to get June on a sleepover. He planned the break-in for when you'd be home.'

'No,' I push back, refusing to accept it.

'You were the target, Ava. He unset the alarm.'

'To put out the trash.'

'He didn't put the trash out. The trash was empty.'

I shake my head, confused.

Nate's eyes burn into mine as he waits for the penny to drop. And then it does. Robert told me he turned the house alarm off to put out the trash. He lied. What else has he lied about?

21

Robert shuffles into the room with his head down, looking like a man who has just been given a terminal diagnosis. He doesn't look at me. Is that a sign of guilt, or just embarrassment? He's wearing a too-big orange jumpsuit and a pair of white paper slippers. His hands are cuffed. I glance at the door, checking my escape route, realizing with a shock that for the first time ever I'm afraid of the man I married.

He slumps into one of the plastic seats opposite me and I stare at him. Who is this man in front of me? Have I ever really known him? I leaped so readily to his defense earlier with that lawyer Horowitz and with Nate – but did I speak too soon? Is Nate right? Did my own husband conspire to have me killed? It's such a horrifying thought, but even worse is the knowledge that I just don't know.

Robert casts a glance at the door and then at the two-way mirror.

'No one is watching,' I tell him. 'The lawyer told me we're not being recorded. So you can tell me the truth.'

He turns to me with a queer expression on his face.

'Did you do it, Robert? Did you organize the break-in? Did you pay those men to do it?' My voice trembles.

Robert glowers at me.

'They told me that you planned this,' I say, trying to read him. 'That you pawned all our things, you planned the break-in, paid people to do it . . . that you wanted me dead.'

Robert puts his clasped hands on the table and bows his head. He takes a deep breath then looks up at me. 'Is that what you think?' he asks.

'I . . .' I break off. I don't know what I think.

'Do you believe it?' he asks, startling me with the anger in his voice.

'I don't know,' I admit, shaking my head and fighting back tears.

The look he gives me could slice through flesh.

I swipe at my tears. 'I've seen the evidence, Robert. What were you doing with those men? How do you even know them? Why did you increase the insurance premiums?'

He just stares at me and his expression is impossible to fathom. I'm the one who has to look away first because I can't bear it. It reminds me of the time we went to the Grand Canyon for our honeymoon. One glance over the edge had me scrambling back to safety, away from the abyss. I couldn't look down again. I was too afraid of how it made me feel.

For a minute Robert and I sit in silence, the fissure between us widening.

'How's June?' he suddenly asks.

I look up. How are we talking about June? 'She's the same,' I hear myself answer. I close my eyes again. Did he do it? If he did, then he's the one responsible for what happened to June. It's on him.

'And Gene?' Robert asks.

'I don't know,' I snap. 'I haven't seen him. I had to call him and leave a voicemail telling him about you, just in case he hadn't seen the news yet. I've had to leave a hysterical Hannah with Laurie. She's asking me what the hell is going on and what do I say? What do I tell her?!'

Still more silence.

'For God's sake, Robert . . . talk to me! Tell me what you were doing with those men. Tell me the damn truth!'

He snorts a little at that. 'The truth? That's rich, coming from you.'

'What?'

'Asking for the truth. When all you do is keep secrets.'

I draw in a sharp, stabbing breath and stare at him, alarmed.

'You think I didn't know?' he says, crossing his arms over his chest.

'Know what?' I ask, my back stiffening, my pulse skittering.

'About you and the Sheriff.'

The air is punched out of me. 'There's nothing to know.'

'Really?'

'Yes, really.'

He presses his lips together so tight they bleach and nods thoughtfully. 'So before you saw the Sheriff in the hospital you hadn't seen him in over twenty years – is that right?'

Blood pounds in my face as though someone is beating on a drum. 'I . . . no . . .'

'Don't, Ava,' he growls. 'Don't lie.'

'I'm not,' I protest.

'Yes, you are. I know about you and him.'

My mouth is dry and my heart has started galloping. What does he know? And *how* does he know it?

'You told me you were going to book club. There was no book club. I saw you together in that restaurant.'

Oh God. 'Robert—' I start to say.

'I don't want to hear it,' Robert spits and he gets up, crosses to the door and bangs on it with his fists.

'Robert,' I say, standing up on legs that threaten to give way, the floor sliding beneath my feet.

'I want to get out!' Robert hollers.

A key rattles in the lock.

'Robert,' I stammer again. 'You can't just go. We need to talk. We need to . . .'

Robert turns around. 'Save it for lover boy,' he sneers. His eyes narrow. 'Is he the one who sent you in here for a confession?'

I don't answer and he shakes his head at me in disgust. 'It was, wasn't it?'

The door opens and a uniformed cop takes Robert by the arm and starts leading him back to the cells.

'Robert!' I shout, following him out into the corridor. He can't just leave like this. We need to talk.

'Tell the kids I love them,' he calls over his shoulder, and then he's gone.

22

18 MONTHS AGO

It's just coffee.

I keep saying that to myself. It's just coffee. But if it's just coffee, why did I lie to my family and tell them I was going to a book club meeting? If it's just coffee, why did I take extra care with my makeup and wear the perfume I save for special occasions? Why did I spend three hours trying on different outfits and then, exasperated at how middle-aged I looked in all of them, drive fifty miles into Santa Barbara and spend almost a thousand dollars on a new dress, a pair of Spanx, and a cripplingly high pair of shoes? If it's just coffee, why did I delete the text invite from my phone?

I keep telling myself that it's just coffee. Except it isn't. And the moment I walk into Coffee Connection and see Nate, rising from his seat to greet me, I know that.

Two days after we ran into each other he sent a text message asking if I wanted to grab a coffee. He'd got my number from one of the forms I'd filled in prior to them releasing Gene. I hadn't expected him to call. I thought the comment about owing him coffee was a joke, just one of those throwaway comments you make, like when I tell Sam, Abby's mom, that I'd love to go to her church fundraiser, or tell the PTA women that of course I don't mind running as chair again.

Is it wrong to admit that my heart skipped a beat when I saw the text? Hannah tried to peer over my shoulder to read it and I quickly dropped the phone to my side and then busied myself in the kitchen, tidying up.

There was nothing going on – I hadn't done anything wrong – so why was I feeling so guilty? I think it's because from the moment I saw Nate again I've been feeling a low-level hum of electricity coursing through me; a buzz that emanates around my belly button as if a swarm of bees have set up a hive in there. And it's been a long while since I've felt that kind of charge with anyone. Of course I'd had that with Robert – back before we had three children and conversations turned from what we wanted to do to each other to what we wanted the other to do about the washing up or the mess they'd made in the kitchen.

I should have said no. I shouldn't have replied. But I did. Robert's been locked in his study for what feels like months, never present even when he is and, truthfully, reaching forty has sucked.

After picking up Gene from the police station Hannah insisted on going shopping, as we'd intended, so I drove her to Santa Barbara. Walking down State Street with her, I realized that I was invisible. Everyone was looking at her. I was prepared for the menopause but not this. It's too soon. There have been no warning signs. I've been shoved over the line from visible to invisible without even the chance to protest.

You don't realize how much you've spent your life being validated by the male gaze until that gaze bounces right off you and lands on your daughter. And while the feminist in you rears up in anger that you've allowed that gaze to define you and your worth, nonetheless you feel a jealous little stab in your gut.

As we walked, every male eye snagged on Hannah as if she was magnetized. She wasn't oblivious, far from it. She tossed her hair over her shoulder and swayed her hips and strolling beside her I felt a sharp pang. It's not that I wanted to be her, but I envied the choices and the opportunities she had in front of her. Life was a runway and she was strutting down it with a confidence I had never had at her age and still didn't possess. And now I knew I never would.

It's not an excuse but it's where I was at when Nate texted me. Suddenly I was visible again.

As I walk towards him I notice he's wearing a pair of jeans and a black sweater with a little star logo on it which makes me wonder if it's something off-duty Sheriffs wear. It reminds me of his football sweater back in high school and how he used to wear it even after he graduated, as though it was a badge of honor.

'Hi,' I say nervously as I reach him.

He leans forwards and kisses me on the cheek and I feel a flurry of butterflies. I tell myself to stop being stupid.

'You look great,' he says, appraising me.

Oh God. I immediately fluster and warm under his gaze.

'Thanks,' I stammer.

'You want some dinner?' he asks before I've had a chance to sit. 'I just got off duty and I'm starving.'

'OK,' I say, and he grabs his jacket and ushers me towards the door.

As we walk onto the street I find myself glancing around, worried that someone might see me. It's Ventura, which is a bigger town than Ojai, but even so I know a lot of people. There's nothing illicit about two old friends going for a bite to eat though. At least that's what I tell myself. But then why do I feel so nervous, like I'm doing something wrong?

Nate leads me around the corner to a quiet little Italian restaurant, nothing romantic, but not too pedestrian either. There are candles on the table but a couple of boisterous families seated beside us, and I glance around to make sure I don't recognize anyone. Nate pulls out my chair and I remember he was always a gentleman. He summons the waiter and orders wine and, quickly checking that it's OK with me, orders for both of us, telling me he's a regular and that I won't be sorry.

After the first sip of wine I start to relax. There's a lot to catch up on: June's illness, Hannah's academic success, our inability to shoehorn Gene out of the house, how much Hannah and Gene fight, my mom's long, drawn-out death and my dad's sudden one, Nate's failed marriage to Kathy, a cosmetologist from Kentucky whom he married in a shotgun wedding when she fell pregnant nineteen days after they first met at a casino.

He grins at me, his blue eyes flashing, and I shuffle a little in my seat, feeling awkward under his gaze. My own keeps dropping to his lips, remembering the first time he kissed me, remembering too the first time we slept together, the first orgasm he ever gave me.

'How about you?' he asks, jolting me out of my memories.

'What?' I reply.

He studies me, a half smile on his face. 'Are you happily married?'

It's such a direct question that immediately I start to stammer. 'Yes, I mean . . . for over twenty years, I guess . . .' I tail off. Nate's still eyeing me with a curious smile, and now an arched eyebrow.

'Twenty years? You got married in college then?'

'Actually, I dropped out to get married and have Hannah.'

'Wow,' he says. 'Twenty years, that's a long time. You're not bored?' The look in his eye is testing, inviting and I feel a response in the deepest part of my core, a little spark of life. I shake my head, looking down at my plate. I feel disloyal to Robert. I should be announcing loud and clear how happy I am, how satisfied . . . but I can't. And when I look up at Nate I feel a kick in my chest as my heart bangs against my ribs and a jolt of adrenaline rushes through me. I want to kiss him. I imagine what it would be like to sleep with him after all these years. Before I can stop myself, I'm thinking about him stripping me naked and fucking me. I'm imagining it in glorious detail. Oh God.

'You still painting?' he asks.

I shake my head, trying to banish the image. 'Not really,' I say.

'What happened?' he asks as the waiter sets a panna cotta in front of him. I remember how proud I was to get into the New School, how I told Nate I'd come home and visit him in the holidays. He was staying put in Ventura, helping in his dad's construction company.

'Life,' I mumble, thinking of all the dreams I had at eighteen. Where did they go? Down the drain when I had Hannah, that's where. I've got no one to blame but myself for that. 'I probably would never have made it as an artist anyway,' I say.

'What are you talking about?' Nate asks. 'You were really good.'

I shrug, pleased at the compliment.

'I think I still have a few of your paintings, you know. I kept them.'

I look up at him, astonished. 'You did?' I ask.

He nods, picking up his spoon. 'Couldn't bring myself to throw them away.'

I cringe once more. 'I'm sorry,' I say, shaking my head with a sigh.

It's his turn to shrug. He gives me a wry smile.

'I was a bitch,' I say, thinking of how heartless I had been.

'No,' he says. 'We were kids. I get it. You had a whole life ahead of you. Making new friends. Big city and all that. It's all right,' he laughs. 'I'll forgive you for breaking my heart.'

I look down, feeling awkward. Did I really break his heart?

Nate holds out a spoonful of panna cotta. 'Tempt you?' he says.

My stomach falls away. Are we crossing a line? It's been so long and I'm so out of practice I'm not sure. I swallow hard and then I open my mouth very slightly and he eases the spoon between my lips. I taste the panna cotta, let it slide down my throat, and he takes the spoon back, smiling.

'Seriously though, you breaking up with me – it gave me the kick up the ass I needed. Figured I needed to get my shit together. I joined the army. Was in the First Armored Division out of Fort Bliss. Did eight years then came out and joined the Sheriff's department.'

'You did well, Nate.'

He spreads his palms wide. 'This high school jock didn't turn out too badly huh?'

He puts his spoon down and signals the waiter for the check, refusing to let me put my card down. 'I got this,' he says. 'You can get it next time.' He stares at me directly as he says it and there's a glint in his eye. A challenge.

My pulse leaps. Next time? I know I should get up and leave. I should tell him it's been great to catch up but that we should probably go our separate ways. But my tongue is tied and my feet stay planted firmly to the floor.

Nate signs his name on the receipt and then stands. I follow suit, nervous as he helps me with my jacket. What happens now? As we walk out of the restaurant he rests his hand on my lower back the way he used to when we were dating, and there's a feeling of possession in it, of being desired, that sets my nerves jangling. He walks me towards my car and the whole way I feel shot through with an electrical current. We stop and I rummage in my bag for my keys, procrastinating, not wanting to confront Nate.

'I'm not sure I should let you drive,' Nate murmurs.

'I really should get home,' I say, too nervous to look at him.

'Ava,' he whispers, stepping closer, so he's almost touching me. I can smell the woodsy, musky scent of him. My stomach gives way and I look up. He takes my face in his hands and then pulls me closer and kisses me. And I close my eyes and let him.

PART TWO

23

DAY 5

There's no deputy Sheriff on duty outside the ICU, guarding the door. A nurse buzzes me through the double doors and I ask her if she knows where the police officer might have gone. She says she doesn't know and then quickly hurries off. I don't fail to miss the sideways look she gives me, and as I walk to June's room I can feel the heat of shame prickling my skin.

Robert's arrest is all over the news, but they haven't yet released information about the second charge – the conspiracy to commit murder charge – so everyone thinks I'm complicit in some way. *But I didn't know anything!* I want to yell after the nurse. I still don't. My husband might have wanted to kill me!

Laurie told me it can't be true. She kept repeating it to me over and over in the car. Of course Robert didn't do it, of course they're grabbing at straws, of course he'll be proved innocent. But the fact is . . . what if he did do it? What if he is guilty? What if he did want me dead?

The door to June's room is shut and I pause before opening it, readying myself for the sight of her. It's only been five days but she seems to be getting paler and smaller by the hour – some essential light fading in her. As I step inside I see a doctor in a surgical cap and gown standing over the bed, reaching for the IV line running into June's arm.

'What are you—' I shout, stepping into the room.

The doctor turns, startled, and then bolts towards me, shoving me forcefully aside as he sprints for the door and then down the hall.

'Hey!' I yell after him.

He doesn't turn.

In a panic, I turn to June and glance at her. What did he do to her? The machines are still beeping. Her chest is still rising and falling. She seems OK. But who was that man? And what did he want? I race back into the hall, just in time to see him disappearing through the fire exit at the end of the hall.

I run after him, reaching inside my bag for my phone, but before I can pull it out, the door to the relatives' room further down the hallway flies open and Hannah and the deputy Sheriff who should have been on duty rush out. The nurse yells, directing the Sheriff's attention to the fire escape doors, which are slamming shut behind the fleeing man. The deputy starts sprinting towards them, drawing his gun as he goes.

'What is it? What happened?' Hannah asks, racing over to me.

I ignore her and keep running down the corridor towards the fire escape, following the deputy. Hannah runs after me. 'Stay with June,' I shout at her over my shoulder.

I carry on, past the nurse, who is already on the phone calling for security, and push through the double doors. I lean over the stairwell, out of breath, and see the deputy three floors below, thundering down the stairs in pursuit, gaining on the man fast. They reach the bottom and I hear the screech of a metal fire door being flung open and the smash of it hitting a concrete wall and then they're gone. Was it the journalist from the other day? Or someone else? What was he doing in June's room?

'Mom?'

A hand on my arm makes me jump. I turn and find Hannah standing in front of me. 'What happened?'

I glance over her shoulder. 'I told you not to leave June,' I hiss, pushing past her, panic surging through me.

'It's OK. The doctors are in with her.'

Hannah tails me as I rush back to June's room. The doctors are buzzing around her, checking the machines, calling out readings.

'It's fine, she's fine,' the nurse tells me, patting my arm. But even though she reassures me, I can't drag my eyes off June. What was that man doing in her room? What would have happened if I hadn't shown up?

There's a tap on my shoulder. I wheel around and find Hannah standing there, eyes wide with shock.

'What were you doing?' I demand angrily. 'Why wasn't that police officer watching the door? What the hell were you and he doing—'

'The machine ate my money.'

'What?'

'I was trying to buy a Coke and the machine ate my money and he heard me yelling and came in to find out what was happening. He was just trying to help me, that's all.'

'He shouldn't have left her,' I say, fury lighting me up.

Hannah's eyes brim with tears. 'I'm sorry.'

My anger leaches away at the sight of her tears. I drop my arms to my sides.

'His name is Jonathan. He bought me lunch the other day because I had no cash,' Hannah says, starting to cry. 'My cards won't work. And I didn't want to ask you for money because I know you don't have any and . . .' She starts to sob loudly, big choking cries, and I open my arms and she falls into them. I hold her and stroke her hair, feeling more than a pang of guilt that a stranger has been taking care of my daughter because I've been too absorbed with other things. I'm a lousy mother. A familiar guilt drenches me like ice water. The same thing happened when June was in the hospital. Hannah and Gene became secondary to everything. If it hadn't been for Laurie and Dave helping to take care of them and feed them, I'm not sure how we would have managed. They would probably have been taken into care.

'I'm sorry,' I mumble, kissing Hannah.

She hugs me back tightly. 'I love you,' she says.

'I love you too.'

I haven't thought about Hannah at all in all of this. When did I have time? There's been too much else going on. But of course this is affecting her the same as it's affecting me. Probably worse, in fact. Who has she got to turn to? To talk to? And what is she going to say when she finds out about the other charges – *oh by the way, Hannah, they're also charging your father with conspiracy to commit murder.* I need to find a way to tell her and Gene soon, before the media finds out. I can't have them hearing it on the news.

Loud voices pull us back out into the hallway. The deputy Sheriff is back, sweating and out of breath. He's talking to the hospital's head of security and another officer, and he's shaking his head. Clearly, he didn't catch the man. Damn it.

He looks my way then, his expression abashed. He ducks his head unhappily as the other deputy scowls and gestures angrily at the door. He's getting bawled out.

'Oh no,' whispers Hannah, watching it happen. 'This is my fault. I should say something.'

I glance at her. Her face is flushed and her shirt is undone so that her bra is showing. A thought occurs to me. Maybe it was the flustered look on her face when she ran out into the hallway, or something about her concerned expression as she watches the Sheriff get reprimanded now. I look at him more closely. He's late twenties I would guess, and good-looking in a clean-cut way. I can see how Hannah might find him attractive, especially wearing his Sheriff's uniform. I've seen him a few times with Nate. I wonder if Hannah's been turning to him for comfort and think about tackling her about it as he's far too old for her, but before I can say anything Nate arrives on the scene.

He's obviously been apprised of the situation, as he strides into the ICU with a scowl on his face and makes a beeline straight for his deputy. He glances briefly our way and nods his head by way of greeting before leading the deputy away, further down the hall, where they stop and Nate pulls out his notebook and starts interrogating him.

'Come on,' I say to Hannah, pulling her back into June's room.

24

DAY 6

Hannah's problem becomes my problem. A day later I'm standing beside the newsstand in the lobby of the hospital, trying to withdraw cash from the ATM and the machine is refusing to play ball. I've tried every single card and I'm aware that there's an impatient nurse standing behind me tapping her foot and sighing loudly.

I turn around, stuffing my wallet full of redundant cards back into my bag.

'I can lend you money,' Laurie says, seeing my face when I walk back over to her by the coffee stand.

'How am I going to pay you back?' I ask, taking out my bottle of painkillers and dry swallowing several.

Laurie smiles at me and links her arm through mine. 'Don't worry about it. That's what friends are for.'

Yes, I think, sure, but at some point I'm going to exhaust the limits of her generosity. It's not like she and Dave can afford to keep supporting me. But what am I going to do? How am I going to get money to pay for our living costs? How am I going to find a place to stay or pay our hospital bills, let alone a lawyer? I don't know what to do.

It's been two days since they arrested Robert. His arraignment happened this morning but Horowitz failed to tell me, so I missed it. He entered a no contest plea, something which

I had to Google. It means he's neither denying nor admitting the charges against him, but is willing to accept the punishment. The pundits on the news are all proclaiming this a surefire sign of guilt. Even Horowitz. The only charge he refused to plead guilty to was conspiracy to commit murder.

I've called Nate to ask if I can see Robert again but apparently he's refusing all visitors, including his lawyer. Another sign of guilt? I'm so angry that every time I think of him I feel like I might burst into flames. He lied to me about the bankruptcy and yet had the nerve to accuse me of being a liar, as though he's so goddamn innocent!

Hannah wanted to know how I could doubt his innocence, how I could believe for an instant that her father was guilty. *Because the evidence is so insurmountable,* I wanted to shout at her. Because he had a motive, several in fact, though I can't tell her all of them. I've seen enough crime shows to know that money and jealousy are two of the biggest motives in homicide cases. And yes, I thought I knew Robert, better than anyone in the world, but how well do you ever know anyone, really?

'Why won't he see you?' Laurie asked.

I just shrugged. I can't tell her either.

'Where's Gene, by the way?' she asks now, as we make our way across the hospital lobby.

I shake my head. 'I don't know. He came by yesterday to see June, stayed five minutes, then disappeared. I haven't seen or heard from him since. I'm worried.'

'What did he have to say about his dad being in prison? About the charges? Is he doing OK?'

'I don't know,' I say. 'I don't know anything. I've been living in a state of complete ignorance. My whole life was a lie.'

'Where's he staying?'

'He's not staying with you?' I ask, turning to her.

Laurie shakes her head.

'Oh. Well . . . at the house, I guess, or maybe with a friend.'

'Dave drove him somewhere the other day but I haven't seen him either since then.'

I frown at that. 'Why did Dave have to drive him?'

'I think Gene sold his car. Didn't he tell you?'

'What?' I stare at Laurie in astonishment but she just shrugs.

I wonder if he's sold it in an effort to help out with the bills, and for a moment my heart softens towards him. But then I remind myself it's Gene and he's probably just used the cash to replace his stolen laptop and buy weed. He certainly hasn't bothered to call or offer money. It does give me an idea though. Perhaps I can sell my car, or Robert's. And we own some good pieces of furniture . . .

'How long have you got to move out of the house?' Laurie asks as we walk to the elevators.

'I don't know,' I say. I probably would know if I checked my messages but I've been ignoring all calls and letting them ring through to voicemail. I only answer if it's the kids, Laurie or Nate. I'm tired of having to repeat myself endlessly to friends and family seeking updates on June and more recently looking for an inside scoop on Robert's arrest (though they disguise their rabid curiosity as sympathy). My voicemail is also filled with pleading messages from journalists, all asking for an exclusive interview. I gave up deleting them after the first two dozen.

I stop in front of the newsstand and scour the front pages. Immediately a headline leaps out at me from the *Santa Barbara Herald*. TWO MORE SUSPECTS ARRESTED OVER HOME INVASION. There are mugshots splashed across the front page and I recognize them as the two men in the photographs Nate showed me; the ones Robert was paying off, supposedly to break into the house and murder me.

'Did you know about this?' Laurie asks. 'Did the Sheriff tell you they were arresting them?'

I shake my head dumbly. 'I knew they were wanted for questioning, that's all.' I scan the article. There are few details about the suspects, other than their names and ages. I study their faces. One is a solid slab of a man. He's staring at the camera like he's facing off with an opponent in a title fight, his eyes so heavy-lidded they're almost slits. The other one looks like he could be a friend of Gene's from school – he's preppy with clean-shaven good looks and a neat side parting. Could either of them be the men who broke into our house? I stare at the one with the shaved head and instantly I'm back in June's room, seeing her there, on her knees in front of him, the man turning towards me with the gun in his hand.

Dots start to dance frantically in front of my eyes and a sheen of sweat breaks out all over my body. I feel as if I've been hit all at once with flu.

'Are you OK?' Laurie asks.

I take a few deep breaths, waiting for the dizziness to pass. Laurie throws some dollars at the newsstand guy and we walk a few paces away to study the photograph under the light.

'Is that them, do you think?' Laurie asks.

I shake my head. 'I don't know. They were wearing masks.'

My phone rings and I pull it out. It's Nate. I take the call as Laurie and I enter the elevator.

'Did you see the news?' he asks me, straight off the bat.

'Yes.'

'We found the guys. We've brought them in for questioning. Can you come down to the station? We need you to do an ID.'

'I told you, I didn't see their faces.'

'But you heard their voices. We want you to see if you recognize them by their voices.'

Can I remember their voices? I don't know anymore. It all feels like it happened so long ago. There's something though – something that keeps nagging at me – something in the foggiest part of my brain that I know I've forgotten and that I need to remember.

'Ava?'

'Yes. I'll be there.'

'Great.'

I make to hang up but I stop because I can hear Nate on the other end of the line, hesitating. 'Ava?' he finally says.

'Mmmm?'

'How are you doing?'

His voice is soft as a caress, low – as if he's trying not to be overheard. He's not asking as the Sheriff.

'I'll see you later, Nate,' I say, and then hang up.

25

'In your statement you said that when you were in the kitchen the second man said the words *"Get over here"*.'

'Hmm?'

I glance at Nate. He's been talking and I haven't been listening.

Nate looks up from his notebook. 'Sorry, I know this must be hard.'

I study him and in my head I'm thinking, *You have no idea. No one does. No idea at all.* 'What happens?' I ask, turning my attention to the two-way glass and trying to compose myself. 'I give a correct ID on these guys and you arrest them?'

'We're checking their alibis. If you can ID them and we can find a hole in their alibi, then yes, we've got enough to charge them. If we can match DNA to traces left at the house, then we've got an even stronger case. The lab are running tests but they'll take a month, maybe longer, to come back with results.'

I stare through the glass at the empty room on the other side. It's the same room I sat in with Robert when he told me he knew about me and Nate. I can't tell Nate that Robert suspects something is going on between us, as I'm sure Nate would use that as further evidence against him – another motive – and until I know for sure that Robert isn't guilty, I'm not about to give Nate more evidence to use against him.

'Did they admit Robert hired them? Did they say he hired them to kill me?' I ask.

'They haven't admitted to anything,' Nate says. 'But that's because they're lawyered up better than OJ and their lawyer's counseling them to say nothing.'

So they haven't admitted it. 'And if I manage to identify them by their voices, then what?' I ask.

'We can't hold them. It won't be enough for the DA. The defense will punch a hole right through it in court.'

'So what's the point of this then?' I ask.

'Because it's something,' Nate says. 'If you can ID them, at least we know we're looking in the right direction. We can discount other lines of enquiry. We're looking into their alibis for the night of the break-in right now. If we can tear those apart and put them at the scene with DNA evidence, we've got enough to charge them.'

'And Robert too.'

He gives an awkward shrug. 'Don't you want to know the truth?' he asks me.

I nod. I do. I need to know if Robert is guilty. I wish I could swear blind that he's innocent, but I can't. If he lied to me about the bankruptcy and the fact he'd blown through three million plus dollars, then what else could he lie to me about?

'Let's do this then,' I say impatiently to Nate. 'I need to get back to June.'

Nate bangs on the door. An attractive Latina woman strides into the room wearing an expensive suit, stiletto heels and a slash of red lipstick. She gives me a once-over that makes me shrink about three inches. If I had balls they would have ridden up somewhere inside my body.

'Their lawyer,' Nate whispers under his breath to me. I eye the woman with a frown. How the hell can they afford a lawyer who looks like she just walked off the set of *The Good Wife*?

A minute later six men, all wearing ski masks that cover their faces, troop into the room on the other side of the glass. I take a deep breath, feeling a tremor run through me. I sense Nate glancing at me out of the corner of his eye. I wasn't expecting the masks but of course it makes sense. Nate and I watch as the men are lined up in front of a height chart. I immediately discount number six because he's tall, almost six feet one, but the others are all shorter.

'They can't see or hear us,' Nate reminds me.

I scan the men in turn. With the masks over their heads it's almost impossible to tell which two I saw in the paper. But it's just as hard to know if any of them were the two men who broke into the house.

Nate leans forwards and presses a button on the desk in front of us. 'Number one, if you could repeat the line on the piece of paper.'

I notice now that they're all holding a small scrap of paper. The man holds his up in front of his face. 'June,' he mumbles. 'Get over here.'

'Louder please,' Nate orders.

The man repeats it. I close my eyes and try to focus on the timbre of his voice. He sounds too gruff, too old and the words are too muffled through the mask to hear well. When I open my eyes I find Nate watching me. I shake my head.

'Number two please, step forwards and repeat the line,' says Nate.

Number two takes a slouching step forwards, glaring in our direction. Even though there's mirrored glass between us, I can't shake the feeling he can see through it and is fixing his gaze right on me. He talks quietly at first and Nate has to ask him to speak up.

'June, get over here,' he says louder, a hint of amusement in his voice as though he's smirking beneath the ski mask.

I study him hard. He's about the right height but he's stockier than either of the men who attacked us. He reminds me of a pit bull. And the man who took June upstairs, the leader, he said *get* like *git*.

'No. It's not him,' I say.

Nate makes a mark on a clipboard. I frown and study the man again.

The man who dragged me off the bed and shoved me down the stairs, the man that I hit with the chopping board . . . I remember his hand around my leg – the iron strength of his grip. 'Can you get him to say something else?' I ask Nate.

Nate looks up. 'What?'

'Get him to say: *Where are you taking her?*'

Nate presses the button and leans into the microphone. 'Number two, please repeat the following line: "Where are you taking her?"'

The man pauses and then delivers the line flatly.

Nate's holding his breath and despite her outward cool I can sense that the lawyer is holding hers too. 'Ava?'

I think it's him. I think it's the man I hit with the board . . .

'Is it him? Do you recognize the voice?' Nate asks.

'Sheriff,' the lawyer says in a warning tone.

'I . . .' I stop. If I admit I think it could be, then where does that leave Robert? Will it confirm his guilt? And I'm not sure, anyway, how is it possible to tell? 'No . . .' I say, shaking my head. 'It's not him.'

I glance at the lawyer and see she isn't bothering to hide her smile.

'OK, let's move on to number three,' Nate says, scowling. He speaks into the microphone and gives his orders and we go through two more suspects but now I'm rattled. They all sound similar – muffled and indistinct. By the time we get to the final two I'm more confused than ever. All the voices have blended into one. I admit that I can't be sure about either of the final suspects and Nate dismisses them all.

I know he's disappointed as he sighs loudly, especially as we watch the lawyer stride from the room smiling smugly.

'Which numbers were they?' I ask Nate.

'Number two and number six.'

'Six? The tall one?' I ask.

Nate nods.

'But he's too tall. Neither of them were that tall.' I can feel my heart starting to beat with something like elation, relief filling me with helium lightness.

Nate frowns at me. 'Maybe you got that wrong in the heat of the moment. Witnesses often give confusing statements. Your husband said one of the suspects was between five ten and six feet one.'

I shake my head. 'No. I made a real effort to remember everything I could about them and I know his height because Robert's six foot one, and the man who attacked him was shorter. They were both shorter.'

'Maybe you made a mistake. It happens.' Nate leans against the table, his long legs stretched out ahead of him. He looks tired, I notice, dark shadows beneath his eyes. He hasn't shaved in a while either.

'What happens now?' I ask him.

'We've still got their alibis to check out.'

'So you might still be able to charge them?' I ask.

He gives a non-committal shrug.

'And what about Robert?'

'He still won't talk,' Nate tells me. 'Which isn't helping him any. If he would tell us what he was doing meeting them it would make this easier. A no contest plea means he's going to prison. You realize that, don't you? And he'll still stand trial for the conspiracy to commit murder charge.'

Murder. Every time I hear it I shudder.

'Come on, let me see you out,' Nate says, ushering me to the door. There's no hand on my lower back this time.

'Can I see him?' I ask.

'He still won't accept visitors,' Nate answers.

We reach the door to the reception area. 'I'll keep you posted on what happens,' Nate says.

I nod and make to turn away but then I remember something.

'Remember the guy who said he was a journalist? The one you confronted at the hospital? His name was Euan Shriver. At least that's what he told us.'

Nate nods.

'I Googled him on the way here – he doesn't exist. I called the *Santa Barbara Herald* and they'd never heard of him. And I couldn't find a single trace of him online.'

Nate rubs a hand across his eyes. 'Shit,' he mumbles again. 'OK, well, we both got a good look at him. I'll get a uniform to check the hospital security tapes. See if I can pull something on him. Find out who he is.'

'Don't you think that's important?' I press. 'I mean, what if he's who we've been looking for this whole time? What if he's one of the men who broke into the house?'

Nate nods. 'Maybe, yeah. It's a possibility. But at the same time he could just be a journalist digging for dirt. He could have given a false name so he didn't get into trouble.'

'But what if—'

Nate cuts me off. 'We have our suspects. Robert's pleading no contest.' He looks at me pityingly. He really believes that Robert is guilty, that he's got this whole case sewn up, but I can't just let it go. Not until I'm shown absolute proof.

'Just promise me you'll look into it?' I beg Nate. 'Please.'

He sighs. 'OK. I'll look into it.'

He's about to go back inside when the door opens. It's the deputy who left his post yesterday when he should have been guarding June's room. He sees me and nods. 'Mrs Walker,' he mumbles, tipping his hat in my direction, before turning to Nate. 'Their alibis checked out.'

'Shit,' Nate mutters.

'What does that mean?' I ask.

'Are they reliable?' Nate asks the deputy, ignoring me.

He shrugs.

Nate huffs. 'I'll call you later,' he says as he strides off.

I watch him vanish into his office. That's good, isn't it? If their alibis checked out that means they weren't involved, it means that Robert is innocent . . . doesn't it? But if he's innocent of hiring them to rob us or kill me, what was he meeting with them about?

'Wait,' I say to the deputy, Jonathan, grabbing his arm to stop him from leaving too. I notice his badge, Jonathan Safechuck. 'What happens now?'

He turns to me. 'We have to let them go. We've got nothing to hold them on.'

'What about Robert? Will they let him go too? That proves that he didn't plot any of this.'

'We've still got him on the conspiracy to commit insurance fraud charge.'

'But the conspiracy to commit murder?' I ask. 'Are you dropping it?'

He grimaces. 'You should talk to his lawyer.'

He tips his hat and then rushes off after Nate, leaving me standing there, swaying slightly, wishing the world would stop spinning for a moment and let me catch my breath.

26

DAY 7

The door to June's room opens and I look up in alarm. It's Gene, looking like the vagrants who sleep under the bridge in the park. He's wearing wrinkled, dirt-stained clothes, and looks like he hasn't showered in days. His hair is lank and hangs in his face.

'Where have you been?' I ask.

He shrugs sheepishly. 'Around.'

I narrow my eyes as he shuffles to the bed and looks down at June. Did he see the news?

He frowns and then drops into a chair on the other side of the bed. Is he stoned? He doesn't seem it. His foot is bouncing up and down like he's jazz drumming and his eyes keep darting about the place. If anything, he seems the opposite of stoned. He seems amped on something.

'Where have you been?' I ask. 'Laurie said you weren't staying with her and Dave.'

'I've been at the house,' he mumbles.

'We have to move out,' I tell him.

Gene darts a glance in my direction. 'I know,' he says, his eyes sliding back to June. 'Dave told me.'

I finally checked my messages and the bank have given us *a very generous extra two weeks* before they're sending around the enforcement agency to bodily remove us. I called the bank manager, full of apology, begging for more time, but she was unmoved. I need to sort out all our belongings. I don't know what I'm going to do – sell what I can, put the rest in storage, I suppose, until I figure it out. The irony is that the insurance policy that Robert bought would cover us for all our medical costs and would pay off the bank loans, leaving us well off, but because he's been arrested for fraud we can't get a penny of it.

There's a pause as Gene and I both sit and stare at June, who seems to have shrunk even more into herself. She resembles some kind of macabre doll. Her eyes have hollowed into her skull, the fine bones of her hands and wrists are carving out of the skin as her muscles start to waste away.

'I need your help,' I finally say, wondering why he hasn't asked anything at all about his father or the police investigation. Why doesn't he want to know what's happening? Does he wonder, like me, if his father is guilty and he's just too scared to voice it?

'We need to sell some things,' I say, taking a deep breath. 'The paintings – there's a Simon Caldwell painting that must be worth something – and my car too, maybe the dealer will take it back. I've hardly driven it. I need your help with that.'

'What?' Gene says.

'We need the money,' I tell him, as if it wasn't obvious.

Gene takes that in and then turns back to June. He doesn't react at all, just stares at her. What the hell is going on? Did he not hear what I just said? I need his help!

I'm about to yell at him but I stop myself abruptly, a sudden thought occurring. What if I'm being blind? What if it's something worse than being stoned? I study him closer. His skin is paler even than June's and sweat beads his brow at the hairline. His lips are chapped to the point they're bleeding, and he's fidgeting, scratching fiercely behind his ear as though he's got a bite there. I wrack my brains, trying to remember the signs of meth addiction.

'Gene?'

He looks at me finally and I see that his pupils are fully dilated. 'Are you OK?' I ask him. *Please God. Not this too*, is what I'm thinking. But then I stop my little prayer, cut it short, because it seems that whoever is up there has already decided that I'm his current plaything, like a Rottweiler with a new chew toy, and any exhortation on my part only seems to spur him on to maul me further.

'I'm fine,' Gene says, looking quickly away, scratching again at that invisible itch behind his ear. He jumps abruptly to his feet. 'I need to go,' he says, making for the door.

'Where are you going?' I ask, getting to my feet. He only. just got here.

'I'll get started on selling stuff on Craigslist, I guess. Can I take your car?'

'Are you OK to drive?' I ask.

He frowns at me. 'I'm fine,' he mumbles, pulling a face like *why wouldn't I be?*

'Gene,' I say, with the tone of a mother who's caught their five-year-old by the empty cookie jar with crumbs down their shirt and chocolate smears all over their face.

'I'm fine,' he repeats impatiently. 'I'm good.' But he won't look me in the eye.

'You don't look good.'

'I'm just not sleeping, is all.' He swipes at his nose. 'I think I might be coming down with something.'

'Gene,' I say, walking over to him. I touch his wrist and he jumps in alarm, pulling away from me, but not before I've felt his skin. He's clammy to the touch and up close I can see the capillary starbursts in his eyes and something else that surprises me. He looks afraid, like he's seen a ghost. His eyes are darting all over the place, refusing to settle.

I glance down, looking for tracks up the inside of his arms, but his sweater covers them. Is he shooting up? Or smoking meth? There's a big meth problem in the valley and I know of one or two kids from his year at school who have fallen into it.

Gene wrenches his arm free from my grip. 'Can I borrow your car?'

'What did you do with yours?' I ask him.

'I sold it,' he says.

'Why?' I ask him.

'We need the money, don't we?' he says.

I think about asking him where the money is, what he's used it for, but I don't because I'm afraid to know. I can't handle hearing he's on drugs. I have too much else to deal with. So I let Gene snatch the car keys from my hand and watch him scurry out the door.

27

Dave meets me outside the hospital to give me a ride home so I can start packing our things and sorting out items to sell. Laurie, he tells me, has had to get on with some school work. Of course. I'm embarrassed at how reliant I've become on her. I should have realized it was too much for anyone, let alone someone who works full time and has her own life and own problems to deal with.

'Don't feel bad,' Dave says, intuiting my discomfort. 'She wanted to come. She just has a backlog of stuff to get through.'

He starts driving, glancing over at me a few times until he finally breaks the silence. 'How are you doing?' he asks.

'Well, you know,' I say, 'I think I'd be doing better if my daughter woke up from her coma and our house wasn't about to be repossessed by the bank and my husband wasn't in jail for trying to murder me.'

Dave winces. 'Yes, sorry, stupid question. I meant how's your head?'

'Oh,' I say, reaching up to touch the thin line of stitches that are hidden beneath my hair. The bruise is still tender but the constant ache has gone. I get the odd slicing pain, as though someone is inserting a red-hot needle into the jelly of my brain, but otherwise it's OK. 'I'm fine.'

I sigh and, sinking back in the seat, close my eyes. The car smells as if someone has upended a can of Fanta over the upholstery, but beneath it is the unmistakable whiff of something else, something pungent: weed.

I reach down and grab the aerosol can I've just caught sight of in the side panel of the passenger door. Tropical Tango air freshener. I've found the source of Laurie's paranoia about Dave having an affair. Not cheap perfume at all, but air freshener to disguise the smell of marijuana. I glance around the car. An SUV. Of course. How did it take me so long to figure it out? This is the car I saw outside the house the night of the break-in. The car Gene got into.

'Have you seen Gene?' I ask Dave, keeping my voice casual.

Dave grips the wheel tighter, his knuckles blanching. 'Um, no. Well, earlier this week I drove him to the hospital. And to the jail to see Robert.'

'Robert?'

Dave darts a glance my way, his eyes round. 'Um, I thought you knew.'

'He went to see Robert?'

Dave nods, eyes on the road. Damn it. Why didn't he tell me? I can't lie, it hurts that Robert agreed to see Gene but still won't agree to see me or a lawyer. What did they talk about?

I'm sick to death of not knowing anything, of getting no answers. Not about June and her prognosis, not about my own husband's involvement in what happened, not even about Gene and why he sold his car. Even Nate has kept things from me. I feel like I'm being swept along by currents outside of my control, hurled against rocks and boulders. I'm barely managing to stay conscious and to keep my head above water. I keep hoping that at some point someone will fish me out and haul me onto dry land and tell me that it's all going to be OK, but perhaps that's the problem. Perhaps I need to stop waiting to be saved and for someone to come along and provide me with answers, and instead I need to drag my own sorry ass to shore and start looking for them.

I stare at Dave out the corner of my eye. Maybe I should start right here.

'Since when have you smoked weed, Dave?' I ask.

He looks at me, eyes wide, before turning back to the road. 'Don't tell Laurie,' he says. 'You know how she feels about drugs.'

Laurie isn't a puritan; it's just that as a teacher she's always had to be careful. Being caught in possession would have cost her job a few years ago, but now marijuana is legal in the state of California. There are two or three dispensaries in town selling everything from infused gummy bears to chocolate brownies to skunk. 'It's legal now,' I say to Dave. 'Why would she care?'

Dave shrugs, apparently not having an answer.

'Gene was with you the night of the break-in, wasn't he?'

Dave startles again, his hands gripping the wheel. 'Yes,' he finally mumbles.

How and when did Dave and Gene become such good friends? There's a twenty-year age gap between them.

'Is Gene smoking?' I ask him, figuring if they're such good friends perhaps he knows what's going on.

'Just occasionally,' he says.

'He told us he quit.'

'Shit,' Dave mutters. 'I don't want to drop him in it. He's a good kid.'

'He's not a kid,' I hiss back. I'm so angry at how I've been duped. Gene and his overnight reformation . . . what a fool I've been to believe his promises that he'd turned over a new leaf.

'It's just some weed, Ava,' he says. 'Come on, didn't you ever smoke, at college even?'

'No.' I've never smoked a joint in my life. I always worried about losing control.

Dave falls silent and I sit there, musing and fuming. 'Is it just that he's doing?' I ask. 'Nothing more serious?'

Dave looks at me oddly, 'What do you mean?'

'Is he on meth?'

Dave almost swerves into oncoming traffic again. 'What? No! I mean, well, I don't think so. Why would you think that?'

'Because he's acting all wired and strung out.'

Dave pulls a face. 'He's just stressed.'

I chew on my lip and look out the window. Would Gene admit it if he were on meth?

'What were you doing the other night?'

'What night?'

'The night of the break-in. I saw you. You picked Gene up and drove off somewhere.'

Dave swallows. 'We just went for a drive, smoked.'

I narrow my eyes at him. His face has gone the color of a strawberry and his Adam's apple is bouncing around like a live animal as he swallows repeatedly.

Dave's a terrible liar. I glare at him and he shrinks beneath my gaze like a turtle retreating inside its shell. I won't get anything more from him. I need to confront Gene.

28

I stand in the hallway, looking at the stairs. Fingerprint smudges dirty the bannister, and a trail of blood snakes down the steps – mine or June's?

I guess Robert never got around to cleaning up the house and the idea of cleaning has never occurred to Gene before, so why would he start now? Hannah hasn't been back since that first visit. Alone, I stand there and think through what's happened, forcing myself to go back over that night. My brain tries to resist it but I know if I'm to get to the bottom of this I need to face it. I need to walk through the events of that night and see if I've forgotten something important, something that could help shed light on the truth.

I came in through the garage door, following June. I walk into the cold kitchen and try to picture it. June had left the milk out on the side. I put it away in the fridge. Then I poured myself some wine. Or did I do that after I went to see Robert? After, I think.

I walk out of the kitchen and, shoes echoing on the floor, I cross through the house to Robert's study. The door was closed. I knocked. It was locked. He answered it. How did he seem? Alarmed? Nervous? He was anxious that June was home, I remember that. Is that because he knew what was about to happen and wanted her out of the house so she wouldn't get hurt? God, I don't know. It could be that, or I could be misreading the situation entirely. Maybe he was just worried that she was sick. Which is it? My memory is Swiss cheese. I feel like I have blind spots at the edge of my vision and I'm not seeing the whole picture properly.

Leaning against the door to Robert's study, I close my eyes and try to picture the expression on his face. He was so distracted, desperate to get me out of the room so he could go back to whatever he was doing. And what was he doing? Was he working? Watching porn? Readying himself for the imminent break-in he had himself plotted and planned? Did my arrival throw a spanner in the works? But no, how could it? He had planned for us to be out at dinner that night anyway. None of us were meant to be home.

I bang my hand against the door, frustrated. It doesn't make sense. How can I believe Robert masterminded an insurance fraud or that he was plotting to kill me? That's not who he is. He's a good man. It's why I chose him. He's a kind man. One of the best men I've ever known. I remember saying that to my father when I told him I was quitting school to get married and have a baby.

I cast my mind back. When I first met Robert he was a post-grad at NYU, studying computer science. I liked how nerdy he was, how serious and decent, but also how his shyness gave way to passionate discourse about politics and history and books. I loved how I could talk to him about art and literature, whereas whenever I talked about those things to Nate he'd glazed over. I liked how when we made love it was less about conquering and more about sharing. He was gentle, sweet, skilled. When I told him I was pregnant Robert offered to marry me straight away. I often wondered if he regretted it but the few times I asked he always reassured me no. I don't think he was lying. Robert always tells the truth. I find it infuriating at times. I asked him not long ago if my crows' feet were visible and he said yes. He didn't seem to understand why the truth wasn't what I was looking for.

And yet, he lied to me about our finances. Not outright, but by omission. Was I wrong to think of him as honest? What if he's lied to me all along about other things that I don't even know about?

And he knew about you and Nate, the voice in my head whispers. Is that enough of a motive combined with the fact he was bankrupt? Perhaps it is. How else does it explain what he was doing in Oxnard, meeting those men and giving them money?

Goddamn it, I'm going around in circles. I open the door to the study and scan the room, my gaze falling on the blood spattered all over the cream rug, dried now to a dark brown the color of rust, before moving on to the safe. It's set into the floor, normally hidden seamlessly beneath the floorboards. The door is open and I take a step closer and peer inside.

It's empty, of course.

I don't know for sure what happened in here – I haven't been allowed to read Robert's statement. All I know is what he told me before he was arrested, which was only the barest details.

Robert opened the safe for the man – of course he did. June was there and the man was pointing a gun at them. He was hardly going to refuse. Besides, all our things, like my jewelry, were insured. The man punched him and then hit him with the butt of his gun and knocked him out, all because he was moving too slowly, his hand shaking too hard as he opened the safe. The bloodstains on the floor are evidence of the savageness of the beating, as if Robert's face isn't testimony enough.

Robert's laptop has been taken away as evidence and the filing cabinet drawers are all flung open, the files emptied.

The police must have taken everything. Everything except for a painting on the wall – another one of mine, a landscape view of the valley, and a couple of framed photos on the desk. One is of Robert and me taken a few years ago on our wedding anniversary, just after we moved into this house. The glass is broken but the photo is intact. We're looking into each other's eyes, both of us grinning. The happiness shines out and seeing it now causes a sharp stabbing pain in my side. We were happy. Weren't we?

My gaze drifts to another photo of all the children, taken last Thanksgiving. June is pulling a funny face at the camera, Hannah stands behind her, pouting. I remember her sighing and telling me to hurry up and take the damn photo already, she had to be somewhere – I can't remember where – yet still managing to strike a pose like a pro. And there's Gene, arm flung loosely around June's shoulders, staring slightly over her shoulder into space. He was probably high at the time, now I think about it.

I pick the photograph up, swiping at the tears that spring to my eyes, and study the children's faces, wishing I could step back in time and hit pause on that day, wishing I'd have known to treasure that moment, every imperfect second of it.

29

My hand is bleeding. Absently I watch the drops fall like tears onto the kitchen floor for several seconds before it dawns on me that they're coming from my hand. I've somehow walked from the study to here, gripping the photograph of our wedding anniversary in my hand so tightly that my palm has been sliced open on the broken glass.

I set the photograph down and pick up a tea towel, wrapping it around my hand to staunch the blood. It doesn't hurt – even though the cut runs deep – but it makes me woozy to see the blood welling up. I haven't eaten in I don't know how long. I'm not hungry anymore. And I can't remember the last time I slept for longer than an hour or two. Whenever I do fall asleep I wake with my heart pounding, the image of the man in the razor-teeth mask burned like a sunspot onto my retina. The effect is to make me feel as if I'm wearing virtual-reality goggles – I am sluggish and disconnected from everything around me, dizzy and clumsy too.

Throwing down the tea towel I start gathering up the fragments of glass from the frame. I wrap them in the stained cloth and then cross to the trash can but then stare down at it, confused. There's a bin liner in it, but it's new. I remember wiping up the milk that June had spilled and then throwing the wet kitchen towel into the trash along with the empty milk carton. It had been three quarters full.

Nate said Robert hadn't put the trash out. He claimed Robert lied about it, so why is the can in the kitchen empty? Perhaps Robert emptied it the day we came home from the hospital. Or perhaps the police did after their search.

I open the back door and cross over towards the big wheelie trash containers parked at the side of the garage. Both of them are empty. I dump the broken glass wrapped in the tea towel and then stand there, hands on hips, for a few seconds, puzzling over what happened to the trash from the kitchen. Where did it go?

I wander around to the stairs that lead up above the garage to Gene's apartment. When I got home thirty minutes ago I texted him to see where he was and he told me he was out buying groceries. I make for the stairs, deciding to take advantage of his absence and search his room for drugs. I should have thought of it sooner. I'm an idiot.

As I start up the stairs, I catch sight of a flash of white out of the corner of my eye. Looking closer, I see it's a plastic garbage bag, half hidden behind the stairs as though it's been dropped there and forgotten about. I pull it out and then sit down on the bottom step to open it. The empty milk carton sits on the top, along with the soiled kitchen towels.

Robert did put the trash out then, he just never put it in the cart. Why? The only thing I can think is that he was walking over to do it but got distracted – maybe by Gene coming out of his apartment and disappearing like a thief down the drive. Perhaps he went to investigate. But why didn't Robert just tell Nate this? Why let them make a wrong assumption? This one small detail could help clear his name. He wasn't lying about it. But, I think to myself, dampening my own excitement, even if he isn't lying about that, he did still meet those men – there's no denying the photographic evidence – and what the hell was that about?

I head back inside, holding the trash bag. I need to call Nate and let him know.

As soon as I walk back into the kitchen I hear a creaking sound from overhead, which makes me freeze mid-step and stare up at the ceiling. It's coming from June's room.

It can't be Gene as I would have heard him coming back in the car, and Hannah has been staying at Laurie's, having refused to set foot in the house again, so I know it's not her. My heart smashes into my ribs, trying to escape my chest. *Get out of the house,* the voice in my head commands. I put the trash bag down and tiptoe to the back door, then remember that I don't have a car. Gene has it.

My eyes land on the knife block and I draw a knife from it – not the carving knife, which is no longer there, but a small meat cleaver Robert uses for hacking up slabs of steak before he puts them on the grill – and then I pull out my cell phone and start to dial 911.

There's only silence overhead now and I wonder if I'm going mad, hearing things, echoes from before. Another creak followed by a loud, high-pitched shriek – a girl's shriek – interrupts me. Dropping the phone, I run to the bottom of the stairs, and haul myself up them.

'No!' a girl screams and I recognize the voice. Hannah!

I skid to a halt on the landing outside June's room. Hannah's standing with her back to me in the middle of the room, but when she hears me she turns in alarm.

'Mom,' she says, putting a hand to her heart. 'God, you gave me such a fright.' She double-takes. 'Why are you holding a meat cleaver?'

'What? What are you doing?' I pant. 'I heard you scream.'

Hannah holds something up in front of her face.

My hand flies to cover my mouth. 'George.'

The hamster dangles by its tail from her thumb and forefinger. His little body is limp, his mouth open in a tiny rictus grin. 'We forgot to feed him,' she says.

Big fat tears start falling down my face. 'Oh God,' I sob, collapsing down onto the bed. 'George. Poor George.'

Hannah is right there, arms around me, hugging me, as though I'm the child and she's the mother. 'It's not your fault, Mom,' she whispers. 'You were in the hospital. I told Gene to feed him.'

I look at the dead hamster lying on the carpet and start to cry even harder. 'What will June say when she wakes up?'

'We'll buy her a new one,' Hannah tells me. 'She'll never know.'

Of course she'll know, I think to myself. She's not five. We can't pull the wool over her eyes like we did that time with the goldfish.

I lean against Hannah. 'What kind of a mother am I?' I ask her.

'It's not your fault,' she says. 'It's Gene's.'

'Stop blaming him for everything.'

'Stop excusing him for everything.'

'I don't . . .'

Hannah huffs and her arm drops from my shoulder. She stands up and crosses to George's cage. 'It's not like we could have taken him when we leave here anyway,' she mutters, and for a moment I think she's talking about Gene before realizing she means the hamster. 'I mean, we don't even know where we're going.'

'You're going back to college,' I tell her.

Hannah looks at me. 'How? I can't pay my rent, let alone the tuition.'

'We'll figure it out,' I tell her.

She shakes her head. 'How?'

'We'll take a loan.'

She shakes her head. 'What's the point? Unless I become a lawyer, which I have no intention of doing, why would I get myself over a hundred thousand dollars in debt? I'll never be able to pay it back.' She puts her hands on her hips. 'I'm not going back to New York.'

'Yes, you are,' I say angrily.

She shrugs at me, mind made up. 'I'm not taking a loan,' she says, crossing her arms over her chest. 'And besides, I can't leave you here with June in the hospital and Dad in prison. How can I go back and pretend like my life is the same when it isn't? Nothing's the same. It's never going to be the same again.'

I open my mouth but she cuts me off. 'I've decided, OK? So don't bother trying to talk me out of it.'

I close my mouth. It's her life, I suppose, and what am I going to do? Force her to go? I'm too tired to even try. 'OK,' I say quietly. 'We can talk about it again later, when everything is back to normal.'

Normal. As though that's ever going to happen. There is no normal anymore. There never will be. I sink back down onto the bed and for a few moments we both just contemplate the room. It's still an utter pigsty, and now it smells of one too, the gut-churning stink of rotting hamster filling my nostrils. My head drops into my hands. When June wakes up we'll have to tell her not only that her hamster is dead and her dad is in jail but that she can't go home either, that she doesn't have a home to go home to. For once I'm actually grateful she's not awake.

'We need to pack all her things,' I say, taking a deep breath and standing up. I can't sit here crying and feeling sorry for myself, I need to start packing, and start deciding what to sell.

'That's what I was doing,' Hannah answers. 'I've done my room already. I was about to start on June's.' She gestures at a pile of things on the floor. 'I thought maybe we could take a few of her things to the hospital, put them in her room, for when she wakes up.'

'I should have thought about that already.' Another flurry of guilt hits.

I glance at the pile of stuff Hannah has gathered – June's teddy bear, her hairbrush, some gymnastics trophies, framed photographs of her and Abby and other friends, her collection of signed *Hunger Games* books, a photo album, a basketball. The detritus of a life fully but not even partially lived.

I sink to my knees and pick up her bear, bringing him to my face and breathing in deep. He smells musty – of dead animal – and I drop him to my lap. There's no scent of June in this room anymore. No trace of her. Her laughter has faded from my head too. When my mother died I forgot the sound of her voice within a year; the harder I tried to remember it the quicker it vanished, like trying to grab handfuls of smoke. I try to recall June's voice but already it's a struggle, like that lost memory from the night it all happened – the harder I reach for it, the further away it drifts. The doctors said I might have problems with my memory thanks to the head injury, but this fog is driving me mad.

'Have you heard any more from the lawyer?' Hannah asks, snapping me out of my daze. 'About Dad? Are they going to let him out of jail? Has he said anything? Can we visit?'

I shake my head. 'Why?' she asks angrily.

I shrug. I haven't told her that he is refusing to see anyone, except Gene apparently, only that we can't get visitation rights at the moment.

'He didn't do it, he wouldn't do it,' Hannah says, her voice reaching fever pitch. She turns to me, frowning. 'You don't believe it, do you?'

I'm staring at the bear in my lap.

Why is Robert not speaking? Is he hiding his own guilt? What other motive would there be? He knows something and won't reveal it. Think, Ava. What else could it be? What was he doing in Oxnard meeting those people?

'Mom?'

I look up, dazed, at Hannah.

'You don't believe Dad arranged it, do you?' she asks tearily.

I shake my head, because I don't want her to think I do. I'm lying to protect her, as I've always done with all the children, and that's when it occurs to me: is that what Robert is doing too?

What if his silence isn't a sign of guilt? What if he's lying to protect someone? And the only person he'd protect like that, who he'd take a fall for, is one of the kids. I follow that thought, grasping onto it and trying to drag it kicking into the light. The only child he's allowed to see him in prison is Gene. Gene – our possibly drug-addicted son. Is he somehow covering for Gene?

It's like a lightbulb going on.

I remember the feeling I had at the hospital earlier with Gene, that I was talking to a five-year-old who'd been caught pilfering from the cookie jar. But now I realize it might not have been drugs, or flu, or fear making Gene so jittery. What if it was guilt?

What if it was Gene who robbed us? What if it was him dressed up in a fright mask? He could have got one of his friends to help. What if it was Dave?! No. I'm losing it. What am I saying? It wasn't either of them. It couldn't be. I almost laugh at my paranoid delusions, but then I catch myself. Something is niggling at me, trying to push its way into the light. But it vanishes before I can get a grip on it.

I get to my feet. I need to talk to Robert. That's a priority. I need to ask him if Gene had anything to do with this. I would ask Gene himself but he's conveniently gone AWOL.

'I guess I should go bury him,' Hannah says, and I startle, then realize she's talking about the hamster, lying dead on the carpet at my feet.

'I'll do it,' I tell her, feeling sick to my stomach at the thought.

'Are you sure?' Hannah asks.

I nod absently.

'OK, well, I'll go finish clearing up my room then.' She pauses by the door and then comes over and hugs me. 'I love you, Mom,' she says, her breath warm against my neck.

'I love you too,' I say, wrapping my arms around her and breathing in deep.

'Can I come to the hospital with you later to see June?' she asks. 'I want to bring her things.'

I nod and wait until she's left the room before I sink to the floor again. With the bear clutched in one hand, I stroke my other hand over the bloodstained carpet.

There's only one thing I know for sure. Whoever did this to June, whoever is involved, whether it's Gene or a stranger, I'm going to find out and I'm going to make them pay.

30

'Do you really want to do this?' Laurie asks me.

I nod, my eyes fixed on the golden Corona sign hanging in the blacked-out window of the bar we're parked opposite. This area of Oxnard is a no-go zone at night. Under normal circumstances I wouldn't come here even in broad daylight because of all the tweakers and muggings. But these aren't normal circumstances.

'Ava, I'm not sure this is a good idea,' Laurie says as I get out of the car.

I slam the door shut and start marching towards the bar, clutching my purse against my side and wondering if Laurie is right and I'm out of my mind. I'm not totally sure what I'm doing here but I don't know what else to do. I need answers and I don't know where else to get them. Robert won't talk to me, Nate is convinced it's Robert so there is no point talking to him – and besides, if he had any idea of what I'm about to do he'd probably arrest me – and Gene never came home after buying groceries so I had no chance to confront him. My only option, I decided, was to go elsewhere for answers. I'm tired of sitting around and waiting; for June to wake up, for the police to tell me what's going on, for Gene to come home, for the truth to emerge like a springtime flower poking through the soil of its own accord. I need to be pro-active and chase after it.

Laurie thinks I'm mad, but if I can talk to the men who met with Robert maybe I can get them to tell me what he wanted. They wouldn't talk to the police but perhaps, somehow, I can make them talk to me. I can find out what Robert gave them money for and why. I can find out if Gene is involved.

Someone grabs my arm and I whip around in fright, heart leapfrogging into my mouth, but it's only Laurie. 'I thought you were going to wait in the car?'

She arches an eyebrow at me and shoves her arm through mine, and I don't bother to argue. She's not letting me go through with this by myself, or perhaps she just doesn't want to wait alone in the car on a dark street. I don't ask which it is, because when I push open the battered door to the bar and the entire room – two dozen or more men – pivot on their bar stools and look up from their pool games to stare at us, I'm grateful I'm not alone.

Throwing back my shoulders, I make a beeline for the bar, Laurie at my side. A heavy silence has fallen and every eye in the place swivels to follow us. I can feel their gazes on my back like dozens of laser sights. We are so out of place we're like aliens landing on the White House lawn.

The barman, wiping out glasses, watches us approach wearing an amused expression on his face. I can guarantee the last time two white, middle-aged women walked into his bar was ten past never. Two men to our right, slumped on stools and nursing beers, openly stare at us, their faces blank as stone.

'You two ladies lost?' the barman asks.

'No,' I say, staring him in the eye. 'I'm looking for someone.'

'Oh, yeah?'

'You looking for me?'

I turn. A man has appeared and is leaning against the bar right beside me, grinning a lizard-like smile. His thigh rubs up against mine accidentally on purpose. He's forty, maybe, with a pockmarked face and receding, stringy hair that he's scraped into a ponytail.

'No,' I tell him. 'I'm looking for Raul Fernandez.'

He shrugs and pulls a face. 'Never heard of him.'

The barman has turned away, is busying himself with the bottles that line the back of the bar. The men sat on the stools on our other side have returned to studying the labels on their beers. The noise in the bar has started up again, but it's subdued, as if everyone has one ear tuned to our conversation.

'What about James Hill?' I ask, mentioning the second man who was arrested.

'Who's he?' the man asks, frowning.

Did I make a mistake? I knew it was a long shot coming here. When Nate showed me the surveillance photos of Robert handing over the money to James and Raul I made a mental note of the bar that appeared, fuzzy but still distinct, in the background. I figured that if this is their neighborhood, then someone in this bar should know them. Maybe, even, I expected to find them here.

'You cops?'

Another man has sauntered over. This one is in his early twenties. He's short, wearing jeans so baggy they fall halfway down his thighs, revealing his underwear. He's holding a pool cue, rubbing a square of chalk on the end in a gesture that, though innocuous enough, unnerves me. The other man with the straggly ponytail saunters away, making a tssking sound with his tongue and eyeing me through lowered lids.

I turn to face the younger man. Maybe he knows something and will be prepared to tell us.

'Don't I know you?' he says, narrowing his eyes and frowning at me. A second later recognition erases the frown and he nods vigorously. 'You're that woman from the TV. They arrested your husband.'

'Raul Fernandez,' I repeat.

His expression hardens. 'Why you want to see him?'

I leap on that. 'So you do know him?'

He pulls a face. 'Nah, didn't say that, just asked why you wanted to see him.'

'Because I have questions I need to ask him.'

The man glances quickly around the bar and then leans forwards, putting his mouth so close to my ear I can feel the heat of his breath and struggle not to flinch. 'If I were you,' he says, 'I'd turn around right now and walk out of here, while I still could.'

I hear a loud, dramatic sigh. It's Laurie. 'You listen to me,' she says loudly. 'The only place we're going is over there to those bar stools. And we'll stay right there until you go fetch your friends.'

The man looks up at Laurie, startled. He tries glowering at her, but Laurie, towering over him, stares him down unflinching. Before our eyes the man visibly shrinks, his swagger melting away, until he looks just like a twelve-year-old.

Laurie plops herself down on a vacant bar stool. 'Two Coronas,' she calls to the barman. The men sitting to her right swivel their heads in unison to stare at her. Laurie smiles broadly at them until they look away.

The short man turns towards me, scenting an opportunity to regain his dominance. Without missing a beat I hop up onto the stool beside Laurie. She pushes a bottle of cold Corona towards me and I pick it up and take a swig, keeping my eyes fixed on the man the whole time.

'You heard the woman,' I say.

*   *   *

We're on our second beers, sipping them slowly, our eyes continually straying to the clock above the bar. It's almost midnight. We've been here fifty minutes and I'm trying not to show any sign of the anxiety that's gnawing away at my insides. Laurie seems much more relaxed, but twenty years teaching in the kind of schools that have metal detectors and airport-style security at the front gates has given her a Teflon coating.

'Honestly,' she says, eyeing the short man, who has gone back to his pool game and seems intent on ignoring us. 'I've dealt with tougher sixth graders than him. How long do we stay?'

'As long as it takes,' I answer, glancing at my phone. There are no messages from Gene and I wonder where he is and what he's up to. The more I think about it, the more obvious it seems to me that he has to be involved. My mind spins around the possibilities. Did he get into some kind of trouble with these two men – Raul and James – and was Robert trying to get him out of it?

The boy with the baggy jeans is finally finishing his pool game. He pots the last ball and then, after exchanging a handshake and taking money from his opponent, he glances in our direction. Turning his back, he fishes his phone out of his pocket and makes a quick call, looking briefly over his shoulder at us as he talks to whoever is on the other end.

'Here we go,' murmurs Laurie.

Fifteen minutes later my nerves are stretched taut. I eye the tequila bottles lined up along the bar and contemplate getting a shot of one to help steel me but I don't have time. A sudden commotion by the door snatches my attention. The bar falls quiet as two men enter, the door swinging shut behind them.

I recognize them instantly from their mug shots. Raul and James.

They scan the bar, their eyes falling on us. One nudges the other and they weave their way towards us, the tall one – James – stopping to slap the young man on the shoulder by way of greeting.

Everyone in the bar is now staring at us, collectively holding their breath. My heart starts racing and I wonder for the thousandth time what on earth I was thinking coming here.

'Are you fucking stupid?' the man with the shaved head, Raul, hisses the minute he reaches me, as though he's read my mind.

'I . . .' I stutter.

'Did the cops see you come in here? Are they following you?' His mouth twists into a snarl that shows his gums and a gold tooth flashes where his canine should be.

'No. No, we made sure,' I say, my voice quavering. Laurie and I did some rudimentary spycraft learned from the movies, taking an early exit on the freeway and then circling the block a few times before parking.

'No one knows we're here.' I instantly regret making that known.

Raul studies us, eyes roving our bodies, his mouth tightly pursed. 'Maybe you're working with the cops.'

'Oh please,' says Laurie, scoffing loudly. 'Really? Do we look like police informants? Do I look like I'm wearing a wire?' She gestures to the tank top she's wearing.

'Why are you here?' the second man – the preppy-looking one, James – says to me. He seems agitated, glancing over his shoulder nervously and keeping his voice low.

'I need to talk to you.' I glance between the two of them. 'I know it wasn't you who broke into my house.'

'Tell that to the fucking detectives,' Raul snarls. 'Cos they still seem to think it was.'

'I did tell them,' I say, taking a deep breath.

They glance at each other, then back at me. 'So what are you doing here?' James asks. 'What do you want?'

'Why did my husband meet with you?' I say. 'What was he paying you for?'

'Why not ask him?' he answers.

'I have. He won't tell me. He won't speak to anyone and I need to know what's going on. I figured maybe you might be able to tell me something.'

Raul stares at me for a beat and then he's suddenly in my face, looming over me, baring his teeth, fists coiled tight at his side, his mouth a mean, tight slash. I flinch.

'You fucking bitch,' he spits. 'Coming here, who do you think you are? You think just cos your husband don't want to speak to you, that I will?' He laughs, shaking his head, and looking around the bar. 'You realize the shit you could get us into?' he asks, gesturing at the room. 'Everyone seeing us here together. Cops already think we're connected to you. They're looking for any excuse to nail us. Now you're giving them one.'

I shrink backwards on my stool, my heart pounding and my mouth dry, but then a switch flips inside me. All the fear and anger that's been building since it happened explodes and I'm up off the stool, pointing my finger in Raul's chest. 'Listen,' I spit, 'I'm sorry you're pissed but here's the thing: my husband's in prison, my daughter's in a coma, the bank is about to take my house and I'm so in debt I couldn't pay it off even if I worked for the next hundred years.' I lean even further into Raul's personal space. 'You think your life is fucked? Believe me, mine is way more fucking fucked than yours. You have a lawyer who looks like she eats prosecutors for breakfast. Meanwhile my husband is stuck with a public defender who last won a case in 1987. The cops are convinced that it was you who broke in to my house and shot my daughter and put her in the hospital.'

Raul looks like he's about to interrupt at this, but I don't let him, my voice rising to cut him off. 'I don't believe it was you. But if it wasn't you, then it was someone else, and I really need to find out who it was, and you two are the only people who might be able to help me because the police couldn't find their own assholes if they were sitting on the toilet shitting diarrhea.'

I take a deep, shuddering breath in and then let it out and now everything comes back into focus – my field of vision widening to take in the almost silent bar and the two men standing in front of me, mouths agape, and Laurie behind them, turning paler by the second. Did I go too far? Oh shit. I don't know what just came over me. All I know is that it came from somewhere deep and guttural inside me and that now it's unleashed like a genie from a bottle, there's no way of putting it back.

I look at Laurie. She's clutching her keys in her hand like a homemade knuckleduster and her eyes are darting wildly from them to me and back again.

'All right,' Raul says, and just like that he pulls up a stool and sits down beside us.

I topple backwards onto my own stool, legs suddenly amorphous as jellyfish.

James sits on Laurie's other side and signals the barman who pulls a bottle from under the bar, lines up four glasses and then proceeds to pour shots of what I assume is tequila.

'Drink,' says Raul, nudging the glass towards me with a tattooed knuckle.

I pick it up and throw it down my throat, slamming the glass down on the bar. Fuck, I needed that. Raul guffaws and signals the barman to refill my glass. I down that shot too. The alcohol strips a layer off my throat but brings an instant hit of warmth and settles my nerves. I wait for Raul to pick up his glass and drink, his eyes fixed on me the whole time as though he's still trying to get my measure.

'Do you know who broke into my house?' I ask.

He splutters, coughing. 'Look,' he says, crunching his shot glass down on the bar and wiping the back of his mouth with his hand. 'We can't tell you shit about the break-in. Wasn't us and we don't know who it was.'

He leans in close and I study his eyes – inches from mine – the golden halos at the center burning bright. Can I believe him? I look at Laurie, who shrugs.

'What did my husband pay you for?'

Raul and James exchange a look. 'Like we told the police, no comment.'

I sigh loudly. 'He gave you money. What for?'

They exchange another look. James finally nods at Raul who leans forwards so his lips are right by my ear.

'If you must know, your son Gene owes us eighty thousand dollars.'

I reel backwards to stare at him. What the hell? 'I don't understand,' I murmur. 'What for?'

'What do you think?'

'Drugs?' I say.

'Shhh,' he hisses, darting a glance over his shoulder at the bar, but all the customers are studiously looking everywhere but at us.

'That's a lot of money,' I say.

'Was a lot of drugs.'

I stare down at the filthy, unswept floor, trying to gather my thoughts. What was Gene thinking? He must be dealing to be buying such large amounts. Even he couldn't smoke that much weed. The damn stupid idiot. I look up. Raul and James are watching me.

'What kind of drugs?' Laurie asks, before I think to.

'Meth,' Raul murmurs.

'Meth? He's dealing meth?' I screech so loudly that Raul growls at me to keep it down. I think back to how Gene was at the hospital and the pieces slot into place like the cylinders of a lock. 'Oh my God.' Gene's not just dealing. He's using.

'It's a huge problem in the valley,' Laurie breaks in, looking and sounding as shocked as me. 'I read about it in the paper.'

I feel suddenly dizzy, the tequila making my head spin. 'Robert was giving you money to pay off the debt,' I stammer.

'He gave us thirty grand. Gene still owes us eighty. You don't happen to know where he is, do you? We've been trying to find him.'

'Join the club,' I murmur, all the while trying to wrap my head around the enormous number he just mentioned. Eighty plus thirty. One hundred and ten thousand dollars! What was he thinking? And what was Robert thinking bailing him out like that using my pawned jewelry?!

'Why does he owe you so much?' Laurie asks, and I can tell she's suspicious that they're lying to us.

'He's meant to pay commission on what he sells.'

'You take a cut?' I ask.

Raul eyes me. 'Us, and the people above, the people who provide the product and allow him to distribute it.'

People above them? It's a chain. I look at Laurie who's figuring it out too. Raul and James are only the middlemen.

'Who are these people?' Laurie demands.

Raul cocks an eyebrow at her. 'You don't need to know.'

'But he owes them too?' I say, dully.

He nods.

'If it wasn't you who broke into the house, could it have been them?'

Raul gives a non-committal shrug. 'Could be anyone. Gene pissed off a lot of people. Could be one of the people he dealt to – figured he had money on the property. Or maybe they were looking for his stash.'

'How long has he been dealing for you?' Laurie asks.

'Six months.'

I take that in. My stepson is a drug dealer. Gene, the little boy I raised, is a drug dealer, and not a small-fry one either. I can't look at Laurie. I'm too ashamed.

'Why couldn't Gene pay you the money?' I ask. 'If he's been dealing for six months and making profit, why couldn't he pay you?'

'He claims it was stolen.'

'Stolen?' I ask, frowning. 'What? When?'

'About a month ago. All his cash vanished, conveniently just before he was meant to pay us. Told him I didn't give a shit, he still owed us the money. That's when your husband showed up with the thirty Gs.' He scoffs. 'Like that was gonna do it.'

'Bought him some time, that's all,' says James.

I absorb this new information and muse on what he just said. Something about it didn't track but I've forgotten what it was. Gene must have gone to Robert and told him. And Robert, instead of telling me, or telling his criminal son to go to hell, pawned my jewelry to help Gene get these men off his back, only it wasn't enough money to clear the debt. Not even close. Is that why Robert adjusted the insurance? Was he planning on filing an insurance claim for the jewelry he pawned, so he could use the payout from the insurance company to pay off Raul and James? It looks that way. I think about Nate and his hypothesis about Robert. If he actually knew the real story he'd use it as even more evidence against him. But then I realize something else – Robert wasn't meeting them down some dark alley to arrange a hit, as Nate would have it. He was trying to help his son.

James leans close, elbows on the bar, and I notice the incongruous Virgin Mary tattoo on his arm. 'We told your husband he and Gene had three more weeks to find the money or . . .' He tails off, leaving the threat to hang nebulous in the air.

'Three weeks?' Laurie asks, doing the math. 'So that makes the deadline a week ago. The exact date that the break-in happened. Seems like strange timing.'

'What are you saying?' James asks.

'What if you didn't get the money, so this was your way of threatening Gene and Robert? Maybe you thought you could rob the house and steal enough to make up for it.'.

'She didn't ID us in the line-up,' Raul says, jerking his head at me.

'Maybe you paid some associates to break in,' Laurie presses.

'Look, it wasn't us, lady,' Raul growls, his eyes sparking with fury at the suggestion. 'I already told you.' He glares at me and I study him. I think he's telling the truth, but if it wasn't them who broke in, who was it?

'You said you owed money to other people,' I interrupt.

James glances at me. 'Yeah, and they're not the kinds of people you want to owe money to. They're tired of waiting for it.'

'Who are they?' Laurie asks.

James shakes his head and gives Raul a warning look. He's not telling.

'Could it have been them who broke into the house?' I ask.

Raul shrugs, giving nothing away. Goddamn it, the suspects keep multiplying. I stare around the bar, dazed, as though I'll find the truth sitting at a table sipping a beer. 'You need to tell me who they are,' I say, my voice rising. 'These men you owe – what if it was them? What if they come back? I need to know so I can protect my children.'

Raul shrugs. 'The best thing you can do is pay up, then you won't have to worry.'

I press my lips together. Why should I have to pay up? This is Gene's debt not mine. That's probably why he's fucked off, isn't it? Goddamn him. If I ever see him again I'm going to kill him myself. I'll tear him limb from limb.

'Where are we meant to find eighty thousand dollars?' I hiss, my throat hoarse. 'I can't. I don't have that kind of money.'

Another shrug. 'I'm sorry you got problems, but this one ain't mine.'

I'm starting to feel like I'm in a pressure cooker and my skull is about to implode. There has to be a solution to this. But what? Unless . . . what if . . . an idea starts to form in my head.

Raul laughs under his breath. 'I know what you're thinking. You're thinking you could just go to the police. Maybe Gene could provide testimony, cut some kind of deal with the DA's office. He's a rich white boy after all. The system's already rigged in his favor.' He lowers his voice, draws nearer so his face is level with mine and I can see the glint of gold in the depths of his mouth. 'But you do that,' he says, 'and I promise you and your family you're going to be looking over your shoulders the rest of your lives.'

My lungs scream for air but I can't breathe.

He leans forwards and whispers. 'The cops aren't going to help you.'

'And your husband,' James adds. 'I can tell you this, he opens his mouth about Gene or about any of this, he's a dead man.'

A cold shudder runs up my spine. They must have friends in prison, friends who could reach Robert and threaten him or hurt him. Is that why Robert has been so silent? Did they threaten him already?

Guilt eats at me as I realize everything Robert has done has been to protect us, his family. How could I ever have doubted him? It makes my anger at his financial mismanagement dissipate, not completely, but somewhat.

Raul and James slip off their stools and Raul pulls out a wallet stuffed with bills. He selects one – a hundred – and throws it down onto the bar. 'We got this,' he says to me with a slight smirk. 'But you better find Gene and that money. Clock's ticking.'

I watch the two of them turn and saunter out of the bar.

31

Laurie's hands are white-knuckled on the steering wheel. All the blood has drained from her face. 'What are we going to do?' she whispers.

I shake my head, staring at the glowing Corona sign in the window of the bar.

'You need to go to the police.'

I shake my head again, this time harder. 'You heard them! I can't.' The truth is I would happily hand Gene over – he's the reason June's in the hospital and his father is in prison – but I can't risk Hannah getting hurt, or Robert.

'But how are you going to find that kind of money?' Laurie asks.

I chew on my lip. 'They said Gene said the money was stolen from him. But who stole it?' My mind is racing. 'If we can find out who stole it, maybe we can steal it back.'

'What?' Laurie gasps. 'Are you crazy?'

I pull out my phone. 'I need to find Gene.'

I hit dial but the call goes straight to voicemail and his mailbox is full. I swear loudly and hang up. For months and months Gene's been impossible to lever out of the house and now, when I need him, I can't find him anywhere. Damn him. This is all his fault. 'He's run,' I say, furious. 'I know it. He's run away and left me to deal with it all. I'm going to kill him if I find him.'

I'm aware of Laurie eyeing me nervously and realize my

hands are fisted and my voice is a growl. She thinks I mean it and I think I do too. I force my hands to unfurl.

'I wonder who they buy their drugs from,' I say.

'I do not want to know,' Laurie mumbles.

'What if it was them who broke in though? Maybe they thought they could scare Gene or threaten him, or maybe they wanted to rob us in lieu of payment.'

'It's possible,' she says.

'More than possible,' I shoot back. 'It's the only thing that makes sense.'

My phone suddenly jerks to life in my hand and I jab at the button, hoping it's Gene. It isn't. It's Hannah. She's at the hospital. There can't be a good reason she's calling so late. I put the phone to my ear with a shaking hand.

'Hannah?'

'Mom?' she says, her voice strangled.

Oh God. Something is wrong – I can tell at once.

'You need to come,' she sobs.

32

DAY 8

Dr Warier meets us at the door to the ICU. He gives a very brief smile and then ushers us into the pastel-hued relatives' room, where two other doctors and a woman in a sharp blue pantsuit await us, grim-faced as undertakers.

'What's going on?' I ask, the bones dissolving in my legs as I drop down onto the sofa opposite them. 'Where's Hannah? She said there was some kind of emergency but said she couldn't tell me over the phone. What is it? Is June . . .?'

Laurie puts her arm around my shoulders. The first doctor, who I know is in charge of pediatrics, stands up and clears his throat, which is never a good sound, I've discovered, when it comes from a doctor. 'I'm afraid we have some bad news,' he says.

The ceiling starts pressing down on top of me and with it comes a need to run from the room – but I can't. I'm paralyzed.

'June went into cardiac arrest last night. We performed CPR and we managed to restart her heart.'

My own heart skips several beats. 'She's alive?' I stammer as relief surges inside me.

The doctor nods.

I spring up from the sofa and make instantly for the door. I need to see her. I need to be with her. But someone steps in front of me. It's the woman in the pantsuit. She won't let me pass and, frustrated, I glare at her.

'Someone interfered with her oxygen line.'

'What?' I look between her and the doctor.

The woman gestures for me to sit back down and I do, dropping like a stone. Laurie sits too and takes my hand. 'What are you saying?' I ask again.

She takes a deep breath. 'Someone made a deliberate attempt on June's life.'

'How?' I ask, staring at them. 'Who?'

'Someone bypassed security with a stolen pass and came in via the stairwell. He was wearing a white coat and surgical scrubs. He hid out in the supply closet and then he lit a fire in there. The cop on duty left his post for a few minutes to help put it out.'

The woman darts a look at the doctors. The first doctor, the surgeon who operated on June, takes over the conversation. 'We're sorry,' he says to me. 'But June's score on the Glasgow Coma Scale has slipped. As you know she was an eight. Now she's scoring a five.' And there it comes, the moment that tips me over into the darkness.

'Now, what that means is—'

'I know what it means,' I cut in. I've Googled it. It means a severe brain injury. Anything below a three is brain dead. She's deteriorated.

I look around at the other doctor to see if he's going to contradict him, because someone has to. He can't be telling me the truth. But everyone is silent, grave-faced, deliberately avoiding my eye.

'The likelihood of June recovering is now less than one per cent.'

'No, no, no,' I mumble, shaking my head harder and harder until it feels I might dislocate something. Where's Robert? I need Robert. I can't do this alone.

'What does that mean?' I hear Laurie asking. 'You're not giving up on her!'

There's a pause and then Dr Warier starts talking, his voice soft and calming. 'We don't feel there is any point in keeping June on life support. Even if she were to regain consciousness, there's no telling what damage might have been done.'

I look up, enraged, spitting fire. 'No!' What are they talking about? I'm on my feet, yelling now. 'Someone did this to her . . . someone tried to kill her. This . . . no . . .! You are not switching off the life support. You're not letting her die. I'm not going to let you. You can't.' I move to stand in front of the doorway. I won't let them near her. I won't allow them to do this.

Dr Warier steps forwards and takes both my hands in his. 'I'm sorry,' he says quietly, tears filling his eyes. 'We've done all the tests we can do. The kindest thing to do for June right now would be to let her go, let her die with dignity. Of course, we don't suggest doing it right away. You and your family can take your time, say your goodbyes, prepare.'

Goodbyes? Prepare? The breath is drawn out of me in one long, endless wail. The pain is so immense, so eviscerating, that I think I will die from it. I want to die from it. Because it's too big to contain and I know that this is just the start, that it will grow and grow, like the sun expanding, until it consumes me and the whole, entire universe. There is no way of bearing it.

I collapse to the floor, dragging Laurie with me, and she holds me, rocking me like a child, and all I can do is cling to her and howl June's name over and over and over.

33

'Mrs Walker?'

It takes me almost a minute to break out of my daze and figure out someone is calling me. I'm in the relatives' room still. I don't know how long I've been sitting here, on the floor, in Laurie's arms. I'm no longer crying or wailing and the doctors have all left but I don't recall them going or what was said or what comes next. Goodbye. They said we should say goodbye. Prepare. My head throbs and my body is broken. My heart too – beyond repair. I'm all exposed raw nerves, and someone is holding a blowtorch to my body. How is it possible to live through this? To stand up? To keep breathing?

'Why?' I whisper, half-crazed, the world pulling in and out of warped focus like a hall of mirrors. 'Why would they do this?'

Was it another warning to pay up? Or did she see their faces? Were they worried she would wake up and identify them?

'Mrs Walker?' I look up slowly. A nurse hovers in the doorway. 'There's someone here to see you.'

Nate enters the room behind her. He strides over and kneels in front of me. 'Ava,' he says. 'God, I just heard. I'm so sorry.'

'How did they get in?' I ask him, swiping at the snot and tears. 'How did they get in? There were police on the door. You were meant to be guarding her!'

My fury takes him by surprise but he doesn't reel away from it. I stagger to my feet and he follows me, reaching for my arm, which I wrench from his grip.

'This is your fault,' I hiss. 'You told me she was safe. I believed you!' I shove him backwards, both hands on his chest.

He falls back a step, holding up his hands in supplication. 'Ava, I'm sorry. We're investigating.'

'Investigating?' I spit, a laugh erupting out of me like some demonic cackle. 'Because you're so damn good at that! You're so focused on Robert, so obsessed with blaming him, you didn't even bother looking for anyone else or for any other motive.' I pull myself back. I can't tell him about the drugs or about Gene, no matter how much it's teetering on the edge of my tongue. 'You didn't even find the damn trash bag!' I yell.

Nate frowns at me, shaking his head in confusion. 'What trash bag?'

'The trash you said Robert didn't put out, but he did! I found it behind the garage. You used that as evidence he was lying and he wasn't!'

Nate frowns. 'What was it doing behind the garage?' he asks.

'I don't know, but the point is you were wrong. Robert didn't lie and if you'd done your job none of this would have happened.'

It's my only chance of getting Robert off the hook – if I can't tell the truth, I can at least provide evidence that could cast doubt on the suspicions.

'Why didn't Robert tell us where he'd put it then?' Nate argues. 'Why is he pleading no contest to the charges? If you were innocent you would deny them until your last breath, you'd fight it all the way. He hasn't. Ava, you need to accept his involvement in this.'

'No,' I shout. 'This isn't on him. He's not the one who broke in here and did this to June. And if you hadn't been so focused on building a case against, you might already have found the people responsible.'

Nate stares at me, clearly taking it in.

I remember the warning I was given – the threats Raul made – and stay silent about the drugs. Whoever did this has already hurt June. What if they hurt Hannah too?

I can't lose another child. I have to find the money to pay them off.

34

June doesn't look any different, that's what strikes me first. In fact, she looks better, her face flushed with color.

Why did I leave her? I think as I stroke her hand. I should have stayed with her. I should have been here, then it wouldn't have happened. I'm to blame too. I glance up at Hannah, who is sitting on the other side of June's bed, hunched over and looking pale and red-eyed.

Feeling my gaze, she looks up. 'I went out to see what the alarm was about. I'm sorry,' she says, her voice trembling.

'It's OK,' I whisper, though the rage is eating away at my insides like acid and it's taking everything I have to hold it in.

'I'm sorry,' Hannah repeats in a whisper.

'I know,' I say, focusing on June. I know it's not Hannah's fault – not exactly – but why couldn't she have stayed with June?

'It's my fault,' Hannah says. 'I shouldn't have left her. I should have stayed.'

Yes! I scream silently, biting my tongue until I taste the hot rusty tang of blood. 'You didn't see them?' I ask after a few seconds. 'You didn't see who it was?'

She shakes her head. 'No. I told the cops. I didn't see anyone. There were so many doctors and nurses rushing around. I was only out of the room for a minute, not even, I don't know how it happened.' I look up and see her wipe her eyes. 'I'm so sorry,' she says, bursting into tears.

'It's not your fault,' I force myself to say. No matter what I feel, I can't let her think it is her fault. How will she live with it if I blame her? It will ruin her life. She will never get over it.

'The doctors said she was OK though, right?' Hannah asks again, her voice filled with hope.

I take a deep breath. 'They don't know.' I can't tell her the truth and prick that bubble. Not yet. Besides, if I say it out loud, then it will make it real.

I take June's hand in mine – limp and heavy, but so warm it tricks me into thinking she's just asleep. How can we turn off the machines? How can I kill my own child? I gave her life. I won't give her death.

I wonder if Robert has been told yet. He was always the one who argued with the doctors when June was fighting cancer. He'd stay up all night researching the latest treatments, making calls to different specialists around the world. He was the one who went tooth and nail against the insurance company when they refused to try experimental treatments and who convinced the doctors to put her on a trial drug that eventually cured her. If he were here, he would know what to do.

'I'm going to get some air,' says Hannah, standing up, shakily.

'Stay inside,' I tell her. 'I don't want you leaving the hospital.'

She frowns but doesn't ask why.

When she's gone I clamber onto the bed beside June, careful not to disturb any of the wires and tubes invading her body. 'Please June, wake up,' I whisper.

The machines keep up their steady beep and the ventilator shushes me.

I close my eyes and breathe in deep but all I can smell is disinfectant and bleach. She was born in this hospital. I had high blood pressure after the birth and a nurse sat with me all night to make sure I was OK. Against all the regulations, she brought me June and laid her down in the bed beside me. We fell asleep like that and I woke the next morning and blinked in astonishment at the sight of this baby swaddled, marveling at her spider-leg lashes, her perfect rosebud mouth, stunned that Robert and I had created something so perfect.

As I lie there, the fog lifts, for just a moment, and I catch a brief glimpse of the picture I've been trying to grasp before it melts away again. I curl my body around June's as I did all those years ago in a bed just like this one, and let out a wracking, soul-splitting sob. 'My baby, my love, please keep fighting.'

35

When I stagger out of the ICU like a zombie ten minutes later to use the bathroom and to check my phone for a message from Gene, who is still AWOL, I run into June's friend Abby and her mom, Samantha, coming out of the elevator.

'Ava,' Samantha says, swooping towards me like a vulture, her arms stretched wide. I stand rigid as she pulls me in for a hug, like an animal already undergoing rigor mortis.

I've never liked Samantha – or Stepford as Laurie calls her – a Christian who judges people more than an Old Testament God. She's perfectly turned out today, as always, in a crisp pink shirt, jeans and blue ballet pumps. She looks exactly how you'd picture the wife of a pastor to look, and I have a sudden, sharp impulse to hit her and wipe that condescending sympathetic smile off her face.

'How are you?' she asks, looking me up and down, her nose wrinkling slightly, before she rearranges her expression back into faux-sympathy.

I'm not going to tell her about June. If I have to watch her doe-eyes widen and hear her pronounce some Bible verse about the will of God or Him working in mysterious ways I will most definitely slap her.

'It's so awful what happened,' she says now, resting a hand on my arm and giving it a little squeeze. 'I hope you know that we're all praying for you.'

My jaw clenches so hard the bone almost shatters. I want to scream at her to take her prayers and shove them up her bony ass.

'Abby's been on at me to visit,' she says, still squeezing my arm with her pink talons. 'But they told us only family are allowed in the ICU. We were about to leave but then we saw you. You know, I've tried calling . . .'

I stare at her blankly as she chatters on, zoning in and out, her words becoming jibberish. After a while I realize that Samantha has stopped talking and is looking at me askance. Did I miss something?

'I was just asking about Robert,' she says. 'We couldn't believe it when they arrested him. It's so shocking. Have you seen him? Have they set a trial date yet?'

My hand clenches into a fist. I'm about to shove it in her face just to stop the questions, but right then the elevator door opens and out steps Nate. He glances in my direction but then sheepishly looks away and starts to head for the nurses' station. I wonder what he's back here for. Investigating? That's a joke.

'Nate?' Samantha exclaims at the sight of him. 'Oh my goodness, I thought that was you!'

Nate turns around. He looks at Sam blankly.

'I saw you on the news the other day and I said to my husband, oh my goodness, I know him! That's Nate Carmichael.'

Nate, frowning, takes a step towards us.

'Sam, Samantha Bridgewater,' Sam explains, grinning at him. 'Or rather, I'm Sam Caskell now.' Seeing Nate's still-blank look, she adds, 'We went to high school together.'

'Oh yes,' says Nate, forcing a smile while walking over to shake Sam's outstretched hand. 'I remember now. How are you doing?'

'Great,' beams Sam. 'I'm doing great. This is my daughter Abby,' she says, showing Abby off like a pedigree dog at a show. 'She's friends with June. That's why we're here. We thought we'd visit and see how she's doing.'

I feel Nate's gaze land on me but I ignore it. 'I'm here to interview the nurse who was on duty last night,' Nate says by way of explanation, then he tips his hat, nods at Sam and takes his leave.

'Bye!' Sam shouts after him.

I glance at the sign to the restrooms, visible over Samantha's shoulder, and wonder if I can make a break for it while she's distracted, but I'm not fast enough and Samantha turns her attention back to me before I can get away.

'Isn't that weird? Him being the Sheriff and all?' she asks.

I cock my head at her, not understanding.

'Well, you two used to date, didn't you?'

I nod, wondering how on earth she remembers that.

'Mom.' Abby tugs on her mother's arm, though Sam ignores her. Abby's wearing a pained expression and I wonder if her mother dragged her here against her will, and then I remember the argument she had with June the night it all happened. If they hadn't argued, then June would have stayed the night at their house. She wouldn't have been home and we wouldn't be standing here now. The realization makes me want to scream.

But then Sam says something that catches my attention. I turn to her. 'What?'

'You didn't know?' she asks, her blue-planet eyes growing round.

I shake my head.

'The whole time you were dating, Nate was seeing Margot Williams, remember her? That girl from Texas. Her brother

Calvin was on the football team with Nate. She was a cheer-leader.' She lowers her voice. 'Rumor has it he was also sleep-ing with her mother!' She takes in my stunned expression. 'Oh lord, forgive me, I mean, that was just a rumor about the mom. I doubt it's true. I'm not gossiping. I thought you knew. Everyone knew.' She gives an apologetic, squirmy smile and once again I want to punch her in the face.

'I didn't know,' I say.

'He was always such a player,' she replies with a shrug, as though I'm an idiot for not realizing it. 'He slept with the entire cheerleading team. Apart from me, of course,' she hastily adds, brushing a strand of hair behind one ear, her face flushing with the lie. 'I thought that's why you broke up.'

I blink at her. Nate was having an affair when we were together? I don't know why it never occurred to me before now. Perhaps because he acted so broken up when I dumped him. But now I see it was just wounded pride on his part, that I left him and not the other way around. My God, I was such an idiot. I've been so blind. I think of how I let him fool me into cheating on my husband, and feel physically ill, like I need to throw up and then rip my skin off my body with my fingernails, scrub myself with bleach.

'Anyway,' says Sam, interrupting my thoughts. 'I guess we should go. Abby has gymnastics to get to.' She puts her arm around Abby's shoulders and the casualness of the gesture threatens to unlock the storm of grief that is raging inside my chest.

'We'll keep praying for June,' Sam says as they head towards the elevators.

I spin away from them, feeling discombobulated and like I might scream or throw up or both, but then something makes me stop and turn around. June had a fight with Abby on the night of the break-in. That's the only reason she came home.

'Abby!' I shout.

She turns, her eyes wide and questioning.

I walk over to her. 'You and June had a falling out, didn't you? On the night it happened?'

Abby swallows hard and nods, her eyes filling with tears.

I soften my voice. 'It's OK,' I reassure her. 'I just wanted to ask what it was about.'

She frowns a little at that and glances, worriedly, at her mother. 'It was silly.' She takes a deep breath. 'It was about stealing.'

'What?' I ask.

'She said the Bible was wrong, that sometimes things weren't a sin, and I said she was wrong . . .' She glances at her mother. 'Because stealing is a sin.'

Samantha smiles smugly at her daughter and squeezes her shoulders before pulling her away towards the elevator. I stare after them, confused, trying to figure out what June could have been talking about.

'Mom? Where have you been?'

I turn around, dazed. It's Hannah. I'm about to shout at her for leaving June's side but before I can, she thrusts her phone in my face. 'Look!' she says. 'Someone just texted me this.'

I take the phone and study the website she has open. It's a gossip site – one of the big ones – and on the front page are several photographs of someone lying in a hospital bed. It takes a few seconds before I realize they're photographs of June, including several close-ups on her face.

The headline shouts: EXCLUSIVE DEATHBED PHOTOGRAPHS OF THE VALLEY INTRUDER'S VICTIM.

'How did they get these?' I say. Dots dance in front of me, blurring my sight. Was it the man in the scrubs who took them or the person who tried to kill her?

'I don't know,' Hannah sobs.

36

Laurie drops me home and tells me she'll be back in an hour to return me to the hospital. I trudge to the front door, feeling numb and exhausted. In the back of my mind is the knowledge that I need to pack up the house and find somewhere to live, but it's so far down the list of things to do it barely registers.

After Laurie drives off I march towards Gene's garage apartment. The blinds are drawn and the lights are off. I know he's not there but perhaps there will be a clue, something that might help me find the money or figure out who stole it.

I've fixated on that and it's probably because it's impossible to fix anything else. I can't do anything about June, I can't find Gene, I can't get Robert out of jail, but perhaps, just perhaps, I can get these people off our backs and prevent them from hurting anyone else.

At the front door to the apartment I search through my bag for my key, but when I fit it in the lock I realize the door is already open. I walk into the kitchen, closing the door behind me and then locking it because I'm terrified of being taken by surprise again.

Dirty clothes, ashtrays and old pizza boxes lie strewn around on the floor, the stale pizza inside growing furry green toppings, and there are piles of dirty laundry that look as if they're about to walk out the door. The closet is ajar and junk cascades out of it: baseball bats, tennis rackets, a snow-board and a few other things we didn't have room for in the garage, including a crossbow I remember Robert buying for Gene at least a decade ago. It looks like he either ransacked the place himself or someone has been here and done it for him. Or was it the men who broke in? Hannah did say they searched here too. They were looking for that money. Or perhaps for drugs.

Was it the men higher up the totem pole? I should make a list of all the people who knew Gene was dealing and had the money. I guess all the people he was selling drugs to – and God knows how many people that was. Hundreds perhaps. That doesn't help narrow it down.

The bedroom door flies open and a man in a black sweater and jeans barrels past me, heading for the door. A split second is all I need to recognize him. It's the man who claimed to be a journalist, the same man who Nate threatened, who gave his name as Euan Shriver. He leaps over the coffee table and dashes into the kitchen.

I follow him, stopping briefly to pick up something I saw in the closet. I find Euan frantically trying the door, pumping the handle up and down, confused as to why it won't open.

I hold up the door keys and see the fear flash in his eyes as he spies the crossbow I'm holding in my other hand. Now I raise it to shoulder height.

'What the fuck are you doing in my house?' I hiss.

The man holds up both hands, palms out. He cowers back against the door and I think to myself once more: *Is this him? Is this the man who robbed us? Is this one of the men in the masks?*

'I was looking for Gene,' he says, eyeing the crossbow with a terror that makes me feel alive.

'Why? What do you want with Gene?'

'Just business,' he says.

Business? Is he one of his clients? Is he a meth addict? Was he here looking for Gene or for drugs, or even for money? 'Who are you?' I demand. 'You're not a journalist. No one's heard of you. You don't work for the *Herald*. What were you doing at the hospital before?' I press, leveling the crossbow at him.

'I'm a stringer,' he finally grunts.

'A what?'

'I was trying to get an exclusive. Pictures.'

I shake my head at him, confused.

'I sell them to the highest bidder,' he explains. 'Normally the *National Enquirer*. A few others.'

'That was you?' I shout, stepping towards him so the bolt is aligned with his chest. '*You* took those photos of June.'

He shakes his head vehemently. 'No, no! It wasn't me. I swear.'

I step backwards. I've left my bag on the table and my phone is in it. Without taking my eyes off the man, I drag the bag closer and reach inside to pull it out.

'I sold them though, yes,' he says. 'What are you doing?' he asks as I pull out my phone.

'Calling the police. You're trespassing.'

'I'm not trespassing. Gene told me to meet him here.'

'Why? When?' I say. 'You've seen him?'

His face bleaches. I inch forwards so the bolt is pressing over his heart.

'I was meeting him here to buy more photographs,' he says.

My mouth falls open. 'That was Gene? Those photos of June in the hospital? Gene took them?'

He nods at me.

'So that wasn't you – in the hospital gown? In June's room?'

'What?' his face furrows. 'What are you talking about?'

I drop the crossbow to my side.

'You fucking crazy woman,' the man yells. 'You can't point that thing at me. I'm just doing my job.'

'Your job? What's your name? Your real name?'

'It *is* Euan, Euan Breslow. Look, in my game, we don't like people knowing who we are. People don't tend to like us much.'

'You don't say!' I yell. 'Get out of my house!' My head spins. The room spins.

He starts trying the door handle again. 'I can't,' he tells me. 'It's locked.'

I scramble to find the keys, dragging them out of my pocket. I unlock the door, but before I let him pass I turn back to him. 'How much – how much did you pay him for the photos?'

'Fifteen thousand,' he says, pushing past me and flying through the door and down the steps.

'If I ever see you again,' I shout after him, 'I'll kill you.'

I fall back against the door, sobbing and panting, struggling to breathe and take it in.

Together with the money from selling his car that makes around thirty thousand dollars. He hasn't run away. He's trying to get the money together to pay off Raul and James . . . but at the expense of his sister.

How could he?

37

I hurry out of the apartment and into the house, my senses prickling like I've stepped inside a mausoleum, with ghosts gathered around me. The first thing I notice is that the paintings on the wall over the mantelpiece, and the one in the hallway by the stairs, are missing. Gene must have sold them.

I feel relieved. He's at least doing something to fix things, not leaving it all to me. Unless of course he's raising the money in order to run off somewhere and start a new life. My mind won't stop conjuring up what-ifs and maybes. Perhaps it's the leaden exhaustion or the paranoia or the drugs I'm taking but my imagination feels amplified, every few seconds conjuring a new theory or suspect.

I head upstairs, deliberately avoiding looking in June's room, and toss everything I'm wearing into the laundry bin, before showering in record time and changing into a pair of jeans and a T-shirt. The jeans fall off my hips and a quick glance in the mirror shows me that I've lost weight – a lot of weight. My face looks gaunt, my eyes dark-circled. I hardly recognize myself and I turn abruptly away.

I let out a scream. Gene is standing in the doorway.

He jumps back in fright. I lunge at him, slapping and clawing at his face, the rage pouring out of me. He staggers away from the onslaught, holding my wrists, but still I come at him. The backs of his legs hit the bed and he tumbles down, holding up his arms to cover his face.

I kick his leg and stumble away from him, forcing myself to rein in the fury. 'You bastard,' I say to him. 'You absolute bastard.'

He peeks out at me from behind the barrier of his arms.

'I met Raul and James. I know everything. I know you've been dealing meth and that some money was stolen – money that you now owe. I know your father was trying to help you and now he's in prison and he won't say anything because he's trying to protect us all. I know that it was you who took the photo of June and sold it to that man, that journalist. I know everything, Gene.'

His face turns ashen.

'Did you think you could keep it all a secret?'

His face crumples. 'I'm sorry.'

'No!' I shout. 'You don't get to say sorry. The doctors want to switch off June's life support.'

His head flies up. 'What?'

'Someone got into the hospital this morning and turned off her ventilator. If you'd been around you'd know this. The police think it was the same person who broke into the house. The same person who shot your sister.'

Gene stares at me. I see the shock waves pummeling him and I relish it. I want to pound him so hard with the truth of what he's done that he collapses beneath the weight of it.

'She went into cardiac arrest,' I tell him. 'They say even if she wakes up she'll be brain damaged.'

Gene takes that in then shakes his head angrily. 'Don't let them. How do you know they're right?'

'Because they're doctors.'

'So? That doesn't mean they can't make mistakes. People make mistakes all the time.'

'This wasn't a mistake, Gene,' I say. 'You knew what you were doing.'

He drops his head and then his body starts to convulse. He curls into a ball on the bed and I realize he's crying, sobbing like a child. I feel nothing except contempt.

'Do you know what you've done?' I say. 'Do you?! This is all your fault. I went to see them – your friends – your drug dealer friends. They threatened me, did you know that? And your father. And your sisters.'

'It's OK,' Gene says in a whisper. 'I'm getting the money together.'

'How? Are you going to sell more photos?'

'No,' he mumbles through his tears. 'I've pooled all my savings, sold my car and a few things.'

'My paintings.'

'I've got thirty-two thousand,' he mumbles, not looking me in the face.

'How are you going to get the rest?' I ask, doing the mental calculation. He still needs to find close to fifty thousand more dollars.

He sits up. 'Don't worry about it. I've got a plan.'

'Yeah,' I snort. 'I can just imagine what kind of plan you have.'

He hangs his head in shame.

'The people who stole the money, Gene – do you know who they were? If you have any idea you need to tell me right now, you should have already told the police.'

He shakes his head, looks up at me. 'You think I wouldn't have told someone if I had any idea who it was?'

'I don't know,' I say, shrugging. 'Would you have? My guess is not, because that means you'd be arrested too and God forbid you ever pay for your screw-ups or that your father or the world ever treats you like a goddamn adult.'

He laughs, a bitter snort. 'You think I care if I'm arrested? You think I'm doing this to save my own skin?' He stands up and paces away from me. Next thing I know, he's whirling back around to face me, fury radiating off him. 'You don't think I wish it was me lying in that hospital bed? You don't think I would trade places with June in a second? I've been trying to fix this! I was the one that wanted to go to the police and tell them, but Dad told me not to.' His voice breaks. 'We didn't plan for any of this to happen.' He looks quickly away, wipes the back of his arm across his mouth as if trying to cancel out what he just said.

'What did you just say? We?'

'Nothing.' He turns his back to me.

'Gene, what do you mean "we"?'

He doesn't respond. I study the back of his head, trying to bat away the impulse I have to throw myself on him and start hitting him. Eventually he grunts something.

'Sorry?' I say, unsure I've heard him correctly.

He turns to me. 'Dave. Dave and me. We were in business together.'

For a few seconds my brain tries to twist itself around these new facts. 'Business?' I ask.

He nods, eyes sliding to the floor. 'I needed some cash up front. He put some money down about six months ago to get me started. It was just a quick buck for him, you know, a good return.'

'Yeah,' I say, 'a *great* return.'

Gene flinches as if I've lunged at him again.

'And then he left you to swing when the money disappeared?' I ask.

He looks up now, startled. 'No. He's been trying to help me fix it.'

'How?'

'He's given me what he had and he's trying to refinance his house.'

Shit. Does Laurie know about this? She'll kill him if she finds out. Should I tell her?

'Look,' Gene says to me, 'Dave was just a silent partner. He gave me a little seed money, that's all. He wasn't involved at all in anything else. He said he really needed the cash. I think he asked Dad for a loan and Dad said no.'

'Sell whatever you can,' I say, sighing and gesturing at the house. 'Furniture, paintings, anything.' I pull off the diamond eternity ring that Robert bought for me last year. 'And this, take this. It's worth at least twenty-five thousand.'

Gene stares at the ring I place in his outstretched palm. 'I can't.'

'Oh please don't let your conscience stop you now,' I tell him. 'I'm not doing this for you.'

'I'm sorry,' Gene says. 'I didn't mean for any of this to happen.'

He's looking at me pleadingly but I can't give him the absolution he's asking for. 'But it did.'

'I'm sorry.'

'Stop saying that. It doesn't make it better. It doesn't change anything.'

'I—' He stops himself, his fisted hand punching his thigh.

'The only thing you can do now is get the money and pay them.'

He nods. 'I will.'

'And after you've paid your debt I want you to leave. I don't ever want to see you again. You're not welcome near this family, do you understand?'

'Ava,' he says. 'Please. It's my family too.'

'Not any longer.'

He doesn't move for a few seconds, but then he slopes towards the door, pausing when he reaches it. 'Don't let them switch the life support off.'

'She's my daughter. I decide.'

'She's my sister,' he answers quietly. And then he's gone and I'm slamming the door behind him.

38

Lies. Lies. Lies.

Laurie drives me to the hospital and I stay quiet the whole way, not telling her about Dave. I think about it – a couple of times it's even on the tip of my tongue – but in the end, I stay silent. I can't be the one to tell her. It should be him.

I find Hannah in June's room where I left her. Jonathan is there too and when I enter, the two of them spring apart like repelling magnets. Hannah looks like she's been crying and Jonathan's face is blotchy red, his Sheriff hat askew.

'Mom,' Hannah says, rushing over and hugging me like I've been gone years, not hours.

'I was worried about you,' she says.

'I'm fine,' I say.

She clings to me and I notice she's trembling. I glance over her head at Jonathan, who gives me a quick smile and then hurries outside.

'Are you OK?' I ask Hannah.

She nods. 'Yes,' she mumbles. She was upset, I guess, and he was comforting her. I keep forgetting that Hannah is going through this too. I'm so caught up in everything, I'm not being a good mother to her.

'I'm sorry,' I murmur into her hair. 'I love you.'

'I love you too,' she says, still clinging to me.

I take her face in my palms and look at her, my first born, my love, older now than I was when I had her.

'Is everything going to be OK?' she asks.

I nod, pulling her back into my arms so she can't see the truth in my expression.

A knock makes me turn. It's the hospital administrator, along with Dr Warier and another doctor I recognize as the neurologist.

'Mrs Walker,' Dr Warier begins.

I eye them all suspiciously. 'Hannah,' I say, 'why don't you step aside and give us a minute?'

She makes to argue with me but I glare at her and she leaves.

'What is it?' I say to Dr Warier.

'We wanted to talk to you about organ donation.'

'What?' I say.

'At a time like this—'

I cut him off. 'I heard you. But we're not discussing it, because you're not switching off those machines.'

The neurologist steps forwards. 'I'm afraid that there's an absence of motor responses and very high levels of enolase in June's system. She is, in my opinion, brain dead.'

'Your opinion,' I say.

The neurologist gives me a steely stare. 'Yes, my opinion.'

I turn to the clipboard-clutching administrator. 'And that opinion is in no way biased by the fact the cost of keeping her on life support is now in the millions and the hospital is concerned about our ability to honor the bill?'

'That's completely ridiculous,' the administrator splutters. 'An outrageous suggestion.'

I death-stare her until she shrivels like a flower cut down by a squirt of Round Up.

Dr Warier steps forwards. 'It's been over a week,' he says in an even tone, 'and the chances of the patient recovering are much less than five per cent.'

I nod. 'Someone once gave June similar odds and she beat them, so next time you tell me my daughter's life support needs switching off, I suggest you give me much worse odds than that.'

The doctors glance between themselves and I can see them trying to weigh up what to do next and whose turn it is to speak. 'And I want a second opinion. This time from an expert.'

Once more the doctors confer silently – a whole language of alarmed looks and twitching eyebrows.

'I don't think—' the administrator starts.

'Well, I know that,' I shoot back before she can finish. 'But we're asking for a second opinion and we're going to get one, and until then you'll care for my daughter as though she's about to come out of her coma, not as though you're about to harvest her for her organs. Do you understand me?'

Nods all around.

'Good. Because we'd hate to add another lawsuit to the one we're already going to file against the hospital and the Sheriff's department and the state for allowing someone to waltz in here and attempt to murder our daughter for a second time.'

Eventually Dr Warier speaks up again, clearing his throat loudly. 'We'll leave you be.'

I watch them troop out of the room then collapse down into the chair by June's side, breathing fast and feeling faint. I take her hand.

'Now prove me right,' I say to her.

39

DAY 9

I head back home at dawn, leaving Hannah in the ICU. We're taking it in shifts to watch over June. I don't trust the Sheriffs to do the job properly and I also don't trust the hospital.

Gene has left. I know it before I even look in the apartment. There's a desolation hanging in the air like it does at ancient ruins, a heavy cloying silence that shrouds the house.

When I open the front door I notice that even more paintings have vanished – though this time I see with surprise that they're all ones I painted. The antique candlesticks on the table are gone, and the silver cutlery my father gave me on our wedding day has been emptied from the drawers in the dining room, which all gape open. It's as if burglars have been again.

As I make my way through the rooms I note that Gene's done a more thorough job than an estate sale. In the bare kitchen there's an envelope sitting on the side with my name on it.

Inside are my car keys and a check for fifteen thousand dollars from a gallery in town.

Ava,
I sold your paintings.
Gene.

I turn the note over but that's all he's written. Fifteen thousand dollars? Does this mean that Gene made more than he needed? He needed close to fifty thousand dollars though, how could those paintings have possibly made that much money? I have to sit down. My name is scattered all over the news, that's probably why they paid that much. It lends cachet to have a painting by the mother of a dying girl and a murderous husband. I can't imagine another reason. They're not that good. Though art, like truth, is subjective, isn't it?

But still, it's money, and I need money right now. This might even be enough to get the bank manager off my back. Or maybe I should be using it to hire a better lawyer for Robert. Horowitz is as useless as a paper condom. But fifteen thousand won't buy a lawyer worth their salt and what would be the point anyway when we need to keep the truth hidden? In that respect Horowitz is a blessing in disguise, I suppose.

I'm about to throw away the envelope when I notice something else inside it. I upturn the envelope over my palm and my ring tumbles out. Gene didn't sell it. I turn it around and look at all the diamonds embedded in it – one for each year of our marriage – before I slide it back onto my finger.

Eternity. Was that another lie?

I trudge upstairs, limbs leaden, and pause in the doorway to June's room. My gaze lands on the hamster cage. I still haven't cleaned it, though George now lies buried beneath a rose bush in the back garden. I can't put it off any longer, the room is starting to smell fusty and fetid and when she comes home, if there's still this house to come home to, I don't want the first thing she sees to be the hamster cage – reminding her that not only couldn't I keep her safe, I couldn't keep her pet hamster alive either.

I grab the trash can from under the desk and kneel by the cage, tugging at the catch and removing the bottom in order to dispose of the clumps of matted sawdust. As I do, something catches my eye. A flat, square plastic container, the kind I use for storing cookies and leftovers, lies hidden beneath the sawdust. I pull it out, dust off the lid and then open it. Inside are a dozen stacks of shrink-wrapped cash.

I rock back on my heels. 'Oh, June,' I whisper.

40

'Ava?'

Heart lurching, I swivel around so fast I almost overbalance. Nate stands in the doorway.

'What are you doing here? How did you get in?' I stammer.

How long has he been standing there? He takes a step towards me and adrenaline pumps into my system. I nudge the container of money behind me with my foot, so it's out of sight. But if he comes one step closer he'll see it.

He doesn't though. He stops, thank God, in the middle of the room. 'I went to the hospital but Hannah told me you were here,' he says.

I frown. 'Oh,' I say.

It's Nate's turn to frown. 'I called but you didn't answer.'

Did he? I left my phone downstairs so there's no way to tell.

'I rang the bell too,' he says, gesturing over his shoulder. 'And you didn't answer that. I was worried,' he adds. 'I thought something might have happened . . .'

'Oh,' I say, a grunt more than a word, desperately trying to figure out how to distract him and stop him inching closer. I could have sworn I locked the door but my mind is on the money. I can't let him see it. How will I explain it? And now he's looking at me strangely, head cocked to one side, waiting for me to stand up because it's odd – it must seem odd – for me to be here, kneeling on the floor at his feet, smiling up at him. 'What did you want?' I ask him, standing up and blocking his view of the cage with my legs.

Nate narrows his eyes at me. 'I wanted to let you know that I looked into that journalist like you asked me to, and I couldn't find any trace of him. I've got a detective trying to find out who he really is.'

'OK,' I say, wondering why he thought it urgent enough to drive all the way out to the hospital and then here to let me know. I could tell him I already know, but I don't want to get drawn into a conversation about Gene selling the photos.

I glance down at the cage behind me. The cash is just lying there, staring up at me.

'Are you OK?' Nate asks. 'You seem very jumpy.'

'I'm fine. Just tidying up a few things.' I swipe at my eyes and my gaze lands on June's basketball trophies on the shelf by her desk. 'She used to play basketball,' I stammer.

Nate obligingly turns to look at the trophies and I take advantage to grab the lid of the hamster cage and slam it down on top of the money, hiding it partially from view.

'What happened to the hamster?'

I swing back around, heart in my throat. Nate's staring at the cage.

'He died.'

'Oh.'

'June will never forgive me,' I say, hurrying past him for the door. I need to get him out of here. 'I need to clean all this stuff out. It's filthy. Probably a breeding ground for God knows what.' I'm rattling away, trying to fill the space, hoping to distract him.

'You shouldn't be doing that. Why don't you let me?' He moves for the cage.

I shake my head. 'No, no, don't worry. It's really fine.'

I stop by the door. Nate's still in the room, looking around. If he looks closer he'll see the money. I do the only thing that comes to mind – I step towards him and fall against him, sobbing loudly, clinging to him. It sounds fake to my ears, put on – especially given only yesterday I was screaming at him to leave me alone.

Nate tenses so I start crying louder, my fingers digging into his shoulders and slowly I feel his arms come around my waist. His hands move up my back and reach my neck. I freeze. But then his fingers are in my hair, stroking. 'It's OK,' he murmurs in my ear.

I inch to the left, managing to make Nate twist around so his back is to the cage. Nate dips his head. I can feel his breath hot against my neck and it sends a shiver down my spine. His arms tighten around my waist and it strikes me how strong he is, how incapable I would be of fighting him off, but then, as though he's reading my mind, Nate pulls away and takes a step backward.

'Let's go downstairs,' I say, striding to the door.

Nate follows slowly, scanning June's room from ceiling to floor before he leaves, his gaze sweeping across the bloodstain on the carpet. Finally, when my nerves are at breaking point, he turns and follows me out into the hall.

I close the door behind us.

'Did you ever remember any more?' Nate asks as we head down the stairs. 'About what happened in there?'

I shake my head. 'No,' I say. 'It's still fuzzy.'

But as I turn around, something jolts loose like a dislocated rib popping back into place – a dizzying sense of déjà vu that almost sends me toppling down the stairs. I get a flash of something. It's not a complete image – just a partial, like someone has their finger over the lens of the camera, and it's only a still frame.

But I see June kneeling on the floor in front of the man.

I only saw it from one angle; she was partly blocked by the man standing in front of her. I made the wrong assumption. I saw what I thought was a man in a mask about to sexually assault my daughter. But that's not what was happening at all. She was kneeling down beside George's cage.

'What?' Nate grips my elbow and when I blink, his face swims sharply into focus and I almost fall; only his hold on me keeps me upright. 'Are you OK?' he asks and there's no disguising the concern on his face.

'Yeah, I just . . . I . . . I'm just a little faint, that's all.'

He frowns at me, his hand still gripping my elbow, and I force a smile. 'I'm fine,' I say.

I make my way down the stairs, holding tight to the bannister, Nate's hand gripping my arm.

41

As we walk down the stairs I can't shake the image of June from my head. Was she already opening the hamster cage when I walked into the room? It was only a split second – lasting only as long as a heartbeat, or the time it takes for a trigger to be pulled and a bullet to travel ten feet.

She took the gunman upstairs on purpose, because she was planning to give him the money. Did she guess that's what they had come for? Did she know who they were? Or was she just trying to give them something – money – to make them go away? But if she told them about the money, or they knew that Gene had money in the house and were targeting us because of that, then they likely suspect that it is still here. They may even know it's in June's room.

So why haven't they been back to look for it?

I stumble and Nate's grip on my arm tightens, as though he's afraid I'm about to run. Could it be him?

No! It wasn't him. He's too tall. My paranoia is getting the better of me. My mind is spewing out what-ifs like a pinwheel throwing out sparks. I'll start blaming the gardener next. If only I could figure out who knew about the money, I'd have a list of suspects.

In the kitchen Nate finally lets go of my arm. 'Can I get you anything before I go? Water? Something to eat?' he asks, looking at me with such solicitousness that I almost laugh out loud at my crazy conjecture. My exhaustion is making me see a suspect in every face I encounter.

I shake my head and my gaze lands on the dark ink stain I tried to scrub out of the wooden island and that, like Lady Macbeth's damned spot, isn't going anywhere.

I turn back to Nate. 'Are the DNA results back?' I suddenly ask, remembering he was waiting on them.

'They came in last night,' he answers.

I wait, holding my breath.

'They weren't able to make any matches,' he says, grimacing. 'There was only one trace found but the sample was too small to get anything from it.'

'Oh,' I say, frowning at the fingerprint ink on the wood. It seems odd, but I don't know anything about how forensics work except what I've gleaned from CSI.

'Actually, Ava,' he says, 'I didn't come here to talk to you about the journalist.'

He scratches his head and looks at me through his lashes, a little rueful, a little boyish. 'They told me you might be suing the Sheriff's department.'

Oh. So this is why he came. Of course.

'I understand,' he says with a sigh. 'And I'm not here in an official capacity, but I wanted to speak with you about it.'

I hadn't given any more thought to what I said yesterday about suing. The threats were spur of the moment. I was channeling Robert. I had no idea if I even had a case but the very fact he's here, wanting to discuss it in an unofficial capacity, suggests I probably do. Interesting.

Taking my silence as an invitation, he carries on. 'I think you have a case,' he says, surprising me. 'Against the hospital,' he finishes. 'It was their security breach that allowed someone disguised as a doctor to enter the ICU.'

'And a Sheriff's deputy was posted outside June's door,' I remark, crossing my arms over my chest.

Nate chews his lip unhappily. 'I know. I'm sorry. I can't tell you how sorry I am.'

'Not as sorry as me,' I answer sharply. 'What do you want?'

He hears the irritation in my voice and exhales. 'My job's on the line. My whole career. They'll look to throw someone under the bus. And that someone will be me.'

I close my eyes in disbelief. My daughter is brain dead according to the doctors and it's partly, if not fully, Nate's fault. And he's come here begging me not to sue in case he loses his job. I always knew Nate was self-centered but this goes far beyond that and into pathological-narcissism territory.

'I can't afford to lose my job,' he says beseechingly. 'I've got kids, a mortgage. This kind of thing sticks to you. No one will employ me.'

I struggle with what to say as he pleads, my hands coiling into fists. Like I give a shit. Thank God, the phone rings, and I race for it, grateful for the interruption.

'Hello?' I say.

'Ava?'

It's Laurie.

'Hi,' I say.

'Do you still need a ride to the hospital?'

'No,' I tell her. 'I've got my car back.'

'From Gene?' she asks. 'Did you see him? Did you ask him about the drugs?'

I whip around, covering the phone so Nate can't hear, but he's gone. Where did he go? I rush to the kitchen door and catch a flash of movement at the top of the stairs. 'I need to go,' I say to Laurie and hang up the phone.

At the top of the stairs I glance right. The door to June's bedroom is open. I walk towards it, pulse skittering. Nate steps out right in front of me just as I reach it. He's holding something in his hand. He smiles and holds it up to show me.

'Forgot this,' he says.

It's his phone.

'Must have left it on the desk.'

I glance over his shoulder at the desk and then at the hamster cage, my throat so dry I feel as if I've swallowed mouthfuls of sawdust. Nate steps past me out into the hallway, and I follow him, but not before craning my neck to see if the money is where I left it. From this angle it's impossible to tell.

'I better be going,' Nate says to me, looking at his watch. 'I'm sorry I came. I shouldn't have. Please forget what I said.'

I follow him, not saying anything, and see him out, my hands shaking with adrenaline. As soon as he's over the threshold I shut the door on him, drawing the bolt and the chain.

After taking a few deep breaths I push myself away and make for the stairs. Did he find the money? I drag myself up by the bannister and rush into June's room. The money is still there, half-buried in sawdust.

I dig it out and count it. One hundred and ten thousand dollars. It's all there.

42

17 MONTHS AGO

The second time I see him I don't even try to kid myself it's just for coffee. I go for a bikini wax. We meet for a drink and I'm so nervous I down two glasses of Pinot in short order and am light-headed when we leave the bar.

Except this time there are no pretenses. When he tells me I'm too drunk to drive and we walk on to his car, I know what I'm walking towards. We end up back at his, a small apartment in a part of town I've never been to before, behind the Vons and the Chinese place, where the houses are all pre-war clapboard bungalows. I'm surprised he isn't living somewhere fancier, but I suppose with the alimony he grumbles about he's on a tight budget.

We enter the small living room and I only get a quick glance around, taking in the bare walls and minimal furniture, before Nate's pulling me into his arms and kissing me. I hesitate for a brief moment then lean in to him, letting the feeling of being desired wash over me.

The initial strangeness gives way to an old familiarity. When he kissed me by my car it only lasted a few seconds, just long enough for me to come to my senses. This time we kiss for a minute or two but no matter how much I want to enjoy it, I can't. The thrill of being desired is numbed. I'm too guilty. It's as if I'm kissing cardboard. I feel nothing.

I don't know if I want to go through with this. Nate's maneuvering me to the sofa, his arms around my waist, his lips on my neck.

What am I doing? The shock of it hits me. Robert would be devastated. I can't do this to him.

He'll never know, the voice in my head whispers.

Nate's hands slide under my shirt and up my back, and with expert ease he undoes my bra. He used to be so proud of that move as a teenager.

I lurch away from him, unsteady on my feet. 'I . . . I just need the bathroom,' I say, and before he can even point me in the right direction I dart towards the narrow hallway.

'First on the right,' he calls after me.

I rush inside and turn to lock it but there is no lock. I sink down onto the toilet, shaking while simultaneously fanning my overheated face. Shit. What am I doing? I glance around at the threadbare towels, Nate's aftershave and razor sitting on the side. This is not a good idea. But how do I get out of it?

I'll just go out there and tell him I can't go through with it. He'll understand.

I stand up and re-do my bra, then stare at myself in the mirror, feeling like I'm staring at my evil twin. I can't believe I almost slept with him.

I wash my hands and dry them on the towel, freezing at the sight of a pink hair tie on the side of the bath with long strands of blonde hair caught in it.

Behind me the door flies open. I jump and spin around to find Nate standing there, a concerned smile on his face. 'Everything OK?' he asks.

I nod but he must see something in my expression as his eyes fly past me and land on the hair tie.

'That's my daughter's,' he says, reaching and picking it up. 'She stayed here last weekend.' Something about the way he says it sounds off. He's too quick to explain it, his voice too high. His daughter's, or another woman's? I wonder. Another reason to be glad I didn't sleep with him.

'I should go,' I say, looking around for my bag. My keys. Oh shit. I left my car in town. Damn. I'll need to call an Uber. Where's my bag?

'Ava.' A hand on my arm. He pulls me gently around. 'My daughters came to stay last weekend. I've been finding their things lying all around ever since. You know what teenage girls are like.'

I nod. 'It's not that,' I say. 'I just . . . it doesn't feel right. I can't do this.'

I grab my bag and rush for the door. I'll call a cab outside.

'Wait,' he says and rushes after me. 'Let me at least drive you back to your car.'

I think about it but I don't want to be rude so I nod. 'OK.'

We drive in silence the five minutes back to where I parked outside the bar. When he parks he reaches over and takes my hand. I turn to look at him, feeling a pang in my stomach. I'm still attracted to him and still feel the buzz of excitement of being touched by him, but he's not what I want and I'm not going to get what I need from him. I slide my hand out from under his.

'Bye Nate,' I say.

'No hard feelings,' he replies.

'No hard feelings,' I answer.

43

I pull up outside a small, shabby, clapboard house in Meiners Oaks. A shopping cart's been abandoned in the front yard – which is a no-man's-land of rubble – and a beat-up old camper van with no tires, decorated with marijuana leaves and Bob Marley stickers, is parked on bricks in the drive. I wonder who on earth lives here and then decide I don't want to find out.

When I beep the horn the front door opens and out slopes Gene. Behind him I catch a glimpse of a girl wearing skimpy underwear and a tatty Bison Lodge T-shirt. Gene hurries over to the car and jumps in the passenger side.

'Is it June?' he asks me immediately. 'Is she OK?'

I didn't tell him anything on the phone, just that I needed him and it was an emergency. I think I took some small pleasure in keeping him on tenterhooks.

'She's the same,' I tell him, tossing a plastic bag into his lap, and stepping on the accelerator.

'What's this?' he asks.

'Open it,' I tell him.

He fumbles with the knot I tied in the bag. 'Holy shit! Where'd you find this?' he asks, eyes wide.

'Hidden in June's room.'

He slams his head back into the headrest, taking a deep breath in. 'Oh shit. *She* took the money?'

I nod. The driver behind honks their horn and I jump. The light's green. I pull onto the 33 towards Ventura.

'She was in my apartment,' Gene says, disbelief in his voice. 'I didn't think about it before but now I remember. A month ago, I guess. I found her. She told me she was looking for her tennis racket. I thought it was weird at the time because she hasn't played tennis in years. But why . . .?' He shakes his head. 'Why would she take it?'

'I don't know,' I tell him honestly. I've been wondering myself. June wasn't a thief. Why would she take it?

Gene exhales, punching the seat and swearing. 'She must have thought I was going to use it to buy drugs . . . She caught me smoking a few times.' A quick glance my way and he holds up his hands. 'I know! I'm sorry. She lectured me about it one time – sounded just like you and Dad. They did some talk at her school about drugs being bad. Gave out these flyers. She left them on my bed.'

It comes back to me then, the conversation I had with her the night she was shot. She asked me what I would do if I knew someone had done something bad but that telling the truth would get them in trouble. She was talking about Gene, not Abby. She took the money because she was trying to do the right thing.

'Hey, slow down . . .'

The speedometer is flying upwards, nudging ninety. I ease off the gas, my arms rigid on the wheel.

'I'm sorry,' says Gene.

My grip on the wheel tightens as if it's his neck I'm squeezing. We drive in silence all the way to the 101. Gene double-takes as we fly past the turn for the hospital, looking over his shoulder. 'Hey, you missed the exit.'

'I know.'

'Where are we going?' he asks.

'Oxnard.'

44

The Corona bar sign flickers on and off, on and off. I get out the car, Gene scrambling to follow me. The plastic bag of cash is in my handbag. It's almost one in the morning and I know Gene thinks we're crazy coming here at this time of night. He hasn't even heard half of my plan yet though.

'Ava, what are you doing?' Gene says, catching up to me. 'This isn't . . .'

I spin towards him. 'Gene, we're paying these men the money you owe. We're getting them off our back.'

I push the door to the bar open and he stops talking.

I'm only vaguely aware of the instant drop in volume and the faces turning towards me. Gene sticks close to my side as I march towards the bar. The barman takes me in with an expression that moves from amusement to annoyance in the space of a second. Sighing, he turns his back on us and reaches for the phone on the wall.

I pull up a stool and sit down. Gene stands beside me, jittery and nervous, until I push a stool towards him and glare at him until he sits down too.

The barman finishes his call and pulls a bottle of Tequila from under the bar. He pours us both a shot. I leave mine untouched but after a minute of waiting Gene picks his up and downs it, wiping his mouth with the back of his arm.

'Tell me,' I ask him. 'Did you get fired from the Bison Lodge for dealing?'

Gene doesn't answer, which is answer enough. I sigh and turn away, sick to my stomach, and catch sight of myself in the mirror behind the bar, my face all blurry as though someone's hurriedly taken an eraser to it but given up halfway through trying to make me disappear. It's only when I focus hard that I realize that the mirror is burnished metal and is distorting everything reflected in it. I look over at Gene, head hanging morosely over his empty tequila glass.

'Why did you do it?' I ask him. 'We gave you everything you ever asked for.'

He nods, not looking at me. 'I know.' There's a pause and I think he's stopped talking but then he adds, 'You know, I was eight when I first smoked a joint. My mom gave it to me, told me to take a puff.'

I look at him. How did I not know this?

'And then she started dealing – you know, at the bar where she worked. And occasionally she'd get me to courier drugs around on my bike. I mean, who's going to stop a nine-year-old?'

'Oh, Gene.'

He stares down at the bar, toying with his empty shot glass. 'When she dropped me here, you know, when she dumped me, I was so happy. I thought this was my chance to have a new start, but then June got sick and . . . I don't know . . . I'm sorry, that's not fair. June was sick and I guess I just started smoking again to forget about everything.'

'I'm sorry,' I say. I reach across and put my hand on his leg. 'I know we weren't good parents to you when you needed us. And I'm sorry we left you with your mom when you were little.'

He shrugs. 'I'm sorry I was always such a disappointment.'

'What are you talking about?'

He cocks an eyebrow at me. 'Don't lie, Ava, you're terrible at it.'

'I'm not terrible at it,' I murmur. I'm very, very good at it, actually, but I keep that to myself. 'Are you doing meth?' I ask him, changing the subject.

He looks at me, wearing a wounded expression. 'No. I never do the hard stuff. I saw what it did to my mom.'

I frown at him. I didn't know his mother was on meth. I knew she was a drunk but I realize how little I ever knew about his life with her. It's amazing how we focus on only what we want to see and what we want to believe, even when the truth is staring us right in the face.

'And you still deal it,' I say, unable to keep the harshness out of my voice. 'After seeing what it did to her?'

'I'm sorry.' Gene darts a glance my way, looking for my reaction. Does he want forgiveness? From his tone I'm guessing that he does but I can't find it in me. How can I ever forgive him? He may as well ask me to give him the moon. He didn't pull the trigger but the gunmen were only in the house because of Gene and the stupid decisions he made. I can't even think of the other countless lives he might have ruined by supplying meth.

'I didn't want Dad to get involved,' he continues, his voice low, the words tumbling out of him in a rush. 'I didn't know he was going to come here and try to speak to them.' Gene reaches for my tequila and downs it.

'When did he find out?' I ask.

'Just after the money disappeared. I was freaking out. I needed to pay it back. I didn't know who else to ask, so I went to him.' Again, he darts a nervous glance my way.

'You told him?' I ask.

'I told him that I was in trouble with some people. That I needed to borrow money to pay them back.'

'And he agreed, just like that, no questions asked?'

Gene shakes his head. 'No, he refused to help unless I told him what it was for.'

'He knew?' I can't believe he knew the truth and still offered to help, and that he pawned my jewelry in order to do it.

'I told him that if I didn't find the money they'd kill me.'

My eyebrows shoot up. 'What? Raul and James told you that?'

Gene shakes his head. 'No, not them, but they said the people they owed the money to would hunt me down and kill me, as a warning.'

I draw in a shuddering breath. Was that what happened? Did they break in looking for Gene? Was the robbery a punishment? The room swims in front of me. It has to be them. The people Raul and James get their drugs from.

'I'm going to go to the police,' Gene blurts. 'I should have gone to them in the first place.'

'No,' I say, alarmed, turning to clutch his arm. 'You can't. They can't know any of this. Your sisters are in danger. Everyone would be if we talked. You know who these people are. You just said they threatened to kill you!'

'But Dad,' he chokes. 'I can't let him go to jail because of me.'

I press my lips together hard and nod. I know. But what if the police can't keep us safe? So far they've done a lousy job of protecting June. How can I trust them?

'Do you think Dad will get off?' Gene asks.

'I don't know,' I say, and then I close my eyes and take a deep breath. One thing at a time. When I open my eyes I see myself again – a stranger – reflected in the burnished circus mirror.

Beside me Gene signals the barman for another shot. I watch him down it. There's so much of Robert in him, in his eyes and the set of his mouth, and for a moment my heart softens, but then I remember that he's the reason Robert's locked away and the iron shutters slam down before I can stop them. I turn away from him and back to my own reflection.

The problem is that if June dies I won't ever be able to forgive him – or Dave or Robert for that matter. I will want to destroy each and every one of the people involved, for lying, for their complicity, for their stupidity, for not thinking of the consequences.

The door opens before I can get lost in any more dark thoughts. I don't have to look. I know by the drop in noise that it's Raul and James.

Gene, who has been playing with his shot glass, freezes. I still don't turn around. I wait for them to come over to us, and only when they're beside me do I swivel to look at them.

Raul's shoulders are rounded, his nostrils flaring with every angry breath. Behind him James hovers, tense, eyes darting around as though he thinks maybe we've brought the cops with us.

'We brought you the money,' I say, handing Raul the plastic bag of cash. He can't hide his surprise when he opens it.

'It's all there. You can count it.'

'Nah, I trust you,' he says, looking up now with a smile. 'So, I guess we're done then. Just tell your husband to keep on keeping his mouth shut.' He nudges James and jerks his head in the direction of the door.

'Wait,' I say, before they can leave.

Raul pauses and turns back to look at me over his shoulder, the smile gone, a wariness descending as though he's worried he's stepped into a trap.

'I need a favor.'

Raul cocks an eyebrow at me and glances at James. 'You need a favor, from us?' he asks, an amused look on his face.

I take a deep breath, then reach into my handbag. After paying them back what Gene owed, minus what he'd already pulled together, I've got seventy thousand extra dollars in my pocket. I don't know how much it will cost, but I'm willing to pay whatever it takes.

45

DAY 10

The media camp outside the hospital has whittled down. It's less an army now and more a scrum. I can't help but scan the parking lot as I walk towards the doors, holding my bag close to my body and preparing to use it as a battering ram if I have to. Before, I was terrified to run the gauntlet of all those journalists and news crews but now I barely notice them.

Elbows out, I shove my way through, tuning out the shouts and barrage of questions. There's a blur of blue and white up ahead – a cop tunneling his way through the flailing arms and microphones to reach me – but I dig in and forge my own path forwards.

I'm almost in the center of the scrum when someone tugs sharply on my handbag strap. I whirl around in an instant, shoving them away. It's a woman – a reporter. She stumbles and trips over a cable snaking along the ground, dropping her microphone. But another reporter rushes in to fill the gap, thrusting her mic in my face. 'Is it true that June's life support is going to be turned off?' she shouts.

I turn to the camera. 'No,' I say, loud enough for them all to hear. Silence falls. It's the first time any of them have heard me speak and so they hush, jostling to get their microphones nearer. 'Her life support is not about to be turned off.' I smile to the cameras. 'She's doing great. The doctors expect her to wake up any moment.'

The cop materializes right then at my side and takes my elbow, ready to accompany me out of the crush. I shrug him off. I don't need him. The media have sensed that they've got all they're going to get from me anyway – their morsel, their pound of flesh – and they're already backing away, desperate to be the first to file a report.

The elevator is empty. I slip my hand into my bag and find my phone. It's eleven already. There are five missed calls from Laurie, probably about the specialist she was trying to arrange to come and give a second opinion on June, but no new voice-mails, which is strange. But then I remember Sam telling me my mailbox was full. I need to find the time to go through it and delete my messages. The bank manager, who I met with first thing this morning, was most understanding. It helps when you hand over twenty thousand dollars in cash. There's debt still of course, more debt than I can wrap my head around, but it's temporarily keeping the wolves from the door.

I told Gene to use the money he'd raised to buy back his car, pay back Dave and then put the fifteen thousand he made from selling the photograph of June into June's bank account for when she wakes up. I also told him to speak to his father – seeing as he's the only one Robert will see – and update him on everything.

When I reach the ICU I'm met by two men in Sheriff uniforms, one of whom is Jonathan. He waves me through with a nod of the head and a smile and I can see why Hannah is attracted to him. He's a good-looking guy, and she's always gone for the athletic, all-American types. I'm glad she has him supporting her at a time like this.

As soon as I walk through the door into the ICU I see the hospital administrator walking out of June's room. Today she's wearing a tailored black pantsuit and heels, her trusty clipboard still welded to her chest. My stomach muscles contract at the sight of her, like armor locking into place, and I look around desperately for escape routes. There are none.

'I was just coming to find you,' she says, noticing me.

'Oh,' I answer, and for a brief moment hope soars in me. Is it June? Have they done another MRI?

'If we could just take a seat in here,' she says, gesturing towards the relatives' room, and I follow her, pulse quickening.

But if it was good news about June I'd expect the doctors to be present, and there's no one in the room. The wind taken out of my sails, I turn back to the door. I have things to do. The specialist is due any moment and I want to check in on June first, relieve Hannah from duty.

'You know what?' I say to the woman. 'I don't have time for this.'

I make to move past but she stops me. 'This will only take a moment.' She gestures at a seat but I stay standing.

She sighs. 'As you know we're sorry there was a lapse in security that allowed what happened to happen.'

I open my mouth to tell her it wasn't so much a lapse in security as a total fucking fuck-up but she keeps going, obviously rattling off a pre-prepared statement that she must have learned by heart.

'While we recognize our limited role . . .'

'Limited?' I hiss, eyes bugging.

A muscle by her eye twitches in response. 'In respect of the situation the hospital board has drafted the following contract, which we would appreciate you looking over.'

She hands me a sheaf of paperwork and I take it, bewildered. I scan the pages, the words bouncing nonsensically in front of my eyes. Concentrating hard, I'm able to put together the gist of it and after a few minutes I look up. 'You're trying to buy us off?'

The muscle starts to ping by her eye again as though someone's tugging on it. She gives me a polite but pained smile. 'I wouldn't call it that. We are aware of what our liabilities might be and we also know what your liabilities are, as regards the health insurance situation. If you sign this contract all those liabilities go away. You won't have to pay a single dollar for June's care, retrospectively or going forwards.'

'*If* we agree not to sue the hospital.'

She nods.

I look at the number with six zeroes after it, and the dotted line where I'm supposed to sign. When I glance up she's holding out a pen. On seeing my expression she quickly withdraws it. 'Of course, take your time, speak to a lawyer.' She stands up. 'But the offer is only on the table for twenty-four hours.' She crosses to the door and starts to open it.

'I can give you your answer now,' I say. I slowly rip the contract in two and then drop the pieces to the floor. Stepping over them I walk towards her, stopping when I'm just a few inches away. 'The thing is, my husband is innocent. And when he's released from prison our insurance will pay out and cover all our medical bills. And then,' I say, reaching for the door handle, 'we'll take great pleasure in suing your asses into the ground. Here.' I pull a card from my pocket and give it to her.

She looks down at it, frowning.

'If you have anything else to say to me you can say it through my lawyer.'

I got the business card from Raul. It's their lawyer. The woman in the thousand-dollar suit. Now, happily, our lawyer too. And it turns out I didn't even have to pay her a retainer. I just offered her a percentage of the payout.

I don't bother to wait for the woman's reaction. I stride past her and out the door, slamming it behind me. Let her stew in that.

I find Gene asleep in a chair beside June's bed. He wakes with a start when the door closes behind me and leaps to his feet, disorientated.

'Where's Hannah?' I ask him, looking around.

He shakes his head. 'She wasn't here when I got here.'

'What?' She was meant to be here, watching June. Where did she go?

'The nurse said she left about midnight, just after Laurie.'

'Laurie was here?' I ask, even more confused.

Gene shrugs again. 'That's what they said. I didn't see either of them. But I only got here an hour ago. It took me a while to arrange a time to visit Dad.'

I nod, pulling out my phone. 'Did you try calling her?' I ask.

'I couldn't. I can't make a call from here and I didn't want to leave the room. You told me not to.'

I nod. Damn. 'OK, I'll be back in a minute,' I say, casting a quick glance at June. I head back out of the ICU to find Jonathan.

'Have you seen Hannah?' I ask him.

He shakes his head. 'No. Why?'

I glance at him, wondering if he and Hannah are still seeing each other. She hasn't said anything about it and I haven't asked as I've been too preoccupied. 'Are you two . . . dating?' I blurt.

He blanches. 'No,' he says, shaking his head furiously and blushing. 'We're just friends.'

Friends. I suppose that's the lingo these days. No one dates anymore. Hannah did try to tell me that once. They hook up or hang out or Netflix and chill. They don't date.

'If I see her I'll tell her you're worried about her,' he says.

I nod and hurry off into the stairwell, propping the door open with my foot. I try Hannah's phone. It rings through to voicemail. I hang up and try again. This time it doesn't even ring. She's switched it off. Strange.

'Hannah?' I say, when her voicemail kicks in again. 'It's me. Call me back as soon as you get this.'

Where could she have gone? And why did she leave June – she knows the rules about not leaving her alone, not even for a minute. I fumble through the buttons to my own voicemail and start playing old messages, not even listening to them all the way through before hitting delete on each one, trying to clear space. They're mostly from journalists anyway, a few from friends sending love and best wishes for a speedy recovery. Delete. Delete. Delete.

The phone rings in my hand. Hoping it's Hannah, I'm disappointed to see it's Dave. 'Ava, is Laurie with you?' he barks, the moment I pick up.

'No. Why?'

'She hasn't been home all night. I've tried calling but she's not picking up. And now her phone's switched off. Do you know where she might be?'

'Gene says she was at the hospital yesterday evening and left around midnight.'

'OK,' he mumbles.

'I know about you and Gene being in business together,' I snap.

There's a silent hum on the end of the line and I wonder if he's hung up but then he stammers. 'Oh God, Ava, I'm so sorry.' He pauses, then adds, 'You didn't tell Laurie, did you?'

'No,' I tell him, 'but you need to.'

'I know,' he half sobs. 'I just . . . she'll leave me . . .'

'You need to tell the truth,' I say, though a part of me wonders at the irony of me saying that.

'I can't,' he cries.

I close my eyes. 'I know,' I whisper.

46

Still worrying about Hannah, I hunt down Dr Warier in the ER. His scrubs are blood-spattered and his face is no longer smooth and clean-shaven but darkened by a day's worth of stubble. 'Dr Warier?' I say, chasing after him.

He turns. 'Mrs Walker,' he says, surprised to see me outside of the ICU. 'How are you?'

I shrug. How am I meant to answer that question?

'Has the specialist been?' he asks, pulling off his latex gloves and ditching them into a nearby medical-waste container.

'He's on his way from the airport,' I tell him. 'My friend Laurie knew him in college, that's why he agreed to come at such short notice.' And without payment, I think to myself, though perhaps now I can at least offer him something.

Mentioning Laurie reminds me of my call with Dave. I wonder where she is. Perhaps she's gone to the airport to meet the specialist? He was meant to land at eleven this morning and spend the afternoon running tests on June.

'Well,' Dr Warier says, 'I hope he finds something we couldn't. He's one of the finest neurologists in the country, so if anyone can give you hope it will be him.'

I nod my gratitude. Dr Warier is the only person who didn't take offence to our insistence on a second opinion about June, who actually seemed to welcome it. A nurse comes over with some paperwork for Dr Warier and when he's done signing whatever needs signing he looks up and sees me still hovering by his side.

'Is there something I can help you with?' he asks.

'Yes,' I say. 'Yes, there is actually.'

We exit the elevator together and hurry towards June's room. In my absence the specialist has arrived and is standing over June's bed, alongside Gene and a nurse. There's no sign of Laurie though.

'Dr Philips,' I say to the specialist, a man in his early fifties with salt and pepper hair and an intimidating air of authority, 'this is Dr Warier. He's the ICU physician who took care of June and me when we were first brought in.' I turn to Dr Warier. 'Dr Warier, this is Dr Philips.'

'I know,' says Dr Warier, shaking the older man's hand vigorously. 'It's a pleasure, sir. I've read most of your papers.'

'Is Laurie with you?' I ask.

He shakes his head. 'No, she was meant to meet me at the airport but didn't show up. I thought we'd had crossed wires and that I was meant to meet her here.'

That's strange. I give an anxious smile. 'I'm sure she'll turn up.'

He nods and turns back to June. 'I've just been looking through all her notes,' he says, flicking through the papers he's holding. 'I've ordered an MRI, a CT and a PET scan as well as new lab tests. I think we're about to take her up for the MRI.'

'OK,' I say.

Two orderlies in green scrubs wheel June's bed out into the hallway. There's a nurse in charge of her ventilator and heart monitor, and both the doctors, and Gene and me. We flank the bed on all sides, June's own Praetorian guard. I stroke her hair out of her face. It's looking lank and greasy and I wonder when it was last washed or if she'll ever be able to do something as mundane as shower ever again. I can't go there so I push the thought away.

'We're taking her up for an MRI,' Dr Philips explains to Jonathan, who is still guarding the door. He looks at me. I nod at him to reassure him.

'OK,' he says tentatively.

'You don't need to come,' I add when he looks like he might be about to follow us down the hallway towards the elevators.

He pauses, looking troubled. 'Oh . . . um . . . I think—'

'Don't worry,' Dr Warier says in his usual soothing manner, 'she won't be let out of our sight.'

Jonathan backs off.

We crowd into the elevator, squashed around the bed, and I glance over at Gene, who is chewing his already bloody lip.

The MRI takes an hour. June is in a separate room to us, visible through a thick glass window. Gene and I sit with Dr Philips as he watches the computer screen in front of him in silence. I do too, mesmerized by the rainbow color segments of June's brain.

I bite my tongue to stop myself from asking how it looks. He'll tell us if he finds anything. Instead I twist my fingers around and around, playing with a loose thread on my bag, watching through the glass as the machine haloing June's head does its work, and I pray, I pray that this doctor sees something the others don't, that the colors bursting on the screen speak to him in a language the others can't understand.

When I was pregnant with June I went for an ultrasound. A part of me was hoping that perhaps it was all a mistake, that the little blue lines on the pregnancy test were a trick and that the scan would reveal a big black void. Instead a perfectly formed baby materialized on screen. There was her head, the brain a dark mushroom blooming inside the skull; there were her arms and her legs. And in that moment joy swept through me, dissolving all the doubts I'd had. Robert and I looked at each other, grins spreading over our faces. We were so caught up in the shock of seeing a baby on the screen that we missed the silence that crept through the room as the ultrasound technician swiped the wand across my belly in increasingly desperate strokes, poking and prodding at me with a frown.

'What is it?' Robert asked, the first to notice that something wasn't right.

The technician gave us a bright smile and got to her feet. 'I'll be right back,' she said and hurried out the door before we could ask her any more questions.

I looked at Robert. 'What is it, do you think?'

He said nothing and we waited, holding hands, barely speaking, until twenty minutes later a consultant breezed through the door. He introduced himself and then picked up the wand and laid it against my stomach, studying the pixelated image on the screen with a frown. I held my breath the whole time as Robert squeezed my hand. It was punishment, I was sure of it, punishment for not wanting her. I'd come into this room with a sense of dread, only to have that dread wiped out, replaced by sheer wonder and joy, and now that I'd been given a taste of it, it was about to be seized from me. It was so obvious. I should have wanted her more.

'Is there a problem?' Robert asked.

'We're just having trouble finding a heartbeat.'

I pressed my lips together to contain the sob.

The seconds ticked by and the dread I'd been feeling took hold again, only this time a thousand times worse because it came laced with guilt and shame. But then, just as I was about to jump off the bed and run away, the thundering beat of a tiny heart filled the room.

The consultant turned to us, grinning. 'Congratulations,' he said. 'You're having a girl.'

I let out the sob I'd been holding in. 'And she's OK?' I cried.

'Yes, ten fingers, ten toes, everything where it should be, heartbeat's normal.'

'Oh, thank God,' I said, falling against Robert, shaking and laughing and crying all at once. 'Thank God.'

But what if God was just hitting pause, I wonder now. What if this is his punishment – and he was just waiting to deliver it? The cancer was the warning shot across the bow. That's what I can't help but think as I sit here watching another consultant scan June for signs of life.

Beside me Gene is sitting with his elbows on his knees, hands clasped tight, his gaze fixed on the screen.

We both startle when my phone beeps. It's Hannah. At last. A text message. *'Hi Mom, I'm fine. Went home to sleep. I'll be back later. Xox.'* The tension in my shoulders decreases a notch. That's one thing less to worry about at least.

After two hours the doctor stops studying the screens and making notes and turns to us. I wait for him to speak – equally as desperate for him to open his mouth as I am dreading what he's going to say.

'There's some very faint brainwave activity,' he says.

I reach for Gene without thinking. He reaches for me at the same time and we grip each other, squeezing tight, clinging onto the words before the doctor can snatch them away from us.

'What does that mean?' I ask.

'We need to wait for the PET scan and I don't want to speculate about what it might mean in the long run, but I would say that turning off life support is premature.' I look at Gene, who is beaming. 'I don't want to raise your hopes too far.'

'But you think maybe she is OK? That she's alive?' Gene interrupts.

'She's alive. The question is whether she will ever regain consciousness or breathe on her own.'

'Can she hear us, do you think?' Gene asks.

The doctor shrugs. 'Who knows? Some studies suggest talking to patients in comas helps. I've seen patients written off come out of vegetative states, but many more who have passed away, sometimes after months or even years of being kept on life support. So I'm telling you,' and here he gives me a warning look, 'don't get your hopes up.'

'Another doctor told us that same thing once upon a time,' I tell him. 'And she beat all those odds too.'

PART THREE

47

Gene looks at me the moment Dr Philips leaves, and I nod. It's now or never.

Dr Warier puts his head around the door a second later. 'OK,' he says to us. 'We're good to go.'

An orderly wheels June out of the MRI room. Gene, Dr Warier and I follow. By the elevators Dr Warier tells the orderly he can leave us, that he'll take it from here, and once he's out of sight, Dr Warier starts pushing the bed down a quiet hallway, through a set of double doors and down a second corridor, until we finally reach an empty ward that's under some kind of refurbishment, plastic hanging from the ceiling and dust sheets covering the nurses' station. Dr Warier opens the door to one of the rooms and we push in June and all the machines attached to her, sliding her bed in beside an empty one. There's an en-suite bathroom, and a TV still plugged into the wall.

Dr Warier busies himself making sure June's ventilator and IV are working properly and Gene paces nervously. Dr Warier wears a frown the entire time and I know this is going against all his better judgment.

'Thank you,' I say.

He gives me a curt nod, not taking his eyes off June, and I marvel at how I got him to go along with this. When he's done with all the machines, he hands a scrap of paper to Gene. 'If anything happens, anything at all, you dial this number. It's my beeper. I'll come straight away.'

Gene puts the number into his phone.

'Don't leave her, Gene, not even for a moment,' I tell him.

He nods at me, solemn. 'I won't.'

Dr Warier crosses over to me. 'OK, your turn,' he says.

I pull off my sweater and reach for the hospital gown lying on the empty bed.

The doctor and Gene turn their backs as I pull it on. I keep my jeans on, and on second thoughts my shoes too, and then I slip my hand into my bag, checking the gun is still there.

It turns out a gun, bought on the black market, costs a thousand dollars. Once Raul was over the surprise of me asking and understood I only wanted it for personal safety, he sent one of his men to get one and bring it to the bar.

I made him show me how to use it. Now I check that the safety is on before stuffing it and the bag beneath the bedsheet. Everything has taken on an unreal quality as if I'm watching myself from a vast distance.

I nod at Dr Warier and he starts attaching wires to my chest and then linking them to the ECG machine by the bed, which begins beeping loud and fast, out of time with June's.

'What's the time?' I ask.

Gene looks at his watch. 'Four p.m.' He reaches for the TV remote and flicks through the channels until he gets to the local news.

There I am on the screen, almost unrecognizable, so thin and old and tired that at first glance I could be my mother.

Gene cranks up the volume. I watch myself fidgeting on the TV studio sofa, trying not to look directly at the camera.

48

11 HOURS AGO

'Jesus, Ava, this is crazy,' Gene mutters as Raul and James drive off.

'Now give me the number.'

Gene glowers at me but I can tell he doesn't dare argue. He can't. 'This is crazy,' he mutters again as he pulls out his phone.

He scrolls through the contacts list and then reluctantly presses dial and hands it to me. I hand it back to him. 'You need to set it up. He won't trust me.'

Gene sighs loudly but puts the phone to his ear. 'It's late. He's probably asleep,' he grumbles.

It's nearly five in the morning, it took longer to do business than I thought it would, but I'm betting on the fact Euan, the stringer, picks up the phone whenever it rings if he thinks there might be money involved.

The call connects. 'It's me,' Gene says. He glances at me. 'I have something might interest you.' He starts pacing the alley – explaining what we need.

'Maybe Santa Barbara – whichever news outlet can do it – but it needs to be one that can guarantee secrecy.'

Euan starts asking questions. 'She needs the money to pay the lawyer for my dad,' Gene explains. 'So she's offering an exclusive to the highest bidder. An interview where she'll tell all.'

Gene hangs up shortly after.

'Well?' I say to him.

'He's calling back in five.'

We hurry to the car and get in. Gene glances at me, hope flaring in his eyes.

'This doesn't absolve you, Gene,' I mutter, switching on the engine.

'I know,' he says quietly.

When Euan calls back five minutes later it's with directions to a studio in Santa Barbara – a local TV station. I put the directions into the GPS and start driving. Gene tries to talk to me but I cut him off. 'I need to concentrate,' I tell him, thinking of the lies I'm about to tell.

49

And here I am now, on screen, telling the lies to an audience of millions.

The presenter, whose immaculate makeup and hair is in marked contrast to my own, sits with her legs crossed and smiles at me. 'So the doctors say that June is going to make a full recovery?'

I nod. 'Yes. She's awake and she's starting to talk.'

Even I'm blown away by how convincing my smile is, by how true the words sound as they pour out of my mouth. I am indeed an amazing liar.

The presenter beams. 'That's wonderful news. What a miracle. And has she been able to remember anything at all about that night? Have the police talked to her yet?'

'No, not yet. But soon. She's starting to talk and she remembers . . .' I glance quickly at the camera. 'She's remembering everything.'

I reach forwards and take a sip of water from a glass on the table beside me and the camera zooms in. Can everyone see the faint tremble in my hand? I watch myself rapt as the interview continues. It's an out-of-body experience, as though I'm watching a stranger. I'm so convincing I start to believe my own lies about June being better and having woken up and it's with a jolt that I remember the truth.

The scene cuts back to the newsroom and to a different

presenter, who starts talking about a car accident on the 33 which is causing ten-mile tailbacks.

Gene switches off the television and silence falls like snow. There it is, it's done.

My phone rings almost instantly. It's Nate. He must have seen the news. I don't answer, just shove the phone in my bag.

'Come on, let's hurry,' I say to Dr Warier, who has been patiently waiting this whole time.

With pursed lips Dr Warier fits a surgical cap on my head. I tuck my hair inside it, making sure all the blonde strands are out of sight.

'OK, now the oxygen.' He attaches a breathing mask over my mouth – helpfully obscuring half my face – and then presses a button on the ventilator machine. It starts to pump air. 'Ready?' he asks me.

I nod and he pushes the bed towards the door.

A hand grabs mine. It's Gene. 'Be careful,' he says.

My instinct is to snatch my hand out of his, but then some reflex buried deep stirs to life, and before I can stop myself I roll my palm over, take his hand and squeeze it.

Dr Warier wheels me down the hallway towards the elevators. The only sound is the squeak of his shoes and the rapid beeping of my heart monitor.

I'm pushed into the elevator and after what feels like forever the doors shut and then open and we're off again, bumping down a hallway. If anyone thinks it strange to see a doctor wheeling a patient through the hospital they don't say anything, and I pray it stays that way.

'Could you get the door?' Dr Warier calls as we approach the ICU. I daren't open my eyes. I just hope we don't run into Nate or the administrator or a nurse who looks too closely. I wonder if Nate is on his way here – and how the hospital are responding to all the journalists calling up asking for news on June. They must all be so bewildered, but I only need the confusion to last for long enough to draw out the person who did this, the men who want June dead.

I know they'll strike. I'm counting on it.

Dr Warier leans over me, obscuring my face, as he pushes the bed through the doors to the ICU and I hear a nurse offer to help but he waves them away, telling them it's all under control. He pushes me into June's room and I finally let out a breath and open my eyes.

'OK,' whispers Dr Warier as he hurriedly starts unplugging me from the machines, switching them off first so they don't flatline and cause an army of medical staff to rush in. I pull off my oxygen mask and surgical cap and climb down from the bed and as I'm undoing my hospital gown Dr Warier's beeper goes off. 'They need me in the ER,' he says, glancing at it.

He crosses to the door. 'I'll tell the nurses that the police have put the room on lockdown and that I'm the only person allowed in.'

'OK,' I say. 'Thank you. I know this was a big ask.'

His hand is on the door. 'I'll check in on June as much as I can.' And then he's gone and I get dressed, sit back down on the bed, and reach for my bag.

50

Fifteen minutes pass and I count each one down, my hands sweating so much I have to wipe my palms on my jeans. On the other side of the door I hear footsteps and I stare at the door handle.

There's a voice. I crane to hear. It's a woman. The hospital administrator, it sounds like. She's arguing with the cop on the door.

'Sorry ma'am, we're under strict instructions,' the cop says. 'No one goes in.'

'That's ridiculous,' she says. 'What about her doctors?'

'Oh, they're allowed in,' he answers. 'And family, but that's it.'

She huffs loudly and then I hear her walking away. I relax back against the wall but then, after a few seconds, the footsteps return.

'What are you—?' the cop says, but he doesn't get to finish his sentence. Instead there's a loud thud.

I flinch backwards in horror. What was that? Oh my God. Even though I'd instigated this, I realize in this nanosecond as I watch the door handle turn that I didn't really believe it would work.

The door starts to open. Because I'm behind it, all I can see is an outstretched arm and a hand holding a gun. My heart gallops into my throat, I freeze in abject terror – I hadn't thought this far, hadn't truly considered this eventuality, even though I'd hoped for it.

And then a man enters the room, takes two quick steps towards the bed and, without even pausing, holds up a gun with a silencer on the end, and shoots twice into the pillows that I've stuffed beneath a sheet in a pretty useless attempt at faking a body.

Before the second bullet has even hit he's turning – realizing that the bed is empty. Somehow I've brought my arm up and somehow it doesn't shake. I don't pause. I pull the trigger before he can, my brain registering just as I shoot that it's Jonathan.

The bullet smacks into his chest below his right shoulder. He lets out a cry and his gun goes flying out of his hand as he crashes to his knees. He lunges sideways for his weapon, but I dive for it at the same time and kick it out of his reach.

It skitters across the floor and smacks into the wall and Jonathan makes a grab for my legs. I jump backwards, bringing my foot up and smashing it as hard as I can into his face. This time he goes down properly, grunting hard, blood streaming from his shoulder and from his nose.

I leap towards the bed, yank on the red emergency cord and start screaming for help.

Jonathan grimaces at me, one hand gripping his shoulder, blood seeping through his shirt and flooding down his arm. It was him. It was him all along. He was one of the men who broke into the house. Which one was he? How can I not have seen it? I've been so blind. He's been standing guard on the door this whole time. He's been hanging out with Hannah.

I train my gun on him. 'Who else? Who else is involved?' I shout.

He glares up at me, lips pulled back against his teeth, fighting the pain.

'Tell me who else!'

I shove the muzzle of the gun into the bullet wound in his shoulder. He lets out a high-pitched scream. I press harder and sweat pours down his face. My free hand tears at the buttons on his shirt, ripping it open and pulling it away from his shoulder until I can see the top of his arm. It's there. An angry red slash running the length of his arm. It was him I fought off in the kitchen.

'Who was the other person?' I ask. 'Who else was involved?' Was it Nate?

He grimaces, blood spilling down his lips, coating his teeth. He sinks to his knees. I sink with him. 'My daughter. Hannah. Have you seen her? Where is she?' Was she part of this? It's impossible – another paranoid delusion.

'Hannah,' he grunts.

I squeeze his arm so hard his eyes fly open.

'Where is she? Do you know?'

'. . . Took her . . .' he slurs.

'Took her? What do you mean?' I shake him. 'Who took her? Where?'

In the background I hear an alarm start to blare, people starting to shout.

'Where's Hannah?' I scream.

Jonathan's eyes roll back in his head. His body slumps. I stare down at him and the spreading pool of blood around us. Is he dead? I shake him.

'Wake up!' I yell hysterically. 'Tell me where my daughter is!'

The door crashes into the wall behind me and next thing I know I'm being shouldered roughly aside.

'What the—?' Nate, out of breath, looks at Jonathan on the floor and at me kneeling in front of him, holding the gun.

'It's him. It was him,' I stammer, staggering to my feet.

Nate's gaze flies from the gun in my hand to the bed, his eyes widening in surprise and shock at the situation he's just walked into. 'Where's June?' he shouts, noticing the empty bed.

'She's safe,' I say. 'But Hannah—'

Nate cuts me off. Striding over to Jonathan, he kneels down and checks his pulse. I'm about to ask if he's dead when people flood into the room behind us, a swarm of them, police and nurses and doctors, uniforms everywhere, people yelling things, rushing to give aid to Jonathan, elbowing Nate out the way. Nate refuses to budge. He starts rooting through Jonathan's pockets and finally pulls out his phone.

He rushes towards the door and I rush after him, quickly stashing the gun back inside my bag. In the hallway outside it's utter chaos. The downed cop who was guarding the door is lying in a lake of blood as nurses and a doctor tend to him. Someone yells for a crash cart.

'Lock the fucking place down,' Nate yells at two hospital security staff, who startle and then start shouting into their radios.

Nate grabs another man in a police uniform. He points through the doorway at Jonathan who's now surrounded by doctors and nurses. 'Don't let him out of your sight,' he shouts. 'He's under arrest.' Then he takes off, running towards the elevator.

'What for?' the cop calls after him.

'Attempted murder and that's just for starters.'

Nate reaches the elevator and hits the button. I chase after him.

'Nate!' I shout, grabbing him by the arm. 'Someone has Hannah.'

He spins to me, a look of alarm on his face. 'What?'

'That's what I was trying to tell you. Jonathan said someone took her.'

Nate looks at me blankly. 'What do you mean?'

'She's missing. She's been missing since last night. And—'

'Why didn't you tell me?' he interrupts.

I shake my head. 'I didn't know. She texted. I thought she was OK but—'

The doors to the elevator ping open and another wave of cops and doctors spill out and go swarming past us. I realize with a start that the cops will be wondering who shot one of their own. I need to get out of here. I can't be arrested or held for questioning. Not now. Not with Hannah out there, God knows where. Nate darts into the elevator and I rush after him, jumping inside as the doors seal shut.

'What are you doing?' Nate asks.

'Where are you going?' I answer back.

'To Jonathan's place, to see if I can find anything there that might give us a clue as to who he was working with, or where Hannah might be.' He has Jonathan's phone in his hand and he tries to open it but it's locked and he doesn't know the code. Annoyed, he shoves it back in his pocket. 'I need to find out who he's working with. That's our only shot right now.'

'I'm coming with you,' I tell him, still shaken from the realization that it's Jonathan. This whole time he's been guarding June, flirting with Hannah, maybe even dating her, acting all concerned. And he was the man behind it.

Nate shakes his head. 'No, you're not.'

He pulls out his own phone and starts scrolling through numbers.

'I am,' I say to him as he puts the phone to his ear.

'I need an address,' Nate says to the person on the other end of the line, who I assume is someone at the Sheriff's department. Nate turns his back on me and pulls a pen from a pocket to scribble something on the back of a receipt, Jonathan's address. Perhaps Hannah's there.

A sudden dread fills me, almost paralyzing me. What if he's hurt her already? Or what if she's not there?

The elevator doors open onto the lobby as Nate hangs up the phone. He darts out, and I follow him, determined to go with him.

'Ava, go back,' he says, spinning around to confront me. 'You can't come with me.' He points back towards the elevator. 'Let me do my job.'

I shake my head vehemently. I've already almost lost one daughter, I'm not going to stand around and do nothing when my other daughter is in danger. 'Either you let me come with you or I'm telling everyone who will listen that you tried to initiate a sexual relationship with me – a witness – the wife of your prime suspect.'

His mouth falls open and he stares at me in shock.

'You want to stay on this case and salvage what's left of your career?' I ask him.

He glares at me in disbelief, and I hold his gaze, refusing to budge. 'OK, fine,' he finally snaps, still glaring furiously.

We start jogging towards the front doors. 'You set it up,' he says, shooting a look my way. 'The interview with that journalist. You lied about June waking up, didn't you? You did it on purpose?'

I shrug. 'It worked, didn't it?' I want to yell at him that I wouldn't have had to do anything if he'd known his own junior officer was the one involved, if he'd done his damn job. I solved the case on my own.

'Where's June?' Nate asks as we reach the door.

'Somewhere safe,' I say.

'It was stupid,' Nate mutters angrily as we weave past patients on our way to the door. 'You could have been killed. You put yourself in danger.'

I shake my head. 'Hannah's in danger. We need to find her. Let's go!'

Reluctantly Nate nods and we hurry outside towards his car, passing a stream of SWAT and police officers, who rush by, storming inside the hospital. They probably think it's an active-shooter situation and I duck my head and clutch my bag containing the gun closer to my side.

'Mrs Walker?'

I think about not turning around but I recognize the voice. It's Dr Warier, running after me. The look on his face is one of shock. *June*. That's all I can think. Something must have happened to her.

'You need to come with me,' Dr Warier says urgently and swivels on his heel to head back inside.

'Why?' I stammer.

'There's been an accident.'

An accident? Is he talking about Jonathan?

'She's in the ER.'

She? June! Something's happened to her. Goddamn Gene. He had one job. I told him not to leave her.

'Come quick!' Dr Warier says, beckoning me over his shoulder.

I look back to see Nate frowning at me and I'm torn for one indescribably awful moment between June and Hannah. It's like *Sophie's Choice*. But my feet make up my mind for me and I rush after Dr Warier. I need to know what's happened.

'What's going on?' Nate asks, racing by my side.

I shake my head. I can't speak, focused only on Dr Warier up ahead, running back inside the building, heading for the ER.

He leads us through the maze of cubicles before stopping outside one and pulling back a curtain to reveal a bloodied, bandaged patient lying on a bed. A nurse is inserting an IV line into the back of the patient's hand while another is drawing blood.

June? I think, in shock. Because it isn't her. I'm confused and it takes me a moment to realize that I'm looking at Laurie, who is almost unrecognizable, her face lacerated and swollen and her neck in a brace.

'Jesus,' I whisper, rushing towards her side. 'What happened?'

'She was in a car accident,' Dr Warier tells me.

'What? When?'

'Earlier today. They only just found the car. On the 33, out towards Rose Valley.'

The 33 is notorious for accidents. It's a winding mountain road and people always take it too fast. But what was Laurie doing all the way out there?

'Someone called it in,' Dr Warier explains, 'but the cops did a drive-by and couldn't see the car at first – it was covered over by trees. They had to airlift her here.'

'Oh my God,' I say, swaying as I take in the damage done to Laurie's face and body. 'Is she going to be OK?'

'We're just getting her ready for surgery. She has multiple fractures, including her hip and thigh. We've notified her next of kin but as soon as I saw her ID I recognized her from the ICU and thought you'd want to know.'

I take Laurie's hand in mine. 'Laurie?' I say, squeezing her palm. There's no answer. 'Is she conscious?' I ask the nurse drawing blood.

'In and out,' she answers, focused on the needle.

'Laurie?' I try again, louder this time. 'It's me. Ava.'

She moans and her eyes flicker open. She stares at me dully, then registers it's me and her mouth twists at the edge. 'Ava,' she whispers through cracked lips, clutching for my hand.

'What happened?' I ask her.

She closes her eyes and murmurs something but I don't hear it, as another doctor has arrived, syringe in hand, and is trying to get between us.

'I'm sorry,' Dr Warier says, trying to move me out of the way. 'We need to get her to the OR. They're waiting. I just thought you would want to see her.'

The woman inserts the syringe into Laurie's cannula. Laurie mumbles something. I reach for the doctor's arm and stop her. 'Wait.'

'What?' I ask Laurie, leaning closer, so my ear is close to her lips.

'Hannah,' she croaks.

'Hannah what?' I ask.

Laurie opens her eyes, forcing out the words. 'I saw her.'

'Where?' It's Nate. He's moved closer too.

'Here, at the hospital.' She licks her cracked lips.

'What did you see?' I ask, my nose almost pressed to hers. I want to shake the answers out of her.

'She was arguing with a man . . . that deputy . . .'

'Jonathan,' Nate mutters, glancing at me.

'I thought at first it was just a lover's tiff but then . . . another man,' Laurie whispers. 'He . . .'

'What other man? Did you see him? What did he look like?'

The anesthetist, oblivious to the importance of our conversation, starts to plunge the syringe into Laurie's IV. 'Stop!' I yell, but too late.

'Laurie?' I shout. 'Who was it? What happened?' I shake her hard by the shoulders. 'What did you see?'

Her eyelids flicker closed. 'Another man. He . . . put . . . van.'

I glance at Nate. He pulls out his notebook and pencil. 'Do you remember the van? Anything about it? Color? License plate?'

Laurie slumps unconscious on the pillow.

'I'm sorry,' interrupts Dr Warier, and I notice the orderlies waiting behind him. 'We need to get her to the OR.'

'Laurie? Laurie?' I shout, but there's no waking her up. The orderlies start wheeling her out of the cubicle. Shit. That might have been our only chance. What did she see? I turn to look at Nate, who looks just as frustrated as me.

As they wheel Laurie past I suddenly catch sight of something.

'Wait!' I say again, lunging towards them, grabbing the corner of the bed to stop it. The orderlies scowl at me but Nate sees what I'm seeing and holds up a hand to keep them at bay.

He takes Laurie's elbow and gently turns it so we can see the inside of her forearm. There, scrawled in lipstick, is a series of numbers and letters.

'What is that?' a nurse asks, cocking her head to read it better.

'The van's license plate number.'

51

I catch up to Nate in the parking lot as a stream of media vans and more cop cars come screaming through the entrance.

Nate ignores them and keeps jogging towards his car, beeping it open as he goes. I race around to the passenger side and get in before he can change his mind and though he gives me a black look he says nothing.

The radio buzzes urgently to life the moment we get on the highway. 'Officer 212.'

Nate grabs for the receiver. 'This is Officer 212. Go ahead.'

'10-5, the van is registered to a Calvin Williams. White male, thirty-four years of age, few misdemeanors on record for petty theft and a couple of DUIs.'

'Address?' Nate asks.

'3598 Lost Canyon Road.'

'10-4.'

Nate hangs up the radio and steps on the gas.

'That's way out,' I say. 'It's off the 33.'

'Yeah,' Nate says.

'That's the direction Laurie was driving,' I say.

'Yeah,' Nate mutters, hunching over the wheel and pressing his foot even further to the floor. More cop cars go flying past us on the other side of the road, heading towards the hospital. I wonder what's happened to Jonathan. Did I kill him? The thought is fleeting. I don't care. But if we don't find Hannah and Jonathan dies, I might never find her. I have to hope and pray they're both still alive.

I grip the car door as we take the entrance ramp to the 101 and swerve in front of a twelve-wheeler before flying across two lanes of traffic. I want Nate to go faster but he's already driving at one hundred ten.

'Hannah must have figured out it was Jonathan,' I mutter, trying to put all the pieces together. 'She must have confronted him.'

But why? Why didn't she tell me instead? Where would they take her? What are they planning on doing to her? What if they've already done it? They're trying to silence her, like they tried with June. What if it's already too late? What if she's already dead and buried somewhere?

Bile rushes into my mouth and I gasp and scramble for the window, trying to open it.

'You OK?' Nate asks, his hand resting on my shoulder.

I shake my head, dizzy. Panic is making me hyperventilate. 'Hurry up!' I whisper. 'Please.'

I clutch the seat as Nate presses his foot to the floor and weaves in and out of traffic, a look of determination on his face. Please God. I can't stop praying. Please let her be OK. Please don't let them hurt her. And Laurie, please let her be OK too.

I can't believe that it was Jonathan. But of course it was staring me in the face the whole time. He's the right height, the right build. He's the man I slashed with the knife and smashed with the chopping board. He hid the injuries under his uniform and Sheriff's hat, but even so, how could I not have seen it?

'I told you it wasn't Robert,' I spit at Nate after a minute, unable to hold myself back.

Nate looks over at me. 'I knew it wasn't Robert,' he says quietly.

I double-take at him, speechless. What the—

'He was covering for Gene.'

I stare at him, my mouth falling open. He knew all along? Then . . . why? Why did he charge him and put him in jail?

'The Oxnard Sheriff's department had already ID'd Gene as a possible small-time dealer,' he says, glancing quickly my way. 'That's what he was arrested for a year back, that time you came to get him from the county jail. Jonathan tried to pull him over on suspicion of possession, he'd been seen with one of Raul's boys doing a deal on the street, and Gene led him on a three-mile car chase. By the time he was pulled over the drugs were no longer in the car. We figured he must have dumped the drugs out the window somewhere en route and then gone back for them later. We let him go because we thought we could keep him under surveillance, see if we could gather more evidence to charge him later for something bigger than a misdemeanor.'

It takes a while to sink in. The whole spiel Nate gave me about being able to get the charges dropped, the way he made it seem like a huge favor – it was all a lie. They already had a plan to let him go.

'When they called me about the break-in at your place,' he says to me, 'I guessed it had something to do with Gene and his drug dealing. That maybe he'd pissed off the wrong people. It's not a big leap of the imagination.'

'So why didn't you arrest him then? If you were so sure?'

He pulls a face. 'What for? We questioned him but he refused to talk and we didn't have enough to charge him. Then along came all the insurance stuff. And suddenly we had enough to arrest Robert. We figured Gene would do the right thing at that point and come forward to get his dad off the hook. But he didn't.'

I stare at him. 'So the whole conspiracy to commit murder charge, that was just a strategy? You knew it wasn't true – that Robert was innocent?'

'I knew it wasn't likely,' Nate says, his eyes on the road. 'Those add-ons to insurance policies are standard. Any good lawyer would have been able to get that charge thrown out or been able to beat it in court.'

'I didn't have a good lawyer.'

Nate shrugs. 'We were going to let him go but he put in a no contest plea.'

I stare at him incredulous. 'But you let me believe my own husband tried to have me killed . . .' I stare out the window. Nate knew Robert was innocent and he still arrested him? And he knows about Gene and the drugs. They've known all along. Everyone's been lying about everything. Nate made me doubt my own husband. Guilt adds itself to the slush of emotions I feel towards Robert.

Nate glances over at me again as I stare dumbfounded out the window. 'My guess is that Gene didn't come forward and Robert isn't talking because Raul threatened you.'

I try to keep my expression blank. Robert might still be in danger if I talk.

'Am I right?'

I turn to glare at him. 'What does it matter? It wasn't Gene. And it wasn't Robert who organized the break-in. And it wasn't Raul either. It was your own damn partner! You need to let Robert go,' I shout. 'He shouldn't be in jail.'

'He'll be out by tomorrow,' Nate answers.

I let my head sink back into the seat and try to put the jumbled pieces together. Jonathan was the deputy who pulled Gene over that fateful day eighteen months ago. He knew Gene was dealing but he let him go so he could keep him under surveillance. But then he must have decided at some point it was more lucrative to rob him than to arrest him.

With a sudden jolt, a memory flashes from that day we went to pick up Gene from jail. Hannah was talking to someone when I came out of Nate's office. It was Jonathan, now I think back on it. They were flirting.

Did they stay in touch? Was something going on between them even before they reconnected in the hospital? I remember the other day, how I walked in on them in June's room, both red-faced. I thought she was upset about June, but what if they'd been arguing? Had she guessed his involvement in the crime and confronted him? Was he threatening her – forcing her to stay quiet?

A deep shudder wracks my body when I think of all the times Jonathan asked me how June was doing – the fake look of concern on his face. I think about the time he was meant to be guarding the door but was strangely absent from his post when the attack on June happened.

It takes us almost thirty minutes, even driving at ninety miles an hour with lights flashing, to reach the turn-off on the 33 that leads down Lost Canyon Road. I spend the entire journey on the edge of my seat, trying not to think the worst about what might have happened. Please let her be alive. That's all I care about.

I place my hand inside my bag and grip the gun. If this man, Calvin, has hurt my baby in any way whatsoever, I will kill him.

It's getting dark as we make our way through the canyon, which is deep in shadow. It's a dead-end road, twenty miles long, ending in a state park and nature reserve where I sometimes hike. Towards the park end of the road there are a few ramshackle old houses hidden away in the trees. There's an air of *Deliverance* about it – dusty pick-up trucks and boarded-up windows, tire swings hanging forlornly from gnarly tree branches. In the summer the risk of wildfires makes it a fairly treacherous place to live, and in winter when it rains there are flash floods, which wash the road away and cause mud slides. On top of that, there's only one way in and out and no cell-phone reception.

We drive in silence, counting up the numbers, until Nate slows to a crawl, his headlights illuminating a mailbox with the number 3598 on it. The name Williams is written there in boxy white letters.

It's fully dark now. Nate kills his lights and pulls the car over to the side of the road. We peer through the trees. It's pitch black, no moon, and it's hard to make out the shape of a house, though a golden light flickers in the distance, indicating something's back there.

'There!' I say, pointing. 'Do you see that?'

About one hundred meters down the dirt drive there's a van parked beneath an awning. We can't make out the license but I know that's the van. Nate seems to be hesitating.

'What are we waiting for?' I urge.

'Back-up. We need SWAT. We don't know how many of them there are or if they're armed.'

'We need to get in there,' I say. 'What if something happens to Hannah? What if she's hurt?' I grab for the door handle. I'm not just sitting here waiting for back-up. Not when my daughter's in that house. Nate grabs my arm and hauls me back.

'OK. I'll go in but you have to stay here.'

I think about arguing but finally nod.

Nate moves to get out the car but then stops and turns back to me. 'You bring your gun?' he asks.

279

I think about pretending I'm not armed but it's too late. He saw me with it back at the hospital. I take it out from my bag.

'Is this registered to you?' he asks, taking it and checking the clip and safety.

I don't answer. He sighs. 'Do you even know how to shoot this thing?'

I raise my eyebrows. I should think Jonathan is proof I know how to pull a trigger.

'Listen to me, you stay in the car, you do not get out, do you hear me?'

When I don't answer, he glowers at me. 'I don't want you following me and shooting me by accident.'

I nod reluctantly. He hands me back my gun.

'Stay here,' he tells me before slamming the door behind him.

He walks around to the trunk. I crane my neck to see what he's doing. He pulls a flak jacket on over his sweater, and then draws his own gun.

'Lock the doors,' he tells me. 'If you hear gunshots I want you to get in the driver's seat and get the hell out of here, OK? I've left the keys in the ignition. When the SWAT team arrive tell them I've gone in.'

'OK,' I say.

Nate darts across the road, keeping to the shadows, and in seconds he's gone, blurring into the woods that surround the house. I wait a handful of seconds before I take the keys out of the ignition and ease open the car door.

52

It's cold, the temperature dropping fast, and I'm only wearing a light sweater. In the trunk I find a Sheriff's department duffel bag and, inside that, another flak jacket – probably Jonathan's. For a brief second I wonder what's happened to him – is he dead? I feel totally numb about it but I suspect that when the numbness fades I still won't feel anything.

The jacket's too big for me but I put it on anyway, pulling the Velcro straps tight until it's as snug as I can make it. I throw Nate's Sheriff department rain jacket on over the top. My sweater is white and I want to do my best to make myself blend into the shadows.

I'm about to close the trunk when I spot a flare gun in the bag and as an afterthought I take that too, slipping it into the jacket pocket.

I close the trunk as quietly as I can, but still the noise echoes through the silence, bouncing off the canyon wall to my right and startling an owl, which hurtles into flight, hooting above me. I run around to the front of the car, ducking low. I don't know what I'm doing – only that I'm not about to let Nate go in there alone. I can't sit there waiting for the sound of gunshots, not when my daughter might be in there, just feet away from me.

I take a breath, and am about to run towards the house, when I catch sight of the mailbox on the other side of the road.

Williams.

It hits me with the force of a boot to the chest. Like stepping from pitch darkness into full, bright light. *Margot Williams.* The girl Nate was sleeping with while he was dating me. Her brother was called Calvin Williams. He was on the high school football team with Nate, that's what Samantha said. They were new to the school – they transferred from a small town in Texas. He had a southern twang and used to get teased about it. She played it up and was thought cute.

The trees sway and for a moment it feels as if the sky is collapsing down on top of me. I have to lean against the car to steady myself.

Nate.

A gunshot ricochets off the trees, like a clap of thunder. I jump and then adrenaline flashes through me. Hannah . . .

I sprint towards the house, slipping into the trees. My feet crunch through the leaves, each step loud as the rat-tat-tat of machine gun fire, but I can't stop running, driven on by the thought of Hannah. What if I'm too late?

I'm close to the house now – can make out the wooden porch running the front length of it, a decrepit lean-to at the side and a mosquito-battered screen door.

A dog barks – a mean, low-throated growl – and I drop to my knees behind a bush, breathing hard, shaking harder. What am I doing? This is insane. I should wait for back-up.

As soon as I think it, another realization dawns on me. No one knows we're out here. There's no SWAT team on the way. Nate never made the call. I assumed he had, too caught up in what was happening, but when? I didn't see him use the radio or his phone.

He's involved. And I let him go into the house.

Fumbling, nerves teetering on a knife-edge as my ears strain to hear what's going on, I dial 911. Nothing happens. I hold the phone up to my face. Zero bars. There's no reception so deep in the canyon.

The dog starts up again but it's cut off mid-bark by a loud blast, another gunshot. Another follows a second later, and now I'm on my feet, zigzagging blindly through the trees towards the house, thinking only of Hannah.

I spring up the wooden steps to the front-porch door and yank it open. Gun held out in front of me, I swing wide into the front room, barely registering anything – except that the room is empty. There's a door to the right, partly ajar, and I edge towards it, gun still clenched in my hands, eyes darting around wildly, scanning the room, jumping at every shadow, ears pricked for any sound but there's only a creeping stillness.

'Hannah?' I whisper.

There's no answer. I nudge the door open gently. The light's off and all I can make out through the gloom are an unmade bed and a dresser.

My feet creaking on the uneven wood floor, I keep heading down the hallway. My heart is hammering so loudly that I can't hear myself think.

At the end of the hallway is a kitchen. A candle in a glass jar sits on the windowsill and a plate of food is on the table. The back screen door is propped open with a brick and a dim light shines over the back verandah, dousing the area a foot from the door, but leaving the area beyond that as black as outer space. Nate could be standing ten feet away and I wouldn't be able to see him.

I blow out the candle on the windowsill and start retracing my steps towards the hall but as I go I hear a sound – a muffled cry. Looking behind the kitchen door I spot another door, this one locked with a rusty bolt.

One hand isn't enough to wrestle the bolt free and I have to put the gun down on the table so I can use both. The lock flies back with a crash, and I jump and grab for the gun, spinning around with it, aiming it at the door.

I wait a few seconds, and then, unable to wait any longer, I open the door. A quick glance over my shoulder and I see that it's the way into a cellar or crawl space. There's a narrow, wooden staircase down – about six steps, but it's dark as a grave.

Cobwebs stroke my face as I move to the narrow entrance. I inch my way down the stairs, fear digging its talons around my chest, my breathing coming fast and shallow.

I reach the bottom step and have to feel my way, hand groping for the wall until I find a light switch. I flick it.

'Hannah!'

She's tied to a chair, her hands and legs bound, a gag in her mouth and a blindfold over her eyes. I run towards her and yank the blindfold down. She blinks at me, squinting, tears rolling down her face.

I rip the gag out of her mouth and she starts choking, sucking in air. 'Mom,' she sobs. Her eyes are alive with terror, dirt streaks her face and there's blood on her lip.

'It's OK,' I say, dropping to my knees. 'Shhh.'

I drop my gun and start pulling frantically at the knots tying her to the chair. I manage to get her hands free and get to work on her feet.

'Quick,' she sobs at me.

'Shhh,' I say, glancing, terrified, over my shoulder. What's happening up there? Where are they? What's Nate doing? Does he plan to kill Calvin and frame him, to keep his own involvement secret?

'Hurry!' Hannah cries.

I dig my nails into the final knot and loosen it, and the two of us wrestle together to undo it. Finally it gives, and I help Hannah get stiffly to her feet.

'Come on,' I say, putting my arm around her as we move towards the stairs.

We creep into the kitchen and I come to a halt, blocking Hannah who is still on the stairs behind me, pushing to get past. The back screen door is now shut. The porch light is off. My eyes dart to the window. Is Nate out there watching us? Or is he in the house with us? And what about Calvin? Are there two of them or just one? Where did they go?

I pull Hannah towards the hallway. She clings to me, whimpering. In the hallway I pause. The noise of Hannah and the noise of my own breathing almost cancel out the sound of a floorboard creaking. He's in here. I can't isolate the sound though. There are two doors – one to the bedroom and another leading I don't know where. Do we hide? No. My instinct tells me to get outside, into the woods where we won't be trapped, where we'll have more of a chance.

I keep heading towards the front room. Hannah stops me with a hand on my shoulder. She points. There's a shadow moving behind the door, visible in a thin band of light. I turn, pushing Hannah back towards the kitchen again, urging her on, panic clawing at my insides, but the kitchen door flies open just before we reach it. There's a blur of movement and a man appears in the doorway pointing a gun. Calvin.

I shove Hannah hard against the wall and aim at him a split second before he fires at us.

My gun doesn't fire and his bullet goes wide and hits the doorjamb, splintering the wood. I shoot again. Nothing happens. And now he's walking towards me, his finger on the trigger. Desperately I keep pulling the trigger. Nate must have done something to it – disabled it in some way.

I hurl the useless gun at him. He ducks and I charge him. He doesn't expect it and stumbles backwards as I launch myself on top of him. I grab hold of his gun and we crash onto the kitchen table, which collapses beneath our weight. The gun goes off again – a deafening blast. I don't know if I've been hit. Calvin is still fighting, kicking and punching and trying to wrench the gun from my grip. But I can't let go. I know this. So I don't. I hold on for dear life and we struggle, breathless, me on top, locking my legs around him and trying to pin him with my weight. He's much bigger than me but suddenly he grunts in pain and buckles in on himself and I realize I've managed to get my knee into his groin. I grind it even harder into the soft space between his legs and his grip on the gun loosens and he grunts and curses some more. I yank the gun towards me, twist it and, my hands clenched over his, desperately press the trigger.

Calvin falls back with a gasp, blood spilling out of his chest, and I scramble off him in horror. A pair of hands grips my shoulders. I panic and lurch around, but it's only Hannah, crying hysterically, pulling me to my feet. We stumble together towards the back door, Hannah's eyes fixed on Calvin, sprawled across the tabletop, dead, still holding the gun in his hand. I hesitate a moment then dart back and grab the gun, trying to ignore the ocean of blood spreading around him and the fact I just killed a man.

The kitchen door flies open as Nate appears. He takes in Calvin's body, then his eyes flash to the gun I'm pointing at him.

'I told you to stay in the car,' he says.

I swallow, trying to subtly push Hannah behind me, to shelter her. I eye Nate's gun. Will he shoot us?

'He tried to kill us,' Hannah sobs, gesturing at the body. She doesn't know what I know. She thinks we're safe now.

Nate takes a step towards us. 'It's OK,' he says gently. 'It's over. You're safe.' He nods at the gun I'm holding in my shaking hand. 'Put the gun down, Ava.' He takes another step towards me.

'Stay back!' I yell, surprising myself.

He startles, pausing mid-step. 'Ava,' he says, frowning. 'It's me. What are you doing? Put the gun down.'

'Mom,' Hannah cries, tugging on my shoulder. 'Don't shoot. It's Nate.'

I stare at Nate. He's poised like an animal about to pounce, his eyes flicking to the gun and then to my face. I waver, not knowing what to do. I could lower the gun, pretend I don't know the truth about his connection to Calvin, laugh at my paranoia and try to get Hannah and me safely out of here with him, but who's to say if I do that he won't just shoot me. The grip on his own weapon is tightening. I catch the movement out the corner of my eye.

'Ava,' Nate says again, beseeching me, but he must see something in my expression – fear, horror. He knows I know the truth. He moves, lunging towards us and I fire, but Hannah is pulling on my arm and it goes wide. Nate ducks and his foot slips on the blood-slicked floor. As he fights to regain his balance I use the opportunity to push Hannah out the back door.

'Run!' I yell as we dive down the steps.

A bullet smashes into the wooden railing by my hand.

'Run!' I scream again and Hannah needs no encouragement, sprinting towards the trees.

I follow her, firing the gun blindly over my shoulder. Another gunshot cracks the night air and Hannah yelps but keeps running. We swerve through the trees, blinded by the dark. I've lost my sense of direction – which way is the car?

I don't see the blur of movement to my right until it's too late. Nate lunges out of the shadows, throwing all his weight onto me, and I trip, falling to the ground, my chin smashing a rock buried in the dirt, Calvin's gun flying from my hand. I hear Hannah scream somewhere off in the distance and I try to lift my head, try to shout at her to keep running, but Nate grabs my head and slams it hard into the ground. Stars burst on the back of my eyelids. Leaves and dirt fill my mouth and I start choking. The next thing I know, he's lifting me up, tossing me onto my back. The air slams out of me and, winded and stunned, I stare up at him, struggling to focus.

He's hovering over me, pointing his gun at me.

The moon has slipped from behind its cloud cover and I can make out the glimmer in his eyes, and just like that I'm blasted back into June's bedroom, to that night. And memories that have been hidden, buried miles deep, break through into the light.

I see June on her knees. I see myself in the doorway, holding the gun I took from the man downstairs in the kitchen. I see myself raise it and fire.

I didn't shoot the man in the skull mask – Calvin. I missed.

Oh my God. It was me. I shot June. Someone came up behind me and hit me around the head just as I pulled the trigger, causing my shot to go wide, hitting June by accident.

I see myself lying on the floor in June's bedroom, fighting against the darkness, eyelids flickering. A shadow falls over me. The man who hit me steps over me. A third man.

The images start to strobe. Past and present merging, memories dancing out of the fog, offering me patchy glimpses of things I don't want to see. The man bends down beside June. His face . . . it's a clown mask. Leering. Grotesque. He shakes June hard by the shoulders. I'm paralyzed to help, to make him stop. The scream chokes in my throat.

He shouts something at her.

Where is it?

Her eyes are wide.

He tears off his mask. *Where is it?*

I remember. It all comes back to me.

June's head lolls back on her neck like a narrow stem has snapped under the weight of a bloom. Blood darkens her T-shirt.

I open my eyes.

Nate stands in front of me, gun pointed at my chest, silhouetted against the moon. There were *three* men, not two. I look at Nate. He was the third man. But where was he? Why didn't I remember him until now? Perhaps he was ransacking Gene's apartment while the others searched the main house.

'It was you,' I say.

'Guilty,' he says.

'Why?' I whisper in shock. 'How . . .?'

I don't get an answer. He shoots me.

The bullet slams into my chest with the force of a freight train, spearing me to the ground. Pain explodes through my body, every nerve ending screaming and writhing with it. Lungs on fire, I stare up at Nate, trying to breathe but it's impossible. 'Hannah . . .' I croak with the breath I've got left.

Nate stands over me. He laughs and opens his mouth to say something.

Whatever he's about to say is cut off by a loud crack. A gunshot. Nate's arm jerks. He staggers forwards, stumbles, but somehow manages to stay standing. Behind him I catch sight of Hannah. She's holding the gun I dropped on the ground when Nate tackled me.

Nate turns around to face her. He's wearing a bulletproof vest. *Shoot him again*, I want to shout at Hannah, but my own chest is on fire. I can't breathe. I realize that Hannah is shooting, her finger pressing the trigger, over and over, but the gun must be out of bullets.

Nate grimaces, then brings up his weapon with a wavering arm and takes aim. Hannah stares at him in horror and starts to stagger away from him. He shuffles forwards.

'Nate!' I try to yell, though it comes out as a gasp.

He turns. Somehow, I don't know how, I've managed to get to my knees, then to my feet, lungs still on fire, vision clouding.

Nate frowns, obviously confused to see me standing. But it's too late for him to react. I've already pulled the trigger.

The flare bursts so bright I stumble, throwing up my arm to shield my eyes from the phosphorescent glare.

A high-pitched scream pierces the night. I can see Nate, dancing like a drunken marionette – the space where his head should be is a fizzing pinwheel, spraying firefly sparks into the dark sky. He collapses to the ground, writhing.

Hannah runs towards me, tripping over the uneven ground, and throws herself at me. I wince, still bruised from where the bullet smacked into my vest, but my arms come up automatically and I hold her and rock her just like I did when she was a baby, covering her eyes.

'It's OK. It's OK,' I whisper, over and over, watching the flare fizz and burn. I can't look away – can't drag my gaze from the horror – not even after the last spark dies.

53

22 YEARS AGO

I count down the days, flipping back through the calendar repeatedly as though if I keep doing it I can find a way to miraculously bend time and alter history, and, more importantly, change the future.

'Ava, you coming?' my roommate Rosie asks.

'Um, in a minute,' I reply in a daze, shoving the desktop calendar in the drawer alongside my hopes and dreams.

'We're going to be late,' Rosie says.

I turn around and see she's dressed for a New York fall in a down jacket and scarf.

'You're not even dressed,' she says to me, looking me up and down.

I'm still wearing my bathrobe. I don't even remember putting it on.

'What's the matter? Are you OK?' Rosie asks, concerned. 'Stop worrying about the IT geek. Let's go out and get drunk.'

'I . . . actually I'm not feeling very well,' I stammer. 'I think I'll stay in.' The calendar is calling to me from its interment in my drawer.

Rosie cocks her head at me, disappointed, but then shrugs. 'Suit yourself!' She moves for the door. 'See you later.'

She's gone before I can say bye. I sink down onto my twin bed and start to shake.

Shit.

I get up, open the drawer and retrieve the damn calendar. I recount the days again and again, then after what feels like an hour I look up and take a deep breath that's like swallowing a swarm of bees.

I could get an abortion. It's not too late. But my hand automatically flies to my stomach and I feel dread. I don't think I can do it. I get up and start pacing the small space between the twin beds. I'm nineteen. This is not how my life is meant to go. I wish I could call my mom and tell her, ask her advice, but I know what she'll say: how could I have been so reckless after everything they've given up for me, after everything they've sacrificed to send me to college?

I could tell him. I sink down onto the bed, gnawing on my fingernails. What would he say? I can't guess. I have no idea. Would he tell me to get an abortion? Would he tell me to keep it, that he'd stick by me?

There's a knock. I get up from the bed and shuffle to the door, opening it a crack. I'm expecting to see one of the other girls from the dorm, but it's not. It's Robert.

'Oh,' I say, bewildered at the sight of him. He pushes his glasses nervously up his nose.

'I was just passing,' he says. 'And I thought I'd drop by.' He glances at my bathrobe and then, flushing, stares at his feet. 'I'm sorry, I should have called first.'

'It's OK,' I say, softening at his awkwardness.

'I was wondering if you, um, fancied going for a drink, or maybe something to eat?'

He looks at me with a hopefulness that makes my heart skip a beat. He's the opposite of Nate. He's serious, bookish, an IT geek, as Rosie joked. He's also not someone I could label a boy. He's a man. A real grown-up. I met him two weeks ago. As a post-grad, he led a group of freshmen on an orientation, and I was one of them. We stopped for coffee afterwards and he asked for my number with the excuse that he had free tickets to MOMA. He called me the next day and we ended up taking in an exhibition. It was nice, but I've been avoiding his calls ever since. He's just too old for me; he's got an ex-wife and a child for goodness' sake. I don't want to get into another relationship so soon after breaking up with Nate. That's what I told Laurie. I want to be single and free in New York. I want to be an artist, like the ones I've read about in magazines and books who drink espresso and wear lots of black and watch art house movies and get invited to loft parties. I want to be someone.

Definitely not a mother. At least not yet.

'It's a little late probably, isn't it?' Robert says, interrupting my thoughts and glancing at his watch. 'I'll go.'

He turns to leave. I make a decision without weighing the consequences but knowing already, some place deep down, that I'm taking a step on a path I can't ever turn back from.

'Actually,' I call out after him, 'that sounds great.'

Robert turns around, beaming, and I feel a pang that makes me hesitate. It's still not too late. 'Let me throw on some clothes,' I say, and turn back inside the room, shutting the door. What the hell am I doing?

Alone in the room, I stand frozen. I see the calendar on the desk, the days marked off. I count backwards and forwards. The indisputable fact of August 18th circled. The last day I spent with Nate. I broke up with him before I left for college. He was upset and we ended up in bed together. One last time.

I shrug off my bathrobe and throw on a pair of jeans and a sweater. Grabbing my keys and a jacket I pause to pick up the calendar and throw it in the trash.

Robert's waiting patiently outside. I take his arm and follow him out into the night.

Sheriff Nate Carmichael guilty of leading brutal home invasion that left a young girl fighting for her life.
The Ventura County Sheriff, 42, was shot dead last night, along with his two conspirators, including deputy Sheriff Jonathan Safechuck, 28.

Carmichael, who had recently transferred to Ventura from Long Beach, was assigned to lead the investigation into the armed burglary that took place in Ojai on the night of May 8th. The victims, Robert and Ava Walker, were home with their 12-year-old daughter, June, when three masked men burst in with guns and demanded they open the safe.

During the assault Robert and Ava Walker were both beaten and their daughter, June, received life-threatening injuries after being shot. While in intensive care and under armed guard two further attempts were made on the young girl's life, both of which have now been attributed to a third suspect, Calvin Williams, a former school friend of Carmichael's. Both men grew up in the area and it's believed that they conspired to target the Walkers, who were well known within the community.

Carmichael, a member of law enforcement for nineteen years, moved swiftly to arrest and charge Robert Walker with conspiracy to commit fraud, claiming that the Internet entrepreneur had hired known criminals to carry out the attack in order to claim on his home insurance policy. The motive appeared to hold water when details of Walker's bankruptcy emerged, however Mr. Walker has since been released from prison and all charges against him have been dropped.

The Walkers' older daughter, Hannah, 22, was kidnapped by Safechuck and Williams after overhearing them discussing an attempt on her sister's life. Details of her rescue have not yet been released by the police. However, Mrs. Walker is believed to have been present at the time and sources indicate that she shot at least one of the suspects. No arrest has been made.

Carmichael had been the subject of at least one internal investigation into corruption, but no charges were pressed. Police believe that Carmichael, who had significant gambling debts as well as unpaid child support, had been shaking down drug dealers and other criminals over the course of his nearly two decades on the job and have begun an investigation. They are also digging through previous case files of unsolved burglaries.

The Sheriff's department is not seeking any further witnesses and declined to comment until a full investigation has been carried out.

Euan Shriver

54

10 WEEKS LATER

The news vans are still gathered outside the hospital. We're the gift that keeps on giving, I suppose. As stories go, it's a good one. Better than OJ, one Hollywood producer told me. Two officers of the law guilty of corruption, burglary, murder, kidnapping; a bloody, dramatic showdown in the woods that left two dead; an innocent man released from prison and reunited with his family; a front-page image that continues to circulate of Hannah wrapped in a foil blanket being helped away from the scene of the crime by paramedics.

I've heard that a cable network is making a true crime show out of what happened and that they're basing it on the article that Euan Shriver wrote for the *LA Times*.

And Jonathan? the FBI asked. What role did he have in all this? Did I know he was having a relationship with my daughter Hannah?

Yes. I was aware. It was my belief that he'd preyed on her, a vulnerable, traumatized girl, so that he could find a way to get close to the family, so he would be the first to know if June regained consciousness and if she remembered anything. What other reason could there be?

When I heard Jonathan was dead I didn't feel anything. I still don't. If I had to do it again I'd aim for his head.

Hannah was interviewed too, of course. They wanted to know everything about her relationship with Jonathan and how it had come about. Did he instigate it or did she? Had he ever mentioned Calvin Williams to her? Had she ever had cause to be suspicious of him or his behavior? Why had they abducted her? What happened to her during the time she was held – a minute-by-minute breakdown. Who was the ringleader? Who sent the text from her phone? What was the dynamic between them all?

I sat with her, alongside our lawyer, as she gave them her statement. She had no idea Jonathan was involved, or Nate. She had never heard either of them mention Calvin. She and Jonathan had been seeing each other casually after meeting at the hospital. Calvin sent the text from her phone.

She found out that Jonathan was involved in the robbery when she overheard him talking to Calvin outside the hospital, saying something about June, about needing to get in there and do it before it was too late. When she confronted them, demanding to know what they were talking about, Jonathan grabbed her and wrestled her into the van.

Yes, she thought they were going to kill her. She overheard them fighting about it while they were driving. She thought she was going to die out there in the woods.

While she was tied up in the basement they must have heard my interview claiming that June had woken up. Jonathan went back to the hospital to finish her off. The police pieced this all together, but Laurie was able to corroborate the details of the abduction. By chance, she saw Hannah being dragged into the back of the van. She had followed, afraid of them getting away, unable to call the cops because she couldn't reach her phone in her bag on the back seat. She hadn't wanted to pull over to get it in case she lost the van. She'd found a lipstick in the cup holder and scrawled the license plate number on her arm and had crashed the car when she eventually tried to reach behind and grab her bag.

Why did they want to kill June though?

Because she saw Nate's face.

Nate knew that I shot her. He witnessed it. But he couldn't press me too hard on it, worried that he'd trigger other memories of the night, ones involving him.

I have no idea what Nate meant to do when he drove me to Calvin's house. Did he plan on killing Hannah? Did he plan on killing us both and burying us somewhere out there in the canyon? The whole way there he must have been plotting his next move, figuring out what to do. He went inside the cabin, alone. It's all conjecture on my part, but I think he planned to kill Calvin in order to frame him. I think he planned on 'rescuing' Hannah. He'd look like the hero. No one would ever know.

That's what the gunshots were. Calvin ran, and Nate chased him out of the cabin, which is why it was empty when I got there. Nate was chasing down Calvin, trying to kill him before he could rat him out.

I wish one of them had survived so we could ask them, so we could know for sure. I guess I'll have to live with the uncertainty.

June is making progress. The lie I told the press came true. It was almost as if she waited until she knew the danger was past, and then she made her move. She blinked. She wriggled her toes. She squeezed Gene's hand. Gene, who spends as much time beside her bed as I do. Gene, who, every day after his therapy and NA meetings, plays her music and reads graphic novels to her, taking the time to describe every illustration in detail. Gene, who tells me every day that she's getting better as though his saying it will force it to be so.

And when she wakes, will she remember? Will she remember that I pulled the trigger?

The thought sends seismic shudders through me. When I sit by her bed and clutch her hand I whisper an endless silent stream of apology and prayer. It's me who put her in that bed. It's me who did this. The knowledge and the truth of that sits in my chest like an unexploded grenade.

Sometimes I think I should pull the pin and tell the truth – tell them all that I am the one who shot June, tell Robert that Hannah, his pride and joy, isn't his – but every time I open my mouth the words evaporate off my tongue.

My family was built on a lie. And lies have broken us apart like bullets ripping through flesh and splintering bone.

But then again, wasn't it the truth that did that? The truth is tricky. You open the door to it, thinking it will act as a salve, that it will set you free.

And instead it leaps at you, teeth bared, and rips out your jugular.

55

Robert is crouched down by the kitchen island. When I walk in, he stands back and smooths the surface. The stain has vanished. He smiles at me and holds up a sheet of sandpaper in victory.

'It came out,' I say, trying to force a smile. I've already started thinking about ripping the kitchen out and putting in something new. Our first instinct to sell was reversed when Hannah pointed out that June will want to come home, not to a strange house.

Robert nods and I notice again the lines carved into his face as though with a scalpel, the pouchy bags beneath his eyes, and the way his shoulders sag under an invisible weight. I feel a sudden pang of love and tenderness. It springs out of nowhere and surprises me.

I don't think he'll ever fully recover from what happened, even if June wakes up, even if she walks or talks again. There's some fundamental shift that's taken place that I don't think can be reversed. His smile fades, and he turns away from me.

We get in the car in silence and drive to the hospital in silence. A fundamental shift has taken place between us too. Ever since the day I collected him from jail we've barely spoken, except politely, and mostly to talk about June. We're like two planets orbiting each other, but every day the gravitational pull gets weaker as though one of us, I can't tell which, is drifting away, pulled by a bigger sun, or perhaps by a black hole.

We talked when he was first released. Or rather, I talked and he listened and said nothing. I told him about meeting Nate for coffee, and then dinner, and what transpired between us, down to my own awkward, shame-ridden flight. He hasn't forgiven me. And I'm not sure he can forgive me either for believing, even for a moment, that he might have arranged to have me killed. That's the bigger betrayal. And yet, he knows that his own reticence to talk to me about the financial troubles we were in, and about Gene, also played a role in what happened.

Can we forgive each other for all the lies? Can we find a way to close the fissure between us? And can it ever be fully closed when the lie about Nate and Hannah sits between us like an invisible ghost?

As though operating outside my control, my hand reaches over and takes Robert's. He's surprised, I can tell, even though he doesn't show it. For a moment he doesn't respond and his arm goes rigid, but then, just at the point I'm about to pull away, his fingers tighten around mine and he squeezes.

It's only the smallest touch, but it feels like a beginning; an offering and an acceptance. He glances my way and as our eyes meet the distance between us shrinks, albeit only by a centimeter or two. It's something though. A start. I banish Nate's ghost.

Laurie and Dave are at the hospital. Dave hugs me, but as if he's hugging a thorn tree. Robert, on the other hand, receives a full bear hug. Dave has told Robert all about his involvement with Gene. The three of them have buried the hatchet, let bygones be bygones. So have Laurie and Dave. I'm happy for them. Of course I am, though envious too.

It bothers me that Robert can so easily forgive his son. No matter Gene's solicitousness of June and his scraping to us like a medieval courtier before his rulers, I can't forget the fact that everything happened because of him. But Robert can't handle the pain of losing June and Gene in one fell swoop, I suppose, and so it seems that we're stuck with one very stubborn wart. I take a deep breath and let it go. I can't hold on to the anger, or that very small start we've made towards fixing things might flounder.

Laurie is beside the bed, brushing out June's hair. Her cuts and bruises are almost healed; only the cast remains on her leg. She smiles at me and I smile back.

Dave and Robert launch into a discussion about a new app Robert's developing to help people who are paralyzed use smartphones with voice technology. There's not much spark to Robert these days, but I see something light up in him when he talks to Dave. We don't need the money of course, not now, not after most of the people we were suing, including the hospital, settled out of court for seven-figure sums, but his way of dealing with grief is by keeping busy.

So yes, Robert's been busy, but I've been busy too. When I'm not here at the hospital, or talking to our lawyer, or the bank manager and the insurance companies, I'm working on paintings for the show I have coming up. The gallery owner could not be more thrilled at the anticipated turnout, and all the press she's already been getting. I feel like a fraud, but I don't say so. I think a lot of people probably feel the same way. And there's something empowering about being in charge of my own future and contributing financially. I don't want everything to be on Robert's shoulders anymore.

Dr Warier comes by with papers for us to sign – patient release forms. He's humbled, hopeful, takes my hands and says he'll pray for us. He tells me that he's sure we'll get our miracle. I whisper my thanks.

The orderlies follow Dr Warier, wheeling June out of the room and down to the ambulance that is taking her to the rehab center. Dave and Laurie go with her.

'Is she going to be OK?' Hannah asks as we finish packing June's teddy bears and trophies into a box.

I nod. 'Of course.' Because what else can I say? What else do I choose to believe? And I don't want Hannah changing her mind and deciding to stay. She's going back to New York tomorrow, back to college, and I want her to live life to the fullest and not have to deal with all the fallout and the media vultures still pecking over the grizzly remains of the case.

It will be easier for me too, though I don't admit it out loud. Now every time I see her, I see Nate. I learned to ignore it when she was little, convincing myself she looked more like me, but her cornflower-blue eyes are his, no mistake. I'm amazed no one else can see it.

Robert starts clearing the Get Well cards from the window-sill, and I pick up the framed photographs from the night-stand. The one of June and Gene and Hannah makes me pause, a bittersweet wave of sadness hitting me before I put the past behind me and drop the photo into the bag along with the others.

'Everything OK?' Hannah asks, putting her arm around my waist and resting her head on my shoulder. She notices the photo and pulls it out of the bag, tracing her fingers over it. 'Look at the face June's pulling.'

I start to smile but then it dies on my lips. I'm not looking at the face June is pulling. I'm looking at Hannah standing beside her. But not her face – at the sweater she's wearing. I never noticed it before, even though it was staring at me all this time.

It's a black sweater with a small red logo in the corner. A mountain lion.

I know that sweater. I recognize it. It's Nate's football sweater. He used to wear it all the time when we were dating. I even wore it on occasion, with a pride I now cringe at. I know it's his because it's the old Matilija High sweater from the '90s, not the new one I see kids in town wearing. I stare at Hannah, who is still gazing at the photograph, and it's as if someone has snatched the veil from in front of my eyes.

Fragments of memory hit me like a spray of bullets, each one impacting with a thud and threatening to knock me to the ground: Nate glancing at Hannah that fateful day at the county jail. *Is this your daughter?* The curious frown Hannah gave him when she shook his hand and said hello. How she questioned me about the timing of the break-up. Did she see it straight away? The similarity, the likeness? Did she recognize herself immediately in Nate? How could she not have noticed the fact they had the exact same cornflower-blue eyes? Is it why she's been avoiding my calls and pulling away from me for the last year, being so secretive? Did Nate know too?

He must have. Why else would she be wearing his sweater? And that pink hair tie in his bathroom – oh my God – he said it was his daughter's. That long strand of blonde hair. Was it Hannah's? She was home then, not in New York. The timing works but even without hard evidence my gut screams 'yes'. He did know. He knew all along.

I think I'm going to be sick. How long have they been in contact? Why did she never bring it up? Did Nate know the whole time he was trying to get me into bed? Was it a game to him? Was he angry and trying to destroy my marriage? Or was he genuinely trying to rekindle something? Given what he did next, I'm assuming he was angry. It would be just like him to include Hannah in his revenge.

More memories assault me. I remember how I found Hannah in June's room – screaming over the dead hamster.

Another veil is stripped away and the image I see is a Gorgon, making me want to throw my arm up and shield myself from the sight. What if Hannah was in June's room looking for the money? Did she know it was there? Did June tell her? If Nate suspected the money was hidden somewhere in June's room, did he ask Hannah to look for it?

Was Hannah part of Nate's plan all along? It makes sense. If June told her about the money she'd stolen from Gene, did she tell Nate? It's true Nate knew already that Gene was a drug dealer. They'd been watching him for months. He may have known that Gene was likely to have cash on the premises.

Maybe I'm clutching at straws. And yet . . .

Hannah had a motive. Isn't it possible that her life-long jealousy of Gene led her to conspire with Nate to rob him? Or her anger at me for lying to her about Nate could have fueled her.

Would she really have done this though? How can I believe it? They abducted her, I remind myself angrily. I found her tied up in the basement of that house, terrified and sobbing. She's the one who shot Nate. I'm losing my mind. It doesn't make sense that she would be involved, that she could ever do something like this. She's not a monster. She's my daughter. I know her . . .

Don't I?

I think back, desperately trying to remember something that will confirm that I'm wrong, that I'm jumping to conclusions, that I'm paranoid and delusional and crazy. But instead all I can dig up are things that further cement her complicity.

Hannah rang Robert the week before the break-in and reminded him about our anniversary, something she's never done before. She encouraged him to book a restaurant and take me out. She called me that night, before I met up with

Laurie and asked, oh so casually, what I was doing and where I was. I remember thinking at the time it was strange of her to call me, so unlike her to check in, and I was so happy to hear her voice. But she rang off quickly when I told her I was going out with Laurie and her dad was at home.

I stare at her, feeling like I'm on a fairground ride that is slowly gathering speed.

Are her grief and tears over June the normal reaction of a sibling in this situation, or is it guilt?

She would never have wanted June to get hurt, I know that. And there's no way she would have gone along with any attempt to harm June either. Maybe that's what she was fighting with them about, outside the hospital. She's been lying – to me, to the cops, to everyone. She didn't just happen to wander past and overhear them talking about June – the very coincidence of that seems unlikely, now I think about it.

What if they were fighting because Hannah was telling them to leave June alone? What if she threatened to tell the truth?

I think of all the times I saw her with Jonathan – how distraught she seemed – the red mark on her arm, the tears. I put it down to grief and stress, but what if they were arguing over how to handle the mess they'd made? What if he was threatening her to keep her quiet?

I remember the way she said his name in the cabin. 'Nate.' It sounded so familiar on her lips, jarring enough that I noticed it, even at the time. Nate – the way she said it with a warning tone.

Is that why they kidnapped her? Because they couldn't keep her quiet any longer?

But would Nate really have harmed his own daughter to save his skin? Yes. Yes, he would. Of that I have no doubt. I think Nate was capable of anything.

I'm staring at Hannah with my mouth hanging open. All these thoughts have taken no longer than a few seconds to coalesce in my mind, and though I try to dismiss them, banish them, unthink them, I can't. Because every single fiber of my body knows I'm right. Hannah played some part in this.

My own flesh and blood. I thought I knew her, and I didn't know her at all.

'Shall we go?' Hannah asks, putting the photograph back in the bag and heading towards the door. She glances at Robert who is collecting the helium balloons banging against the ceiling. 'Come on, Dad.'

Robert follows her, trailing the balloons like a pack of excited puppies. I open my mouth to say something. I need to stop them. I need to confront Hannah, demand to know the truth, tell Robert . . .

Robert reaches the door and glances back over his shoulder at me.

'Ava?' he asks with a faint smile. 'You coming?' He turns back and offers me his hand, pausing when he sees my expression. 'Are you OK?'

I blink at him, swaying slightly, then shake my head.

He steps towards me, concerned. 'What is it?'

I reach for the pin of the grenade. I ready myself for the blast.

Robert takes my hand, frowning.

'Nothing,' I say, shoving the pin back in, before following them out the door.

ACKNOWLEDGEMENTS

Huge thanks are due to my incredible agent Amanda, who opened the door to me writing adult thrillers, after spending the first eight years of my novelist career writing young adult fiction.

I'm also very lucky to have the support and talent of Ruth Tross, an editor with a magic touch, and the whole team at Mulholland, including Hannah, Melanie, Jasmine and Lydia, as well as Lewis who came up with the cover and Helen who was forced to fix my wonky grammar and bastardized spelling. After almost four years living in the US I still mix up wrenches and spanners and pavements and sidewalks.

I moved to Ojai (not a fictitious town!) in 2016 with my husband John and daughter Alula – our third move across continents in as many years. I couldn't continue to follow my dreams so determinedly without their love and support and I count my blessings every day that not only do I get to live in the most beautiful place on earth, I get to do so with the two best people in the world.

Thanks too must go to my dear friend and hiking partner Clarissa who listened to this story when it was just an idea in my head and whose support has meant a huge deal.

And of course, last but not least, thanks to my girlfriends – Nichola, Vic, Rachel, Lauren, Asa, Becky, Karthi, Sara, Clarissa and Theo – who lift me up, love me, laugh with me, inspire me and teach me, and who are the reason I started writing in the first place – encouraging me before I even had my very first book deal. Thanks for continuing to cheerlead me along through all the ups and downs of motherhood, writing novels and working in Hollywood. I honestly wouldn't be here without you.